SLIDING INTO HOME

PLAYING FOR KEEPS - BOOK 3

LAUREN FRASER

CONTENTS

BLURB

Sliding into home isn't easy, sometimes it's a fight to stay on the bag.

Single mom, and tattoo artist, Kia Kamen finally has her act together. Sure, it might be an illusion, but it feels like a pretty good one. Until a chance encounter with Jeff Smith proves it was all a lie. She's not even close to having it all together. But what's a girl supposed to do when her one-night stand from six years ago shows up as her son's T-ball coach? Blurt out he's the father, of course.

As centerfielder for the San Diego Hawks, Jeff 'Smitty' Smith is used to being put in pressure situations. He just never expected that to mean needing to come in clutch as a father. Being a single dad, he could figure out, getting Kia to take a chance on them is proving to be a little more challenging. Thank god, he's a competitive guy, who doesn't know the meaning of the word quit.

But how does he convince Kia it's not a game to him? This professional athlete is ready to play for keeps.

Sign up for Lauren's newsletter and receive a free copy of Undercover Attraction. Join my mailing list for news of my latest release and sneak peeks at upcoming books and special newsletter only content.

Sign up at http://www.laurenfraser.com/newsletter

CHAPTER ONE

WHO KNEW COACHING T-BALL would be so much fun? Jeff clapped his hands to encourage the next batter up at the plate.

"Batter, batter, swing batter!" a little voice yelled from the dugout. The batter turned and scowled at his teammate, then lined himself up at the plate, swung the bat and missed. The boy's shoulders slumped.

Jeff walked up to the plate, crouched beside five-year-old Jeremy. "Keep your eye on the ball," he told the young player. "For right now, I just want you to ignore the pitcher and only focus on the ball. That's what you're aiming for. It doesn't matter what's happening on the mound. It doesn't matter what the players in the dugout are saying." He looked right at Jeremy, who seemed like he was ready to cry. *Oh boy.* "Nothing matters except keeping your eye on the ball."

Jeremy's lips tightened, and he stared at the tee. He looked back at Jeff and nodded.

"You got this." Jeff clapped the little boy on the back and stepped away.

Jeremy lined up and swung the bat. The ball bobbled off the tee, barely clearing the dirt.

"Run!" Jeff yelled.

Jeremy threw the bat and took off. Not the prettiest way to get on base, but it was a start.

Max walked out of the dugout and picked up the bat. He smiled as he walked up to the plate.

"Hey, Max. Couple things," Jeff said. "One, you normally don't want to heckle your own teammates."

Max's little face scrunched up in confusion. "What's heckle?"

"Like tease them or try to throw them off their game."

"What do you mean?"

"I mean, yelling 'batter, batter, swing' at Jeremy. Normally you'd reserve that kind of thing for the other team, not your own."

Max's head cocked to the side, and he chewed his cheek. He looked at Jeremy, who now stood on first base. "But he's on base, so it worked."

Jeff bit back a smile. "True, but not because you were yelling at him. Your cheer made him nervous, and he had a hard time hitting it because you were calling out to him."

"That's dumb. I was telling him to swing cuz he was just standing there doing nothin'."

Jeff pretended to cough to mask his amusement. The kid wasn't wrong. "Okay, but maybe for your own teammates, you want to shout something more encouraging, like 'let's go, you got this,' something like that. You know, the kind of thing you'd like someone to yell when you're at bat."

Max pursed his lips. "That's what I did. He didn't look like he knew what to do."

Covering his laugh again, he dragged his hand over his mouth. "Okay, but still, maybe we could be more encouraging. That cheer you were doing, while a good one, is normally used when you're playing in the field and your pitcher is throwing the ball. It's not normally used in T-ball."

The little boy shrugged. "Okay, Smitty. If you say so, but I think it's a good one."

"I think it's best we table that cheer for this season. Deal?" He shook the boy's hand to seal the deal.

"Deal," Max said as he shook. "But I could yell it at the other team if I came and watched you play, right?"

Jeff grinned. "Absolutely. It would definitely rattle the other team."

"Cool." Max nodded. "Batter up," he called as he walked up to the plate.

This kid cracked him up. When the Hawks had partnered with a local San Diego youth center to run programs for underprivileged children to play sports, he'd thought it was a great idea. He'd never imagined he'd enjoy it as much as he did. Jeff had been coaching the kids twice a week for the past month, and he looked forward to it, especially the T-ball. Introducing these kids to the best sport in the world and watching them fall in love with the game, like he had at their age, was unreal. And kids like Max made it even better.

A woman wandered toward the outfield fence. He couldn't take his eyes off her as she leaned her arms on the railing. Her long brown hair blew in the breeze and she reached out to try to tame it. His gaze lingered on the tattoos on her forearm. Moms sure didn't look like that when he was a kid. But then again, he'd never seen her before, so maybe she was just a babysitter or something. That would be better, for sure, a whole lot less creepy than ogling the mom of one of his players.

He shifted his gaze from her to check his watch. "Alright everybody. Last batter."

Groans rang out from the field and the dugout. Not that he could blame them. There was something magical about playing ball.

With one more bobbled attempt at bat, the game was done.

As the kids filed in from the field, Jeff held up his hand, and each player slapped it for a high-five. "Good job today, everybody. Grab all your gear. You're responsible for your own stuff, so make sure you bring it with you. If I have to bring it in, it's mine."

A high-pitched squeal sounded from his right. He turned, not sure what he was going to find. With this crew, it could be anything from a nosebleed to a butterfly. Max stood on the bench, waving vigorously at someone across the field. He looked in that direction and saw the woman he'd been admiring earlier waving back.

It figures my favorite kid has a hot mom.

Max ran up to him. "Smitty! Smitty! You gotta meet my mom."

His muscles tensed, and his pulse raced a little faster at the prospect of getting a better look at the woman. "Sure, kid." He adjusted his hat on his head. "Just let me make sure no one left anything behind."

Jeff walked with Max toward the dugout. The kid scooped a glove off the ground. "Annie left her glove. Can I have it?" Max looked up at him wide-eyed.

"No, it's Annie's," Jeff answered.

"But you said anything that gets left is yours, and—" He grinned and slid the glove on his hand. "It's not gonna fit you, so...."

"Nice try, kid." Jeff held out his hand for the glove. With a dramatic sigh, Max dropped the mitt onto Jeff's palm.

"That looks like the only thing left behind today. You guys are getting better." Jeff looked at Max and the boy beamed back at him with a grin. His missing front teeth made him look like he was at hockey camp instead of baseball.

Max grabbed his hand. "Come on. You gotta meet my mom."

"I'm coming." Max tugged Jeff's hand, trying to drag him down the field as fast as he could. Jeff resisted. There was no way he was jogging across the field to meet a woman. Not even one as sexy as Max's mom. He could maintain some kind of dignity.

"Mom!" Max yelled as they got closer to the woman. He dropped Jeff's hand and ran toward her. The second he got close to his mom his feet left the ground and he leaped at her. The woman caught him in midair like a seasoned pro. The move was so practiced and easy it was clear they'd done it a thousand times.

Not taking his eyes off the pair, he smiled. Not many kids in the program seemed to have this kind of relationship with their parents. It was nice to see. Reminded him of his family.

"Mom, Mom, this is Smitty."

The woman turned her attention toward him. With her big black sunglasses on, he couldn't see her eyes, but her mouth gaped as soon as she looked at him. "Jeff?" she whispered.

"Yeah?" *What the hell?* How did she know his first name? Most of the players, including the kids, called him 'Smitty.'

"No, Mom, this is Smitty."

"I heard you, baby." She set her son on the ground and then stared to her right for several seconds. Finally, she stood tall, and flipped her dark sunglasses up on her head and stared right into Jeff's eyes.

"Saskia?" Jeff's heart raced. *What was she doing here?*

"Yep." She gave him a tight smile.

"Shit." He winced when the cuss word slipped out. "I mean, wow! Small world." What were the odds a woman he'd slept with years ago in Tucson would show up here, in San Diego, at an inner-city youth program?

"No kidding," she said. "So, you're the infamous Smitty I keep hearing about?" She fidgeted from one foot to the other.

"Apparently." *Why did she look so uncomfortable?* It's not like he was going to tell her kid he'd had a one-night stand with his mom before he was even born. Trying to reassure her, he smiled.

"Wow, Jeff, um...ugh."

Max's face scrunched up as his gaze darted between Saskia and Jeff. "Mom, why do you keep calling him Jeff?"

"Ugh...um..." she stammered.

Jeff decided to help as best he could. "Your mom and I knew each other years ago." That didn't sound so bad, saying they'd known each other.

"You did?" Max's hazel eyes widened, then he turned to his mom. "Why didn't you say you knew Smitty?"

"Um, because I didn't realize I knew him until right now."

Max tilted his head and furrowed his brow. "How'd you not know?"

"Most people call me Jeff. It's only ball players and people around baseball who call me Smitty."

"But I call you Smitty." Max narrowed his eyes at him. His fingers tangled in his sandy blond hair as he scratched his head. Jeff could practically see the little wheels in his head spinning.

"Well, yeah, but you're a ballplayer, right?" Shit. He hoped he was playing this cooler than he felt.

A smile spread across Max's face. "Yeah." He glanced at his mom. "But she's not."

"Exactly." Jeff nodded. "That's why she only knew my name was Jeff."

"Oh." Max's head bobbed in understanding.

"We should get going, buddy. We have to go by Aunty Vika's on the way home."

"Yes." Max pumped his arm in the air, then turned to Jeff. "You want to come?"

Jeff bit back a laugh. Yeah, that wouldn't be incredibly uncomfortable. Saskia could barely look him in the eye. "No thanks, bud."

Saskia flicked a brief look at him. If he didn't know better, he'd think she looked guilty, but that didn't make sense. He glanced at her naked ring finger. No ring. So why the look? What happened between them was one time, years ago. Sure, it had been memorable, but certainly not something she needed to feel bad about all these years later. Weird.

She reached down and grabbed her son's hand. "Let's go, Max."

Max raised his hand. "Bye Smitty."

"Later Max. Have a good week."

Jeff watched as Max and his mom walked across the field toward the parking lot. And maybe his stare lingered on Saskia's ass, but just because she was someone's mom didn't mean he couldn't look.

CHAPTER TWO

KIA PULLED HER CAR up in front of her sister's house and turned off the engine. She really needed her big sister right now. How the hell could the man, Smitty, her son had been gushing over for the past two weeks be Jeff—*her* Jeff? It wasn't possible that the man she'd slept with six years ago in Tucson was here and coaching her son at camp.

What were the odds? She'd looked for him everywhere when she'd found out she was pregnant, and he'd disappeared. Only to show up now. Here. Six years later.

"Why are we at Aunty Vika's?" Max asked.

"I thought you might like to play with your cousins." Kia pushed open her car door then waited for her son to slide out of the back seat.

"They're gonna be so jealous you got to meet Smitty." Max bounced on the sidewalk beside her. Energy vibrated out of him with each hop. He always seemed to have an excess of energy coursing through his body no matter what she did to tire him out. She'd been hoping putting him in the baseball after-school program would burn off some of it, but so far that hadn't happened.

She cupped the back of her son's head. "I don't think your cousins care all that much about a baseball player, honey."

"Nuh-uh, Layla said he was cute." Max bounced on his toes.

Awesome. She rolled her eyes. Her niece was eleven going on sixteen. "How does Layla know what he looks like?"

"She looked him up last time."

Kia squatted so she could look her son in the eyes. "How come you guys looked him up?"

"I don't know." Max shrugged. His little hands splayed out in front of him as his shoulders rose. "I said he was the best baseball player ever. Alex said he wasn't, so we looked him up." Max put his hands on his hips and rolled his eyes. "'Cept Layla kept talking about who was cutest instead of who was the best, then Katya got all mad." He looked at her and huffed out an annoyed sound. "Girls are dumb. Who cares who's the cutest? He can throw the ball so far. He could probably hit our house from here."

Kia bit back a laugh. "I'm pretty sure he couldn't hit our house from here, but I have no doubt he can throw the ball really far."

Max stood on his tiptoes and looked in the direction of their house. She smiled to herself as her son stared at the buildings like he could see through them and over two blocks to their house. Finally, he nodded like he'd come to some conclusion. "I bet he could."

She wrapped her arm around her son's shoulder. "Alright, sweetie, let's go inside so you can hang out with your cousins."

At the front door she rapped twice, then opened it without waiting for an answer. "Hello?" she called as they stepped through the front door.

Her sister's head popped around the corner from the kitchen. Viktoria's eyebrows wrinkled as she looked at them. "Hi, what are you two doing here?"

"Hi, Aunty Vika." Max ran over and hugged the other woman. "Mom picked me up early today and she met Smitty. It was so cool." He turned toward Kia. "Tell her, Mom, wasn't he cool?"

"Yep, he was pretty awesome." She pasted a smile on her face. Cool wasn't exactly how she would describe meeting her son's father again.

How was she going to tell Jeff? What if he didn't want to be a dad? Her son would be heartbroken. "Why don't you go find your cousins?"

"Alex and Katya are in the backyard. Layla's pouting in her room," Viktoria told him.

Max wrinkled his nose. "I'm going outside."

Viktoria shared a knowing smile with her sister. Max had zero patience for anything that ruined his fun. "Good decision. Do you want a snack first?"

"Nah, Mom gave me a bar in the car." He giggled. "Bar in the car." He slapped his leg like he was so funny. "I'm a poet and I know it." Max snickered again.

Kia smiled. "Go find your cousins, you goofball."

"Bye." He tossed up his arm and dashed toward the back door.

The second the back door slammed shut behind him, Viktoria turned to her. "Do we need wine?"

"We definitely need wine." She followed her sister into the kitchen. Feeling completely at home, Kia walked to the fridge and pulled out the bottle of pinot gris her sister always kept on hand, chilling in the fridge door. She set it on the counter beside the two wine glasses Vika had just taken out for them.

With a large glass of wine each, they went back through the house to the living room. Kia dropped onto the worn brown sofa. Vika sat on the old beige recliner across from her. "What's going on?" Vika asked.

Kia took a fortifying sip of her wine. "So it turns out Smitty is Jeff."

"Jeff?" Viktoria looked at her blankly.

"Max's dad."

"What?" Viktoria sat in stunned silence for several seconds. "How is that possible?"

"I don't know." She was still trying to process the information herself. When she'd seen him today, it was like she'd been hit by a Mack truck. Spinning her world out of control.

"I don't get it. How could Max's dad be the same guy he's always talking about?"

Tears welled in Kia's eyes. "I don't know." She didn't understand it herself. "What am I supposed to do?" she whispered. "How am I supposed to tell some fancy major league baseball player, 'Oh hey remember that one-night stand we had six years ago? Surprise.'" She dropped her head against the back of the sofa and looked up at the ceiling. "How the hell am I supposed to tell him that?"

Vika stood up and sat beside Kia on the couch. "You just do, hon. It's not like it's your fault. You tried to find him when you found out you were pregnant. What more were you supposed to do?"

"I know, but still." She blinked away the tears. "He's like this big-shot baseball player. I don't know anything about his life. What if he's married with kids of his own? I can't just upend his entire life."

"Yes, you can. He's Max's dad, sweetie. Now that you've found him, he deserves to know."

"I know that, Vik, it's just...what if he's not happy about it? That would destroy Max." The idea of Jeff finding out he was Max's dad and rejecting him was so much worse than Max not knowing who his dad was. Her son would be heartbroken.

Vika squeezed her hand. "But what if he is happy? Imagine what that would mean to Max. He'd finally have a dad. You know how much he wants that."

"I know." Her eyes burned as more tears rushed to the surface. "It's stupid, but it's always been Max and I against the world. This just ..." She sniffed. "It changes everything."

"True, but maybe for the better."

"Maybe, but maybe for the worse." She swiped her nose with the back of her hand. "What if he's like one of those professional athletes you always hear about? Booze and women and parties. That's not dad material."

"Kia, that's not you talking. You hate it when people take one look at your tattoos and judge you. Don't do the same to him."

"What? I don't know the first thing about this guy."

"Come on, you obviously know something. You slept with the guy."

"Yeah, six years ago, after a shitty day. I had a couple of drinks with a cute guy that I thought worked for a moving company." She stared at the back door where her son had gone outside. "Today I found out he's actually a professional athlete. God, Vika, I wouldn't have slept with him if I'd known we were so different."

"Oh, come on, Saskia, don't give me that crap," she scoffed. "I remember how sexy you thought he was. You talked about that one-night stand for weeks afterwards. About how hot the guy was. How you wished you'd exchanged numbers or at least gotten his last name. You would have slept with him no matter who he was."

"Well, maybe, but..." She exhaled loudly. "What am I supposed to do? Look at me, Vik. I don't exactly run in the same social circles with some fancy athlete."

"Maybe this is a good thing. As Max's dad, he'll have to pay you some kind of child support. You guys can move someplace nicer."

"Jeez, Vik. No. I'm not taking money from him."

"Why not? He's Max's dad. You've been doing everything for five years on your own, busting your ass to make a name for yourself as an artist. Why shouldn't he help out?"

"We're not having this discussion." She picked up her glass of wine.

"Okay, we can table the money discussion. How are you going to tell him?"

"I don't know. I need to figure out what kind of person he is now before I decide if he gets to be in Max's life. I barely knew anything about him when we slept together six years ago. Now that I know he's a professional athlete, I know even less than I thought I did. Just because he donated some sperm to the cause doesn't mean he deserves to be Max's dad. If he's not a good person, he doesn't get to know my son."

"I don't think they'd let him work with kids if he wasn't a good person. Besides, you're normally pretty good at reading people and you liked him enough to sleep with him."

Kia fought the urge to roll her eyes at her sister. She couldn't be that naïve. "Yeah, six years ago, after a night of drinking. Hell, he was still sleeping when I tiptoed out early and went to work the next morning. Who knows what he's like now that he's a big shot athlete with women throwing themselves at him?"

"You threw yourself at him before he was a big shot."

She scowled at her sister. "Shut up. We threw ourselves at each other I'll have you know. It was very mutual. But again, six years ago. A lot can happen."

Vika pulled out her phone. "Okay then, only one thing to do. Let's deep dive his socials."

Kia slid closer to her sister so they could both see the screen as Vika pulled up his social media.

"Holy shit, Kia, he's hot." Vika zoomed in on a photo of Jeff that a photographer had caught of him after a game. In his uniform, with sweat dripping down his face and a smug grin curling up his mouth, he looked really freaking sexy. Had he been that hot when she'd slept with him? She remembered him as being good-looking but not as smokin' as he looked in that picture.

"I told you he was attractive."

"Yeah, but there's attractive and then there's 'here sir, let me give you my panties'." Vika waggled her eyebrows. "Know what I mean?"

Kia looked at the picture again and giggled. "Unfortunately, yeah I do." She grabbed the phone and scrolled through more pictures. How he looked was beside the point. What kind of man was he? That was a whole other issue.

"Max looks like him."

"What? No, he doesn't." She looked down at the picture on the screen. Did he? Maybe a little around the eyes.

"Yeah, that dimple, the hair." Vika tapped the screen. "My god they even have the same little cowlick."

Kia looked at what appeared to be a post-game shot. Jeff's jersey was soaking wet, like he'd had the Gatorade jug dumped all over him. His hair stood up in every direction, and there was the cowlick. The same as Max had when he got out of the tub. She was still staring at the photo when Vika flipped to the next picture.

"Damn, are those his teammates?" Vika fanned herself. "Maybe I could get into baseball. Usually when Ty puts the game on, I just pick up my book, but..." She zoomed in on one of the players. "I think that's about to change."

"Focus," Kia told her sister. She stared at photos of Jeff with his teammates, at press conferences, at various PR events. Everything on his social media was curated for a public image. This didn't show the real Jeff. "This is just what he wants people to see. Check where he's been tagged."

Kia's phone buzzed in her back pocket. She pulled it out and winced when she saw Austin's name on the screen. She flicked the screen to answer the call. "Hey Austin, how's it going?"

"Good, how was your day?" he asked.

"It was good. My last client canceled, so I could pick up Max from camp."

"Oh yeah. He must have been pretty stoked to see you there."

She smiled as she pictured how excited Max had been when he'd spotted her across the field. Hopefully, that kind of excitement lasted for several more years. "He was."

"What are you guys up to tonight? I was thinking maybe I could come by after Max goes to bed and we could hang out and watch a movie or something." The innuendo hung in the air.

How the hell was she supposed to spend the evening with Austin when all she could think about was freaking Jeff Smith? "Not tonight. Max and I are at Vika's place, and we'll probably stay here for dinner. Some other time, okay?"

"Sure," his voice dropped with disappointment. "I'll call you later."

"Sounds good." She hung up the phone and looked at her sister.

"Trouble in paradise?" Vika raised one eyebrow as she studied her.

"I wouldn't say trouble exactly. Just... I don't know, it's complicated. So far he seems like a good guy, but..." She shrugged. "It's just a lot. I introduced him to Max briefly the other day, and you know how Max is with new people, well, men, so I'm taking it slow."

"Honey, you've been dating him for six months. How slow do you want to take things?"

And that was the million-dollar question. Introducing a guy to her son as a friend of hers was one thing. Involving him in their life and routine was something completely different. She didn't want to do that until she knew he had some staying power. "Can we not talk about Austin right now and focus on what I should do about Jeff?"

Vika picked her phone back up. "Right, operation daddy stalk can recommence."

"Operation daddy stalk?" Kia laughed. "Where do you come up with this stuff?"

"Is that not what we're doing?"

The front door opened and Vika's husband, Tyson, walked in and pulled up short when he saw the women on the couch. "What's going on?"

"Nothing. We're just being creepy and checking out sexy baseball players." Vika winked at her husband.

"Oh yeah? You see one you liked at Max's camp?" he asked Kia, then dropped a kiss on his wife's lips. "Hey babe, if you get all turned on looking at shirtless men, you know where to find me." He flicked a glance at the screen, then walked out of the room and down the hall.

"You guys are so weird." Kia watched as her sister's gaze followed her husband out of the room.

"How are we weird?"

"Oh, I don't know. He doesn't care if you get all hot and bothered by some other guy? That's weird."

"No, it's not. As long as he's the one I'm with, what does he care how I get turned on? You should see some of the books Ty buys me."

"Whatever works for you."

Vika grinned. "Oh, it definitely works."

A couple minutes later Tyson emerged from the bedroom, showered, and dressed in a t-shirt and pair of jeans. Any remnants of the day at the garage were long gone. He wandered into the kitchen, then came out with a beer in one hand and the bottle of wine in the other. "Figured if you ladies are ogling you probably worked up a thirst and need a top up."

Vika smiled up at her husband and held out her wineglass. "You know us so well. How was your day?"

"Eh, it was there. Couple of assholes thought just because they're paying me they can tell me how to fix their cars, but I set them straight."

"I'm sure you did, baby," Vika said.

"So, you looking at anyone in particular?" Tyson nodded toward Vika's phone.

"Jeff Smith," Vika replied.

Kia shot her sister a look, warning her not to say anything about who Jeff was yet.

"Hell of a ballplayer." He looked at his wife and wrinkled his nose. "You like that? Really?"

"Honey, all women like that. He's sexy and muscular. What's not to like?" Vika asked.

"You got sexy and muscular right here." Tyson flexed his pec muscles and grinned at his wife.

"I know I do, but Kia doesn't have that at home, so she has to look elsewhere because it'd be weird if she ogled you."

Kia stuck her finger in her mouth and pretended to throw up. "Gross, could you two get any more nauseating?"

"I'm sure we could." Tyson picked up the TV remote. "Cool if I turn this on?"

"Yeah, of course." Kia waved her hand. "Max and I are going to take off anyway and go make dinner."

"You don't want to stay?" Vika asked.

"Nah, but thanks." Kia stood up and her sister followed.

"So, what are you going to do about Jeff?"

Kia blew out a breath. "No idea. Tell him, I guess, and go from there." She looked at her sister. "Wish me luck."

Vika pulled her into a hug. "Good luck. Keep me posted."

"Yeah, will do." Kia walked over to the back door and pulled it open. Stepping out onto the back deck, she watched Max and Alex running around with Nerf guns while Katya sat quietly playing by herself in the tree fort. This was why she'd moved to San Diego, to give Max a chance to grow up with family. Sure, it meant building up a clientele almost from scratch again, but it was worth it.

Finally, after a year, everything felt like it was coming together and now this. Max's bio-dad appeared out of nowhere. And their perfect little world would never be the same. Hopefully, for the better.

CHAPTER THREE

THE FOLLOWING AFTERNOON, SASKIA took a deep breath and walked into Kidsplay. She stopped at the front counter and scanned for someone who worked there. After several minutes, an attractive blonde wandered down the hallway.

"Sorry, I didn't realize anyone was out here. We really need to get a buzzer or something on the door," the blonde gushed. "What can I do for you?"

"This is probably a bit weird. Um, my son Max comes here on Tuesdays for T-ball."

"Okay, right, I thought you looked familiar. I'm Peyton."

"Kia." She opened and closed her fingers as her palms began to sweat. If it was this hard just to ask for Jeff's number, how the hell was she supposed to tell him he was

Max's dad? "Um, my son really loves Jeff. I mean Smitty, as a coach." She shifted her weight. Everything about this situation was so incredibly uncomfortable. "I was wondering if it would be possible to get his phone number."

Peyton coughed, then covered her mouth. "Sorry, you want Smitty's phone number? Unfortunately, I can't give you his number. I'm sure you understand."

"Oh shit, no, I'm not like some weird stalker mom or anything like that." Kia held up her hand. "I just need to talk to him about Max."

"You need to talk to him about Max? Is everything okay? I run the center, so if there's anything I can help you with, I'd be more than happy to chat with you."

Kia winced. How the hell was she supposed to say no, it's got to be Jeff without making Peyton think she really was some crazy mom? "Thank you, I appreciate that, but I was hoping to speak to Smitty since Max talks about him all the time."

Peyton smiled. "Smitty is a favorite around here." Peyton glanced out the front window, then pursed her lips. "For obvious confidentiality reasons, I can't give you Smitty's phone number but um... since you're a parent here. I can tell you he's here on Tuesdays after school to play T-ball with the little guys and he's here around four till six or so on Thursdays working with a group of teens. That's the best I can do."

"That's great, thank you. I'll stop by tomorrow and see if I can chat with him when he's wrapping up. I'd like to talk to him before Max is back on Tuesday." So much for getting this over with today. Now she was going to have to reschedule a client tomorrow so she could come by again. But she needed to get this done. The sooner she told Jeff he was Max's dad, the sooner she'd know exactly what she was dealing with.

Kia looked at her shaking hands and took several deep breaths. She could do this. Everything would be fine. So why did she feel like she was going to throw up?

She stopped at the edge of the ball diamonds and scanned the fields to look for Jeff or 'Smitty' as her son had affectionately been calling him. Peyton had said he was working with the older kids today, but every diamond had teenagers on it. Which one would he be on?

Drawn to the far diamond, she watched as a group performed an elaborate celebratory cheer. The volume and enthusiasm growing with each chant. When they parted, she instantly saw Jeff's muscular frame in the middle of the group of teens. At the first sight of him, her heart did a little stutter step she quickly tried to squash. She could do this.

Slowly making her way down the sideline toward the far diamond, she tried to quell her nerves. When she'd seen him two days ago, it had been a shock. She'd been blindsided, but today? Whole other ballgame. Today, she was purposefully seeking him out after all this time. God, what if he didn't believe her, or didn't care? She didn't think he was that kind of person, but how the hell did she know? She'd spent one night with him six years ago. She didn't know anything about the guy.

One teen pointed in her direction, and Jeff's head turned toward her. A smile split across his face, and he lifted his hand in acknowledgement.

He said something to the teens, then the group disbanded, and the youth began gathering up their equipment. As Jeff walked toward her, Kia's heart pounded in her chest. The closer he got, the more her heart thumped.

Good Lord, he was a good-looking man, with his muscular body and sandy blond hair curling out beneath his ball cap. Her sister hadn't been wrong when she said baseball might be worth watching if she knew the players looked like that. The Hawks were really missing the boat not having billboards of Jeff all over the city.

Ticket sales would skyrocket.

God, between lack of sleep and nerves, her brain was mush that she was even thinking something that stupid at a time like this. What was wrong with her?

Jeff smiled when he got close to her. She sucked in a breath as her eyes landed on the pronounced dimple on his right cheek that looked just the same as the one Max had. She hadn't even remembered he had a dimple.

"Hey, Saskia."

"Hi, how are you?"

His brow wrinkled, the confusion evident on his face. "I'm good. What are you doing here? Where's Max?"

She took a deep breath. "He's at daycare. I was hoping we could maybe talk."

Jeff glanced behind him at his group, then at the surrounding fields. "Yeah, sure. We just finished up our game, so I'm done for the day."

"Oh, that's good." Was it? Shoot. She wasn't ready to talk now. When she'd come here, she'd been expecting him to be busy and need to schedule something on another day. She wasn't prepared. They couldn't have this conversation here, but it's not like she could explain why it would be best to go elsewhere. Shit, shit, shit.

Jeff cocked his head to the side as he studied her. "What's up? Something going on with Max? Is he having troubles?"

"No, no, not at all. He loves everything about coming here." She smiled as she thought of her son. To most people, she was a screwup, but no one would say that when it came to her son. Max was the best thing she'd ever done in her life. Nothing was more important to her than his happiness, which was why she needed to do this. Now. "He's been talking about you for weeks. Smitty this, Smitty that. I didn't realize he was talking about you until the other day. I had no idea."

"He's a cool little guy."

"Yeah, he is." She smiled at a couple of teens who eyed her as they walked past.

"Thanks, Coach," the taller of the two youths said.

"No problem. Good job today, guys. Thanks for putting the stuff away. Appreciate it."

Jeff turned back to her. "You want to talk here, or did you want to grab a coffee or something?" He studied her. "You sure you even want to talk to me? You're kind of freaking me out with how nervous you look."

She laughed and okay yeah, even to her own ears she sounded nervous. Real smooth.

"Saskia, talk to me. What's going on?

"I go by Kia now."

His smile ticked up in the corner of his mouth as he watched her. "Kia, I like that. It suits you."

Her heart thumped again. Damn it. She wasn't supposed to still be attracted to him. She had a boyfriend. A great one...Well, good...Ok, at least. This was about Max. Nothing else mattered. She took a deep breath. "I wanted to call you after seeing you the other day, but obviously I didn't have your number. I came by here to ask for it, but the staff wouldn't give it to me. I guess they thought I might be some crazed fan or something."

He laughed. "You do look a little sketchy."

An overly loud, uncomfortable laugh burst out of her. God, she really was a hot mess. So much for being relaxed. When she glanced at him, heat rose to her cheeks.

Jeff stepped a little closer to her. His blue eyes trailed slowly down her body. "What'd you want my number for?" His tongue dipped out, then swept across his bottom lip like he was imagining doing all kinds of things to her.

"Oh god, not that." She held up her hand. "I have a boyfriend. But um..."

"Just thought I'd check. With how nervous you are, this felt like some weird booty call or something."

"God, no, definitely not." With a shaky hand, she pushed her hair back from her face. She eyed the empty bleachers and flicked her wrist toward them. "You want to sit?"

"Yeah sure." Jeff walked beside her. "It's wild how quickly this place clears out at the end of the games. Considering how many kids are always running around her doing stuff, you'd think they'd linger more on the fields."

She scanned the now empty diamond. "I'm sure the little guys take longer to clear out."

"Sometimes."

Kia could feel him watching her, waiting for her to talk. This was so much harder than she'd anticipated. She dropped onto the vacant bleacher and Jeff sat beside her. He turned toward her. "So, you gonna tell me why you're here?"

"Um yeah." She clasped her hands together in her lap. Took a deep breath and blurted, "Max is your son."

CHAPTER FOUR

"What?" Jeff jumped up. How the fuck could he be Max's dad? Yeah, it was a while ago, but he distinctly remembered using protection. He wasn't an idiot. He never played without a glove. He was always safe. No matter what. A kid was impossible.

"I'm sorry. I shouldn't have just sprung it on you like that." Kia stood up beside him on the bleachers and placed her hand on his arm. "Can you sit down please so we can talk?"

The last thing he wanted to do was sit. He scanned the fields, his body urging him to run, to escape. He took a shaky breath and exhaled. Running wasn't an option. He needed to hear Kia out. He took another deep breath, then sat on the bleacher. Putting some space between them, he slid a few more inches away from her. His body vibrated as his heart pounded in his chest. He couldn't have a kid.

"I know this is a lot. And I'm sorry," Kia said.

"A lot? You think? Jesus, Saskia, what the fuck?"

She winced. "I'm sorry. I meant to ease into telling you. I just panicked and the words flew out."

He angrily dragged his fingers through his hair as he tried to wrestle with everything that was running through his mind. "Maybe you should have eased into telling me when you were pregnant. Maybe that would have been a helpful time to tell me."

"I tried to, but I didn't know how to find you."

"We fucked at my house, Saskia. You knew exactly where to find me." This was bullshit. It's not like he was hidden from public view. She could have found him at any time over the past five years. Jesus. Six years if she'd told him when she was actually pregnant.

"I went to your house. You'd moved and no one knew where you were."

Was she kidding with this shit? "Plenty of people knew where to find me. I wasn't exactly in fucking witness protection. I went to play baseball. I told you that."

She winced. "I thought you were just making it up about playing in the minor leagues. You worked for a moving company, Jeff. That doesn't scream professional ballplayer."

"I didn't lie to you."

"Obviously I know that now." She fidgeted with her hands in her lap. "When I found out I was pregnant, I went to your old place, but you no longer lived there." She looked up at him. Her face pleaded with him to understand. "We didn't exactly exchange last names or phone numbers or anything. It was a one-night stand." She sighed. "I tried to find you. Your neighbors just said you'd moved somewhere. I even called your old boss. All they'd tell me was you quit. That's it. What was I supposed to do?"

"I don't know. Something." He closed his eyes and covered his mouth with his palms like a prayer. What else did he expect her to do? Honestly, it sounded like she'd tried to tell him she was pregnant.

He had a kid. His heart rate picked up the pace again, pounding violently in his chest. He pushed his index fingers into the bridge of his nose as he tried to slow his brain down so he could think.

Kia sat silently beside him.

After several minutes, he opened his eyes and turned to her. "Max is my son?"

She nodded. "He is."

"You're sure he's mine?"

Her eyes flashed with anger. "He's yours." She squared her shoulders. "But we can do a paternity test if you don't believe me."

"It's not that I don't believe you. This is just a lot." He ran his palm across his mouth. "I'm playing catch-up here. You gotta give me a minute."

"Of course." She picked at a piece of loose string on her sleeve. "Maybe we should just table this for today and give you some time to process everything. Give you a chance to figure out what kind of role you want to have in Max's life, and we can meet in a couple of days or something."

"What do you mean, what kind of role I want to have? I'm his dad. That's the role I want to have." His stomach rolled. He felt a little sick. How the fuck was this his life?

"Are you sure? This is a lot. Maybe take a day or so to think about it. Once I introduce you to Max as his dad, there's no going back from that. You can't decide it's too much and back out."

"Why would I back out? I'm not an idiot, Kia. I know what it means to have a kid. I'm not just going to throw money at him and be done." His spine stiffened. "Or is that what you were hoping was going to happen?" He knew he was being an asshole, but he couldn't seem to help himself.

"What? Of course not." Her hazel eyes narrowed as she glared at him. "I'm not telling you because I see you as some kind of cash cow, Jeff. I'm telling you about Max because it's the right thing to do." She clicked her tongue. "I tried to tell you when I was pregnant and couldn't find you. Now that you've resurfaced in my life, I'm telling you because you deserve to know." She squared her shoulders.

"But nothing is more important to me than Max. It's my job to protect him and keep him safe and that includes from you if need be."

"Why would you need to protect him from me?"

"Hopefully, I don't, but that's what I need to find out. I don't know you, Jeff. So before I explain this to Max, you need to take some time and figure out what you want. Then we can talk and discuss introducing you to him. I need time to prepare Max. He's the only one that matters in all this."

"Of course." What did he want? To meet his son. But what did that mean, exactly? Who the hell knew? There were probably a million things he should say, but his brain felt like it was using two brain cells at the moment, instead of the billions it had at its disposal. Not exactly helpful. Kia was right. It was probably smart to table this discussion till his brain was back online.

Kia chewed on her bottom lip. "I know it's a lot to ask, but can you just behave like normal when you see Max at T-Ball?"

His stomach twisted. How the hell was he supposed to be normal, to pretend nothing had changed?

"Please," Kia pleaded. "That's not the time or place for him to find out who you really are."

As much as it pained him to admit, she was right. "No problem." He stared at her. "When can we meet again to talk about our next steps?"

Her tongue darted out and she licked her bottom lip. "Do you want to meet early next week?"

There was no way he was waiting that long to talk to her about this. "No. What's your schedule like tomorrow?"

"Tomorrow?" She shifted on the bleacher. "I work in the afternoon, so I guess we could meet in the morning."

"Sounds good. Where?"

"Um... Do you know where Bean Scene is on Market?"

"I'll find it. Say 10:30?"

Kia nodded. She stood up and clasped her hands in front of her. "I'll see you tomorrow."

"Yeah."

After she left, he couldn't make himself stand up. His mind raced. He had a kid. He rubbed his sternum to ease the tightness in his chest. It didn't help. Why was it so hard to swallow? It felt like his throat was glued shut.

He steepled his hands in front of his face and tried to breathe. How was he supposed to be a dad when all he wanted to do at this moment was call his own? His fingers itched to pick up the phone, but he wasn't ready for that conversation yet. He could just imagine what his dad would say. *You got yourself in this situation, now man up and do the job.*

But first, he needed to figure out the right way to do that.

Jeff looked around the half empty bar as he waited for his friends to meet him. Ever since Kia had told him about Max, he'd thought of nothing else. He needed to hash it out with his friends because, at the moment, he was pissed. He knew Kia had tried to reach him and it wasn't her fault that he was just finding out about Max now, but he was angry. He'd missed five years of his kid's life already. And he couldn't get that back.

He'd grown up with great parents that were still happily married. In theory, he knew how to be a dad. But in reality, the idea scared the shit out of him. How was he supposed to connect with his son and have a relationship when he didn't know anything about him?

Pete and Ryan strode into the bar together and slid onto two of the vacant seats at the four top.

"Thanks for coming," Jeff said.

"No problem. You okay? You look like you just ate some of Gonzo's cooking." Pete's face scrunched up in sympathy as he stared at him.

"I'm all good." But was he? Not really. He was a mess. His mind was running in a million directions. His first instinct was to figure out where Kia lived and go see his son. The second was to get in his car and head across the border to Mexico.

"What's up? Your text made it seem important," Ryan asked.

"Yeah, it is, but let's wait till Gonz is here, so I don't have to explain everything twice."

"Sure, no problem." Ryan looked around, then flagged the server over. "Can we get a pitcher of pale ale please and four..." He eyed Jeff's glass. "Three more glasses."

"Do you need menus at all?" The server held up a stack of menus.

"Nah, just the beer for now," Ryan replied.

"Coming right up." The server turned and pulled up short when she almost crashed into Gonzo, who was walking up to their table.

"Whoa, easy." Gonzo grabbed her arm to stop her from stumbling backward into a nearby table.

"Thanks."

Gonzo smiled at the server and she ducked her head and blushed, then slinked away. As Gonzo dropped into the last remaining seat, he grinned at the group. "She's cute."

"Can you not turn that off for like five minutes?" Pete joked.

"Hey man, it's a curse. I can't help it that the ladies love me."

"Right." Pete snorted. "Get a hobby."

"I have a hobby, picking up women."

"Get a dog," Ryan added.

"Yeah, that's not even close to the same thing at all."

The server arrived and set the pitcher of beer and glasses on the table. She smiled shyly at Gonzo, then left.

Ryan filled up the glasses of beer, then looked pointedly at Jeff. "Alright, why are we here, Smitty?"

When he arrived, he'd been dying to talk to them. Now that the moment was at hand, he didn't know how to start. Maybe that's how Kia had felt when she'd just blurted out the news. Needing a moment, he picked up his beer and took a sip. He eyed his friends watching him expectantly and took another sip. This was a lot harder than he'd expected.

He took a breath and let it out loudly. "So I had an interesting day today."

"Okay?" Gonzo raised his eyebrow at him, encouraging him to continue.

"This is weird. You know Max's hot mom?"

"Yeah, I remember." Gonzo smiled. "What about her?"

"Well, turns out—" Uncomfortable, he shifted on his chair and his plaid button-up got caught underneath him. He yanked it free and rocked back in his seat. "Max is my son."

Ryan's glass clunked on the table, spilling beer over the edge of the glass. "Say what now?"

Jeff handed Ryan a napkin. "Yeah, that's how I felt when she told me."

"Holy shit," Pete mumbled. "You have a kid?"

"Apparently."

"Are you sure it's yours?" Gonzo asked.

"Pretty sure." Kia had mentioned a paternity test, but he believed her. Not sure why exactly, but he did.

"But you're going to do a paternity test, right?" Gonzo pressed.

Jeff shrugged. "Not sure, but I don't think so."

Pete winced. "Are you sure that's wise? It might be a good idea just to be safe."

"It feels like a dick move to ask for a paternity test. Like I think she's lying." The idea of questioning Kia about it didn't sit right in his gut.

Pete raised a brow. "I don't know, man. Seems a little naïve not to ask. This woman just comes out of nowhere after five-six-years and suddenly you're a dad?"

"I don't know, maybe." Jeff picked at the edge of his paper coaster. "I haven't figured any of this out yet. I'm still processing that I might have a kid."

"But it's possible it's yours?" Ryan asked.

"Definitely a possibility." Jeff picked up his beer and took a sip. The cool liquid hit his mouth but did nothing to ease the dryness in his throat. "We had a one-night thing a few years ago."

"So she was just some random chick you picked up who now is coming out of the woodwork?" Pete asked.

"I wouldn't say random chick." Yes, he'd just had one night with Saskia, but that one night had been unforgettable.

"Did you exchange numbers?" Ryan pressed.

"No, it wasn't like that. We didn't even tell each other our last names, it was just... You know, one of those wild nights."

"Which is all the more reason to ask for a paternity test, man. Not to be a dick, but you make a lot of money. That could be appealing to a lot of people." Gonzo wrinkled his face as he held Jeff's eyes. "Think about it, man. Child support. That's a lot of dollar bills you could be out."

"If it's my kid, I should be paying."

"Exactly, if it's your kid. How about you make sure before you fork any out?" Gonzo took a sip of his beer, then set it down. "I know you want to do the right thing, but just take a beat and make sure it is the right thing first."

"I hate to say it, but he's right." Pete grimaced. "I can think of at least two guys who've come out the other side of paternity tests with it not being their kid."

"Yeah, and a hell of a lot more who have come out as the parent." He was just getting used to the idea of Max being his son. He hated the thought that he now might not be.

"True, so you take the test and if it turns out you're the dad. No harm, no foul, because you wanted to do the right thing anyway. But if it turns out you aren't the dad, you saved yourself from getting hurt." Gonzo nudged his shoulder. "I know you, man, and you'd be devastated if you started down this path just to have it ripped away. Protect yourself, please."

Jeff nodded. Gonzo was right. If he allowed himself to be Max's dad just to find out Kia had played him, he would be destroyed. "I'll think about it."

"That's all I ask." Gonzo's mouth pulled into a tight half smile. "So assuming he's yours, how do you feel?"

"Honestly? Terrified."

"Understandable." Pete nodded. "Kendall and I are just starting to talk about when we might want to have a family, and it scares the shit out of me. I wouldn't have the first clue how to be a dad."

"It's a lot." Jeff pictured hanging with Max for the first time. What if the kid didn't like him? "I don't even have the first clue what my role would be. I mean, the kid doesn't know me. I'm practically a stranger. It's not like I could demand partial custody."

"You probably could if you wanted it," Ryan said.

Did he want it? He didn't know. The idea of being responsible for another human being was terrifying. "That's not really fair to Max. Can you imagine how that would feel? Hey buddy, want to go sleep at this strange man's house?" Jeff shook his head. "Nah, I'll just have to play it all by ear and hope Kia knows how to navigate all this better than I do."

"That's the mom's name? Kia?" Pete asked.

"Yeah, Saskia, but she prefers to be called Kia now, apparently." Jeff drummed his fingers on the table. "It suits her." He smiled. She seemed so different from the girl he remembered. That girl had been so light and carefree, like the world was hers for the taking. Kia seemed harder, more streetwise, with her tattoos and piercings and the whole badass vibe she had going on. Both were sexy in their own way. He took a sip of beer. He wasn't supposed to be thinking about how sexy Kia was. His only focus should be on Max.

"Considering it was a one-night stand six years ago, it's pretty impressive you remembered her name," Ryan said.

"It was a pretty memorable night."

"You hoping to hook back up with the sexy mom?" Gonzo's head cocked to the side in question.

"I'm not even thinking about that at the moment." What a liar. He was definitely thinking about that. But hooking up with a one-night stand again was one thing. Hooking up with the mother of his child was something else entirely. That had complication written all over it. He didn't do complicated. But having a kid was complicated, so apparently that was about to change. This was not what he'd expected when he'd woken up today.

"Probably a good idea not to dip your wick in the mommy well." Gonzo's lips pulled tight as his head bobbed up and down.

"Classy." Ryan rolled his eyes at Gonzo.

"What? I'm just saying. There are lots of other places to get that need met. Hooking up with Kia sounds messy." Gonzo pinned Jeff with a stare. "And confusing."

"No shit." Jeff couldn't agree more. Everything about this day sounded messy and confusing. Hopefully tomorrow, when he met with Kia, he would start getting some answers.

What he needed right now was a distraction. "Who wants to play pool?" Jeff asked the group.

CHAPTER FIVE

THE FOLLOWING MORNING, KIA walked down Market Street a couple of minutes before 10:30. Looking up, she spotted Jeff walking toward her. He flipped her a little wave in acknowledgement.

"Hey," she said when he stopped in front of her.

"Hi." He held open the door for Bean Scene. "What do you want to drink?"

Her nerves were shot. Adding caffeine to the mix was probably a bad idea, but what the hell? "Chai latte please."

"You want to grab a table while I get the drinks?" Jeff glanced at the display case, then back at her. "You want anything to eat?"

"No, thanks." She pointed toward a secluded table by the window. "I'll be over there." The table was the only one in that section. There was a stage set up beside it that was used in the evenings but was always empty during the day. It would allow them to not have anyone else close by while they talked.

Jeff nodded, then walked toward the counter.

Kia slid into the seat against the wall, leaving the other chair open for Jeff. She tapped her foot anxiously on the metal table leg as she waited for him to join her. What was he going to say today? She hadn't been able to sleep at all last night, wondering if he wanted to be a part of Max's life. If he did, their entire world was about to change. If he didn't. Well, that didn't even bear thinking about, but honestly wouldn't alter their current day to day at all. But would make for a tricky conversation in the future.

Watching Jeff as he walked toward her with a drink in each hand, she sucked in a breath. For her son's sake, she hoped she hadn't been wrong to tell Jeff the truth.

He set the coffee in front of her as he sat in his chair. "So, you want to dive right in or—" he asked.

"May as well dive right in." Kia dug the fingers of her left hand into her thigh as she braced for what might be coming.

"Okay, so I'm going to be a dick and get this out of the way first. I talked to my agent and lawyer this morning and they strongly encouraged me to get a paternity test."

Kia's gut clenched. "Makes sense." She'd been expecting him to say that, but it still hurt a little that he didn't fully believe her.

Jeff's foot bounced against the table leg, and the whole table moved. "Sorry." He winced.

As awful as this situation was, it was nice to see that he was as nervous about everything as she was.

"Once we get the paternity out of the way, I'd really like to set up a time to meet Max as his dad. I'll respect however you want to make that happen since you know him best. But I want to do it as soon as possible. My lawyer said the paternity test could be done anytime and we should have the results back the same day, next at the latest."

"Wow, that fast? I just assumed it would take longer than that."

Jeff shrugged. "It's a private clinic that he knows about."

"Sounds expensive," she mumbled. She didn't have money kicking around for things like paternity tests.

"I'll pay for the test since I'm the one asking for it." He rubbed his forehead. "It's just a formality, since I don't think you would have told me Max was my son if he wasn't."

"Thank you. I appreciate you saying that."

"Of course." Jeff shifted in his seat. "Okay, so what's the plan here?"

"You tell me."

"What do you mean? Obviously, I want to get to know him."

"There's nothing obvious about this, Jeff."

He reared back like he was offended that she'd even suggest he wouldn't want to be involved. "Yeah, there is.

If Max is my son, then I want to have a relationship with him, get to know him. But..." He paused. "I'm flying blind here. I don't know what your life is like. I don't want to... I don't want to mess things up for him if he... if he thinks someone else is his dad or something." He scrubbed his hand across his face again. When he looked back at her, the lines on his face made him look as tired as she felt. Maybe he'd lost sleep over this as well. That had to be a good sign that he was taking this seriously.

"He doesn't have a dad, well I mean obviously he does since I'm talking to you, but he doesn't have anyone currently in that role in his life."

"You're not married?"

Kia scoffed. "Not even close."

"That's good."

She raised her eyebrow and looked at him.

"Well, not good exactly. I just meant good that meeting me won't change too much for him that way."

"Oh, it'll definitely change a lot."

"No, of course." He huffed out a loud breath. "I meant. Fuck, I don't really know what I meant."

Kia smiled. "I know what you meant."

"Maybe you could tell me a little about Max and that would help."

Talking about her son was something she could easily do. She pulled out her phone and swiped at her photos. She opened the Max folder where she kept her favorite pics of her son and slid it across the table to Jeff. "That's him. As you can see, he's a bit of a clown. He's always being silly and trying to make people laugh."

"Yeah, I noticed that about him at practice. He's a funny kid."

Kia smiled. "He is."

Jeff swiped through a couple of photos, then laughed. "This is a great shot."

Kia leaned over, looked at the screen, and giggled. "That was Halloween. He wanted to go as my coworker Viper."

Jeff's eyes widened. "You have a coworker named Viper?"

She waved her hand absently. "Stupid nickname. He's very sweet." She looked at the photo of Max, covered in temporary tattoos. "Viper made him his own little fake tattooing machine. Max wanted those fake sleeves you can buy, but they don't come that small, so we had to improvise."

Jeff zoomed in on the screen so he could see the various fake tattoos better. "Why does he have so many on his face and neck? Does your coworker really have that many?"

Kia shook her head. "No, not really. He definitely has some, but nothing like that." She giggled again. "It was funny. You should have seen how horrified Viper was when he saw Max. Changes the perspective a little on how you see yourself when you can see it through a child's eyes. No more scary face tats for Vipe."

"He's seriously not tattooing his face anymore because of this?"

"No, no, I'm sure he'll still do more, but not scary ones. The scary ones are getting tucked away on other body parts."

Jeff looked up from the phone and directed his full attention at her. "You're a tattoo artist now?"

"I am, yeah."

"You didn't have any of those when we met." He pointed to the tattoos on her arms.

"Nope, I sure didn't."

"What made you go into that? I thought you were going to college." He winced. "Sorry, that sounded less judgmental in my head."

"It's fine." She glanced at the flowers on her forearm. Her eyes instantly seeking Max's baby footprint surrounded by various flowers for each of her nieces and nephew. The footprint had been the first tattoo she'd gotten after Max was born. "I was in college but had to drop out when I had Max. I couldn't afford to go to school and be a single mom. Gotta pay the bills."

"Shit, I'm sorry."

"Nothing to be sorry for. It all worked out the way it was supposed to. We'd had this tattoo artist come and guest lecture in one of my classes and they were willing to give me a job." She smiled to herself as she remembered how excited she'd been to have the opportunity to work around art in any capacity. "It was amazing. They let me bring Max to work with me when I came in to clean before the shop opened. Then, as he got a little bit bigger, I worked my way into an apprentice role. They were cool. They let me work my own hours around what worked best for Max."

"That's awesome. I'm glad you had them." He leaned forward and put his forearms on the table.

"They were amazing. And tattooing allowed me to continue my art. Over time, I fell in love with it. And I'm really good at it." Before she'd left Tucson, she'd won several tattooing competitions and been featured in a couple of magazines. That was how she'd met Viper. She'd kicked his ass in a competition.

"When did you move to San Diego?"

"Last year. My sister and her family have been here for a few years and were always trying to get me to move out with Max so we could be closer to his cousins. Then last year I had the opportunity to come out as a guest artist and I clicked with the shop, and Max and I decided to stay."

He shook his head. "You've been here a year and if it hadn't been for Max liking T-ball, I never would have even known he existed."

"I know. The world works in mysterious ways."

"Does your sister help you out a lot with Max? Is that who normally picks him up from camp?"

"No, that's Chelsie, his daycare provider who normally picks him up. My sister Vika works full time, but she helps on the weekends and evenings if I have to work."

"Do you work a lot of weekends?"

"I try not to work too much on the weekend. It's a bit tricky sometimes since the shop doesn't open until eleven every day, so since I want to be with Max, it limits my availability to work a bit."

Jeff shifted in his chair. "And you can afford to work part-time as a single mom?"

Her spine stiffened. "I make decent money tattooing if that's what you're asking. Do we live someplace fancy? No. But I thought it was more important to make less money and be there for Max while he's young. So I made a choice."

Jeff held up his hands. "I wasn't trying to judge you, Kia, honestly. I don't know how you've been doing it as a single mom. I give you all the credit in the world."

"Thanks. Sorry I got defensive." She drew her lips tight. "I work really hard to be a good mom to Max and I know to the outside world sometimes my choices don't seem obvious, but every decision I ever make is with Max in mind."

Jeff reached across the table and squeezed her hand. "I wasn't doubting that at all, Kia."

"Okay." She pulled her hand away from his and placed it on her lap. "My parents aren't the biggest fans of my career, so I can be a little defensive of it sometimes."

"I've got no problem with your career. Certainly not my place to judge." His forehead wrinkled. "Why would your parents not like your career? You're an artist and you get to do art every day. Isn't that the dream?"

She laughed roughly. To her? Yes. To her parents? Not even close. "My parents think I'm basically living a thug life. They're old school, conservative, super religious. Not big fans of body adornment of any kind." She looked at her arms and smiled sadly. "To my parents, only criminals have tattoos."

"Seriously? In this day and age?"

"I know, right? It's strange, but that's how they feel. That's a big part of why I moved from Tucson. It's hard if the people who are supposed to be your support system don't agree with your life choices."

"Understandable. Are you and your sister close?"

"I'd be lost without her." Vika and her husband had been there for her in a way her parents hadn't been. Until she'd moved to San Diego, she hadn't realized just how much she'd been floundering trying to do things on her own. Back in Tucson, she hadn't wanted to ask her parents for help with anything. A simple pick up or drop off was accompanied by a lecture about her life choices and parenting. When she'd moved to San Diego, Vika had immediately offered to take Max in the evenings or weekends so she could work.

"That's nice." He pulled the sugar container closer to him and reorganized the packages. "What does she think about you meeting with me?"

"Um..." How was she supposed to answer that? Her sister thought she was an idiot if she didn't hit him up for child support ASAP. Hell, Vika had texted her the name of a lawyer and a bunch of links to sites discussing Jeff's salary and California law around child support.

And...yes, she knew he should help her out, but there was no way she was talking about that today, no matter what Vika thought.

Jeff stopped fiddling with the sugar packets and focused on her. "She's not happy about you finding me?"

"I wouldn't say that. She's um... she's curious how this will all play out. What kind of role you might want in Max's life?"

"I want to be a part of his life."

"What does that mean?"

"Honestly, I don't know. I've had like a day to process this all." He scrubbed his hand over his face. "I'm not going to lie. It's a lot."

And that was why she wasn't going to discuss child support or anything else yet. "Understandable." It was a lot for her too, so she could only imagine what this was like for him. "So we'll get the paternity test and go from there?"

"Yeah."

Jeff hung up the phone with his lawyer and dropped onto the sofa. The DNA results were back, and Max was definitely his son. Not that he'd ever really had any doubt, but somehow, hearing his lawyer say it out loud, it landed a little different.

He ran his hand across his face. How was this supposed to work? He didn't know the first thing about raising a kid. Sure, he'd had a great role model with his dad, but they were totally different men. His dad had a 9-5 Monday to Friday job. There was nothing traditional about playing ball. He was gone for huge chunks of time during the season. He'd barely be around. How would a little kid understand that? His heart pounded in his chest, and he rubbed against the knot that was forming in the middle of his sternum. How was he supposed to navigate this? How did he want to navigate this?

He pictured Max. The kid was hilarious. Every week, the little guy came up with the craziest stories and was always making everyone laugh. He smiled to himself. He'd been the same kind of clown when he was little. Did he get that from him?

Jesus. Max was his son. He was a dad. Well, not yet he wasn't. At the moment, he was a sperm donor, but make no mistake, he was going to be a father to his son. To do anything less would be disrespectful, not only to Max, but to his own parents as well. Nothing was more important than family.

His lawyer had rambled off a bunch of shit about custody agreements and child support that he probably should have listened to. But his mind was still processing the reality of the fact that he had a kid.

A kid he barely knew.

He grabbed his phone and pulled up Kia's phone number. He dialed, then waited while the number rang. Her voicemail kicked on.

Hi you've reached Kia. The best way to reach me is to send me a text, but if you don't want to do that leave me a message and I'll call you back when I can.

He hung up the phone without leaving a message. He pulled up the messaging app to send her a text.

> **Jeff:** *Hey Kia, it's Jeff. Your voicemail says to send a text so…*

> **Jeff:** *I just spoke to my lawyer. He got the DNA results back and no surprise,*

*I'm Max's dad. I was hoping we could
set up a time for me to meet him.*

Jeff: *Well I know we've already met
but you know what I mean.*

He eyed the text messages and winced. Yeah, real cool
Smitty. He was off to a great start on the first impressions
that he'd be a responsible adult who could look after her
kid. His kid. Fuck, their kid. He dragged his hand across
his face again. Then grabbed his phone and fired off one
last text.

Jeff: *Let me know your schedule.
Mine's flexible so I'll make anything
work. Text me back.*

He looked at the message again. When would she reply? This was painful. There was no way he could just sit
around and wait for her to text him back.

He pulled up the group text with his friends.

Jeff: *I need to workout, who's up for a
run or the gym or anything?*

Instantly, his phone buzzed with a reply. His heart
pounded. Was it Kia? He sighed when he saw it wasn't her.

Ryan: *I could run*

Gonzo: *Screw that I'm not running.
You bastards always want to do hills*

Ryan: *Don't be a pussy. We can get lunch at the top of the hill*

Pete: *And beer?*

Gonzo: *I could run for beer*

Jeff grinned as he watched his friends' text back and forth as they figured out plans. This was exactly what he needed to take his mind off Max.

Jeff: *Usual spot in 30?*

Ryan: *Done*

Gonzo: *Yep*

Pete: ▢

Jeff wandered into his bedroom and changed into his gym clothes. The phone pinged on the mattress where he" dropped it. It was probably just the guys but still his heart jumped.

Kia: *How" Sunday afternoon?*

Jeff: *That works. Just tell me where and when and I"l be there.*

Kia: *2:00pm at my place? I"l text you the address*

Jeff: *Sounds good. Looking forward to it.*

He watched the screen as dots displayed, showing an incoming text. Then they disappeared. Several minutes later, the dots started again. The incoming text from Kia simply had an address. Great. Did that mean she wasn'' looking forward to it? She was? Or maybe she was as wigged out by all this as he was.

Jeff: *Thanks, see you Sunday.*

He flopped back on the mattress and groaned. He needed to become a whole lot more chill before Sunday.

Pushing himself off the bed, he grabbed his phone and wallet and headed downstairs. Thank god for the boys. A run, followed by some beers, would hopefully get his head in a better place, so he didn't make a complete ass of himself come Sunday.

CHAPTER SIX

Sunday afternoon, Jeff sat in his car and stared at the small house in front of him. He looked at the address again. Nothing about this house said Saskia to him. This place was well maintained but nondescript. There was no personality to the house. No porch furniture, no toys in the yard. Nothing that said anything about the people who lived inside.

He glanced down the road at the neighboring homes. It wasn't the best area of town, but the houses on this particular street looked well cared for. He hoped that meant it was relatively safe. He hated the idea of Saskia and Max living in a dangerous area.

He shook out his hands to relieve the nerves. He was meeting his son. Kia had said she'd prepare Max, but what did that mean exactly? Would he be happy that Jeff was his dad? Would he be disappointed? His heart pounded in his chest. What the hell was he supposed to say to the kid? He was a mess.

The front door of the house opened, and Kia walked out onto the front step. Guess he was done hiding out in his car. Opening the car door, he eased out of the vehicle. "Hey." He raised his arm in a wave.

"I was wondering how long you were going to sit out here." Kia flipped her long brown hair off her shoulder as she walked down the steps and onto the walkway that led from her door to the street.

"Sorry. I'm nervous." He pushed open the gate. "How's Max doing with all this?"

"Same as you, I think. Nervous. Excited." She stopped in front of him. "He's scared you won't like him."

"What? Why wouldn't I like him?"

"I don't know. You're a pretty big deal to him." She raised her shoulder and dropped it. "He said he's not the best on the team, and what if you wished Darnell was your kid instead?"

"Darnell?" He waved his hand. "Nah, he's a try-hard. Max is by far the coolest kid on the team."

Saskia smiled. "I agree. You ready?"

He grabbed her arm to stop her from walking away. "Saskia. Is he disappointed I'm his dad? I mean, I don't know what you've told him before about me and..."

"Call me Kia."

"Right, sorry, I know that. I'm just nervous and—"

"Relax, Jeff. This is new for both of you. It'll take some time for you both to feel your way around each other."

She patted his hand on her arm. "I hadn't really talked much about his dad. I told him we'd lost touch before he was born, and I didn't know where to find you. Now I've found you, and of course, you want to be in his life now that you know he exists."

"Okay." He took a deep breath.

"Jeff, don't make me regret introducing you two, please. It will break his heart if he meets his dad, and you don't honestly want to be in his life."

"Kia, I want to be here. I don't know how this is all going to play out, but I want to make it work."

A big truck pulled up to the curb behind his vehicle.

"Seriously?" Kia muttered, then stormed toward the vehicle.

A muscle-bound guy got out of the truck and tried to wrap his arm around Kia's waist. She pushed against the man's chest. Judging from the body language, she was not too happy the guy was here.

Jeff didn't even bother trying to cover the fact that he was checking out the other guy. Seriously? That's the kind of guy Kia went for now? With the souped-up truck, track pants and backwards hat. Jesus, was his ball cap pulled down over his ears? *Come on, Kia, really?*

Kia turned and the Hat Guy followed her into the yard. "Jeff Smith, meet Austin Beck."

Jeff stuck out his hand. "Nice to meet you."

Hat Guy shook his hand and squeezed harder than necessary in some ridiculous big dick display. What a prick. Jeff squeezed back harder until the guy winced.

Kia raised her eyebrow at him, and he shrugged. Maybe her boyfriend shouldn't swing his dick if he didn't have the goods to back it up.

"I take it you're the boyfriend." Jeff stared pointedly at Hat Guy.

"Yeah, I am."

"Cool. But didn't really think we needed an audience for today." He looked at Kia. "Is this what Max wants?"

"No. Austin isn't staying. He just stopped by on his way to the gym."

"Ah, got ya." Jeff stuck his hands in his pockets and rocked back on his heels as he stared down Kia's boyfriend. Dude was obviously feeling insecure, but if he was reading Kia right, this wasn't the way for Austin to stake a claim.

"I'm not staying. I'm a big Hawks fan and just wanted to say hello."

"Right." Jeff watched the byplay between Kia and her boyfriend. Were they serious? If they were, that meant this guy was going to be around a lot, so they'd have to figure out a way to get along for Max's sake.

Kia had mentioned a boyfriend, but the fact the guy felt the need to stop by and introduce himself suggested he didn't think their relationship was casual. A little niggle of regret crawled down his spine. He'd be lying if he said he still wasn't attracted to her. But it was probably for the best she was in a relationship. Hooking up would have complicated things, anyway.

The front door popped open, and Max peeked his head out the door.

Jeff glanced at Kia, then squared his shoulders and walked toward the front door. "Hey, Max."

"Hi, Smitty." Max ducked his head shyly. "Um, I mean..."

"It's cool, bud. We got time to figure out what you want to call me."

Max nodded. "Kay. You want to come in and see my room?"

"I'd love to." He glanced over his shoulder at Kia and Austin. "Austin, nice to meet you. Kia, we'll be inside." He rubbed the top of Max's head. "Lead the way, little man."

He followed Max into the house, past a cozy living room and down the hall. Max wandered into a room with bunk beds along one wall. The floor was littered with Legos. Jeff kneeled and picked up a blue piece of Lego. "So, you like to build stuff?"

"Yeah." Max dropped on the floor beside him and picked up a red Lego.

"You want to build something?" Jeff asked.

"Okay." Max scooped up a big green rectangular base piece. "Why's stupid Austin here?"

How the hell was he supposed to answer that one? "I'm not sure, buddy. I think he wanted to talk to your mom."

Max slammed the piece of Lego onto the base. "He always wants to talk to my mom."

He had a feeling he was walking into a minefield with this conversation. Treading carefully, he said, "You don't like when Austin comes over?"

"No, he's stupid."

"Are you allowed to say that word?"

Max rolled his eyes. "No, but he is."

"Well, I don't know the guy, but your mom seems like she's a pretty good judge of character, right?"

"Yeah."

"So maybe you just haven't gotten to know him very well yet."

Max shrugged but didn't say anything. He just stared down at his green base.

Well, this was off to a great start. They hadn't been together for five minutes and already they'd run out of things to talk about. Jeff scanned the mountain of Legos and smiled when his gaze landed on a Lego baseball bat. "You want to build a baseball stadium?"

Max's head lifted and a grin spread across his face. "Yeah, a really big one, as big as my house."

Jeff eyed the giant pile of Legos on the floor. "We might need to go to the store for more pieces."

Max giggled. "Yep."

"Good thing I brought my credit card."

The little boy giggled again, and Jeff felt it like a shot directly to his sternum. "Good thing." Max pushed a pile of green bases toward him. "Build."

"I'm on it." Never in his wildest dreams had he expected spending a Sunday playing with Legos to feel like this. It should be boring playing with a kid's toy, but he found himself wanting to build the most elaborate stadium just to see the look on Max's face.

They'd just joined a couple of base pieces together when Kia walked in. "What are you guys building?"

"A giant baseball stadium. It's a good thing he brought his credit card," Max gushed.

Kia laughed. "Oh yeah, why's that?"

"Cuz we're gonna have to go to the store." Max looked over at him for confirmation.

"Absolutely. We don't have nearly enough pieces to build a life-sized stadium."

Kia's eyes widened. "Yeah, that's not happening. You can build the biggest stadium you can with the pieces you have."

"But mom!" Max groaned.

"Don't ah mom me." Kia sat on the floor. "Now, do you want some help?"

"Yeah." Max pushed pieces toward his mom.

CHAPTER SEVEN

HAD IT REALLY ONLY been a week since he'd found out he had a son?

Jeff parked his car in front of Kia's small house. He eyed the neighboring houses. Newly planted small planters sat on the front stoop of Kia's place filled with colorful flowers, making it look homey. A forgotten soccer ball lay on the front lawn. The yard looked different from the first time he'd been here. Like maybe she'd cleaned it up for the first meeting and now she'd didn't need to bother. He found the lived-in look comforting.

He pushed open the front gate and smiled as he looked at the chalk drawings along the path leading to the house. Max's stick figures intertwined with Kia's more elaborate artwork. The two blending into each other seamlessly, much like mother and child.

The first couple of visits with Max had gone well, all things considered, but they were strangers figuring out their way. It wasn't fair, but he was jealous of the ease and comfort between Kia and Max.

He put a hand against his stomach. Nausea warred with excitement in the depths, making him regret the breakfast he'd eaten. He could face down a hundred-mile-an-hour fastball with no thought, but the idea of spending time alone with a five-year-old made him break out in a cold sweat. What if they went out today alone and Max didn't have fun? Maybe he should see if Kia wanted to go with them. Maybe it was too soon to go out by themselves. He glanced at the elaborate chalk snake that curled around trees and cars on the sidewalk. He needed to nut up. There was no way Kia would let him take Max out alone if she didn't think Max would be okay.

He jogged up the three steps to the front door and rapped on the screen door. After several seconds, Kia pulled the door open and his stomach tensed again. Except this time it had nothing to do with Max. Would he ever get used to his body's reaction to her? How could a woman look that good in yoga pants and a baggy t-shirt? Her chestnut hair was half-in-half-out of some kind messy bun, making it look like she'd just rolled out of bed and damn if he didn't want to mess her all the way up.

A warm smile spread across her face as she pushed open the screen door. "Thank God, you're on time. Max has been ready to go for the past hour. I was just about ready to force him to organize the Tupperware cupboard, so he'd stop bugging me about the time."

He chuckled. "Ah, I see how it is, child labor to instill order among the chaos."

Kia's amused laughter rang out as she threw her hands in the air. "Gotta do what you gotta do. Just you wait, you'll see." She stepped away from the door. "Come on in." Turning, she yelled, "Max, your dad is here."

The sucker punch that hit him in the gut every time he heard himself called dad landed hard. Running footsteps sounded down the hall a moment before Max barreled around the corner. "You're here," he whooped.

And damn if that sucker punch didn't hit even harder than the last. "I am. You still want to hang out with me today?"

"Yeah," Max scoffed, like the idea he'd changed his mind was ludicrous.

Kia scooped up a toy car from the middle of the living room rug. "Don't forget you gotta clean up your stuff before you go."

"Ah mom, I'll clean it later," he whined.

"Nope, you know the rule. My ears turn off when that tone comes out of your mouth. So if you want me to hear anything you gotta say, it has to be said in your normal voice."

Max huffed, but when he spoke, the whiney tone had left and in its place was his normal childlike voice. "Can you help me, please?"

Kia grinned at Max. "Absolutely." She crouched and began picking up pieces of Lego from the floor. Max scooped up a car from under the coffee table. Unable to stand and do nothing while the other two cleaned, Jeff bent and grabbed the corner of a piece of plastic that stuck out from under the sofa.

"You don't have to help clean up."

"Yeah, I do," he replied.

Kia glanced up at her from her position, kneeling on the floor. "Thank you."

His dick instantly surged to life as he looked down at her. Not cool.

It's not like Kia was doing anything remotely seductive. She was picking up toys. There was a kid in the room. What the hell was wrong with him?

He spun around, looking for something else to pick up just to stop his dick from getting other ideas. If Kia had any clue he thought about her like that she wouldn't be so eager to have him in her house. He mentally berated himself for thinking of her that way. Yes, the woman was gorgeous, and kind and sexy as shit, but she was dating someone, and if that didn't instantly put her off limits, the fact she was Max's mom should.

This new relationship was precarious at best. The last thing he needed to do was screw things up by making her uncomfortable.

With the last of the toys cleaned up, he sat back on his heels and surveyed the room. He didn't have a lot of experience with kids, but watching Kia maneuver Max so effortlessly made him realize just how much he still had to learn. Hell, he'd just assumed Max didn't help clean up. Isn't that why Knight was complaining about needing a new housekeeper, because his wife said she didn't have time to look after the kids and clean?

It sure made sense to him they'd need a housekeeper. He didn't know how Kia managed everything as a single mom. He'd seen the schedule on the fridge. Between taking Max everywhere he needed to go, working, getting groceries, and cooking, cleaning seemed like the last thing she should have time for. Maybe that's why Max helped.

Turning to Max, he watched as the little boy shoved the last of the Legos in the box and snapped the lid on. Max pressed his hands against the edge of the bucket. Jeff bit back a grin as he watched the kid push the bucket of toys across the floor like he was running a football drill. When the bucket thumped against the wall. Max stood up and surveyed his work.

"You ready to head out?" Jeff asked.

"Yeah." He zoomed over to the front door and grabbed a blue sneaker.

"What about your backpack?" Kia asked.

"Oh, yeah." Max hopped off the floor and zipped down the hallway to his room. A second later, he was back with a Marvel backpack slung across his shoulder.

Jeff eyed the stuffed backpack. What the hell was in there? They were only going out for the afternoon. What could the kid possibly need?

He glanced over at Kia, who smirked at him as if to say, just you wait. Christ, maybe he wasn't ready for this.

"What's in the backpack, bud?" he asked.

"Uh..." Max's brow wrinkled as he thought. "Sunscreen, snacks, toys, books, toilet paper."

"Toilet paper?" Jeff blinked at Max, then looked over at Kia, who shrugged. What the hell was he signing on for here? "Why do you need toilet paper?" He was equal parts intrigued and terrified about what the answer might be.

"Cuz you never know?" Max replied.

"What do you mean cuz you never know?" Jeff asked.

Max stared at him in confusion. "Well, you never know when you might need toilet paper."

"True, but I promise there are bathrooms everywhere we're going today." Pleased with himself, Jeff smiled. That should ease Max's mind a little.

Max placed his hand on his hip and stared him down. "But can you promise they have toilet paper?"

Okay, the kid had a point. "No. I assume they will, but no, I can't promise."

Max shrugged. "I better bring it."

"It's always better to be prepared," Kia agreed.

He looked over at her and once again was struck by how damn beautiful she was. Her eyes sparkled with humor as she looked at Max, then back at him.

"Agreed. I'll put some in my car later, so I always have some."

"We got lots." Max dropped his bag and flew back down the hall. He returned a moment later with a roll of toilet paper in his hand. He stopped in front of Jeff and thrust the roll at him.

Smothering a laugh, Jeff looked at Kia. She covered her mouth as she giggled. "Thanks Max." He took the roll in his hand and held it out to Kia in acknowledgment.

"I think you're all set now," she said.

Max slipped on his other shoe and stood back up. Jeff grabbed the backpack off the floor. Weren't there like weight rules about kids' backpacks? This thing weighed a ton. He eyed the offending bag. The kid probably had a Swiss army knife in here somewhere too. There was being prepared and then there was this. Maybe they didn't trust him as much as he'd thought.

Kia smirked at him, then sighed. "He's on a boy scout kick at the moment and I think we've watched every kid's movie ever made about wilderness preparedness, so he likes to be ready."

"We aren't going into the woods."

Kia smirked. "You're going out in the city. It's a jungle out there as well."

He laughed. "True enough, thus the TP."

"Exactly," she chuckled. She stepped up to Max and scooped him into a hug. "Have fun. Listen to your dad."

"I will."

"I'll have him home by five," Jeff said as he opened the front door. He glanced back over his shoulder at Kia. He was surprised by how badly he wanted to ask her to come with them. Because he was scared to be alone with Max or he just wanted to spend time with her, he couldn't say.

His phone pinged in his pocket. Pulling it out, he glanced over at Max. The little boy rolled his eyes. "Is it Mom again?"

"Let's see?" He flipped the phone over and saw Gonzo's name on the screen. "No, it's just one of the guys on the team."

"Which one?"

"Gonzo."

Max grinned. "He's funny."

"Yeah, he can be." He could also be a royal pain in the ass. "The guys are going for lunch and wanted to know if we wanted to go with them."

"Really?" Max's eyes lit up. "I could come?"

"Yeah, they're pretty excited to meet you."

Max's forehead crinkled. "But I met them already."

"True, but that was as a player and coach. This is meeting you as my son, so that's different."

Max's head bobbed up and down. "Yeah, different."

Jeff smiled. Looking at Max now, it seemed impossible that he hadn't immediately recognized him as his son. It was like looking at photos of himself as a child. The resemblance was uncanny. And if he was being honest with himself, it freaked him out a little. He barely knew the kid and yet they were connected to each other for the rest of their lives.

He ruffled the top of Max's head. "Do you want to go for lunch with the guys, or you want to do our own thing?"

"Lunch with the guys," Max whooped and jumped in the air.

Jesus, the kid was loud. Laughing, he shook his head as he watched Max race to gather up all his toys. "We've got time, Max, no rush."

"What if they eat without us?"

"They won't."

Max wandered over and stopped in front of him.

From his place seated on the ground, Jeff looked up slightly and noted the worry clouding Max's eyes. "What's the matter?"

"What if they don't like me as your kid?" he whispered.

Jeff's chest tightened. He pushed up so he was kneeling at eye level with Max. "They're gonna love you. I mean, how could they not? You love baseball as much as they do."

Max nodded. "Yeah, I do."

"I know, plus I showed them pictures of the Lego stadium we built, and they thought that was the coolest thing they'd ever seen."

"They did?" Max's eyes widened.

"Yeah, and we need another guy to round things out in the group. We have an even number, and we need someone who can be a tiebreaker."

"What's a tiebreaker?"

"That's the deciding vote."

Max's lips tightened and he frowned. "Kids can't vote."

"When you're out with the guys, you do. For example, let's say we need to decide on what kind of pizza to order and I want pepperoni and Gonzo wants Hawaiian. You get to vote which one you want and that's the one we have to get because you broke the tie."

Max's forehead wrinkled. "Why don't you just get half and half like Mom does?"

Jeff smiled. "Because we aren't as smart as your mom. Bad example. Okay, how about this? We are going to watch a football game. Ryan and I want to sit at the 50-yard line, but Gonzo and Pete want to sit in the end zone. You get to break the tie."

"I want to sit with you," Max tells him.

"You're sitting with me regardless of what you pick because we're all going to sit together either way."

"Oh." Max chewed on his lip as he thought about the question. "Which seats are better?"

"I think the 50-yard line is better."

"Okay, then we'd sit there."

"Nice. That would be a good choice." Jeff began cleaning up. "Although if we're going to a football game with friends, there isn't really a bad choice."

He eyed Max as the little boy watched him clean. "Grab your stuff," he told the kid.

"I don't want to," Max complained.

What the hell? That wasn't an option. Kia always made it look so effortless for Max to help. He eyed the kid again. "Are you paying me to clean?" Jeff asked.

Max frowned. "No."

"Exactly, so how about you help out, otherwise we won't be going anywhere."

"But you like to clean," Max said.

"I definitely don't like cleaning." He laughed. "This will go a lot faster with both of us helping. Plus, if you want to hang with the big boys you gotta play like the big boys, and unfortunately, that means cleaning up your stuff."

"Okay." Max bent over and gathered up his books.

Huh, that was easier than expected. Maybe he was going to be alright at this parenting thing after all.

With the car loaded, they drove across town to the Greasy Spoon, which made the best burgers and shakes in town.

Max looked up at the restaurant and chewed his lips. "I've never been here before."

"That's part of the fun of going out with the boys. You get to try new things."

"What if I don't like it?" Max asked.

The phone rang in his cupholder, and he scooped it up. He held the phone up for Max to see. "It's your mom."

He hit the button on the steering wheel to answer the phone. "Hello?" he said.

"Hi, Mom," Max yelled from the backseat.

"Hi, Max. You having fun?"

"Yeah. Mom, am I allowed to eat at the... what's this place called again?"

"The Greasy Spoon," Jeff replied.

"That sounds disgusting," Kia said.

"So no?" Max asked.

"No baby, if that's where your dad wants to eat, that's fine. Are there any vegetables on the menu?"

"There's fries," Jeff told her.

"Awesome," Kia mumbled. "Have fun."

"How many more times can I expect you to call before we get home?" Jeff teased.

"Um...not many?"

"You don't sound too sure about that answer."

Kia sighed. "Sorry. I have control issues."

"It's all good, Kia. You're welcome to join us for lunch." He couldn't imagine how hard this must be for her. She'd gone from being a single mom who made every decision to trying to navigate fitting in time and responsibilities for a dad who just showed up on the scene.

"No, she can't," Max chirped. "It's guys lunch."

"Oh sorry," Kia said. He could hear the laughter in her voice even without seeing her face. "I wouldn't want to cut in on that. Have fun at lunch. Try to eat something that resembles a vegetable at lunch."

"Ketchup it is," Jeff joked.

"Har-har, funny man," Kia said.

"Bye, Kia," he sang.

"Bye, Mom," Max yelled.

"Bye."

Jeff hit the button to disconnect the phone and spun in his seat. "You ready to do this?"

"Yeah." Max nodded in agreement.

Inside the restaurant, he scanned the tables, looking for his friends. Spotting them at a flat top by the window, he grabbed Max's hand and wove them through the tables.

"Hey," he called out as they approached.

"Maxie," Gonzo called out. "Glad you could make it."

Max dipped his head and smiled shyly.

Jeff eyed the high bar stools and the cement floor and winced. Was it safe to put a kid on one of those chairs? Did they need a booster seat or some kind of seatbelt situation? Before he decided, Max scrambled up the rail of the chair and plopped onto the vacant seat beside Gonzo.

Guess that settled it.

"Are you and your dad having fun today?" Ryan asked.

"Yeah, we went to the beach and the park and then this afternoon we're doing bumper boats," Max told them.

"Bumper boats? Wow, can we come?" Ryan asked.

"Okay," Max replied.

Ryan grinned back at Max, then looked at Jeff and shrugged. "Sorry man, I know it's Daddy son time, but it's bumper boats."

He snorted. "No problem."

"What's that?" Max pointed to a basket in the middle of the table with a series of colored balls.

"That's a game. Want me to show you?" Pete asked.

Max nodded.

Jeff leaned back in his seat as Pete pulled the wooden boards with an arm sticking up in the middle and began explaining the rules to Max.

"So, you gotta swing your string and get the hook on the end to grab hold of the one on the pole," Pete told him.

Max touched the little hook on the pole with his finger. "Hook it on here?"

"Yep."

Jeff looked around the restaurant, then back at the group. "Max, I need to go to the bathroom. You want to try, too?"

"No," Max shook his head.

"You should probably come with me and try, bud." Didn't kids have to pee like every five minutes?

"I'm good," Max replied as he whipped the string again and Gonzo weaved back to avoid being hit. It seemed Max's strategy was to swing the string as hard as possible and hope it grabbed onto the hook on one of its many back swings.

"You good staying here with the guys while I go?"

"Uh-huh." Max's eyes narrowed and he chewed his bottom lip as he stared at the game like he was willing the string to attach.

Jeff eyed his friends. "I'll be quick."

"No worries, we got him," Ryan reassured him.

Jeff eyed his son, surrounded by his friends. He was being ridiculous. Of course Max was safe with his friends.

"Okay, I'll be back in a minute. Order me a Coke and Max? You want chocolate milk? Juice?"

"Chocolate milk," Max said.

"Got it." Ryan nodded, then turned his attention back to the game.

The little boy threw his head back and laughed when his string almost hit Gonzo in the face again.

After a few seconds, Ryan looked back at Jeff. "You going?"

"Yeah." He stood up from the table, flicked a quick glance at Max, whose attention never wavered from the game. The kid wouldn't even notice he was missing.

After quickly taking care of business, he hurried back to the table. Max watched him walking up and began giggling. What was that about? Gonzo nudged Max's shoulder and his son fought to wipe the smile off his face. Jeff grinned as he watched Max bouncing in his chair. The kid was practically vibrating.

"What's going on?" he asked as he walked up.

"Nothing?" Gonzo replied.

Jeff continued to watch Max as he sat down. The moment his butt hit the seat, a deafening fart sound erupted from beneath him. Every person around them turned to stare.

Max erupted into a fit of laughter, and his traitorous friends all followed suit. Gonzo reached out and slapped a high-five on Max's hand. "Gross, Dad," Max snickered.

He eyed the group of women at the table beside him. The eldest woman glared at him like he shouldn't be let out in public.

At the look of pure joy on Max's face, he smiled and shook his head. Reaching underneath him, he pulled out the whoopee cushion and held it out to Gonzo. "This is yours I assume."

Gonzo blinked innocently. "I don't know what you mean."

"Right." Jeff stared at his friend.

"That was so funny. You let out the loudest fart ever, Dad."

"I didn't fart." He looked at the table of women and reiterated, "I didn't fart."

Max giggled. "Yeah, you did. That lady at the front door even heard you."

Fantastic. He shook his head and glared at his friends, who all wore varying degrees of amusement on their faces.

"Wait till I tell Mom." Max slapped his hand on his lap. "She'll think it's so gross." The little boy erupted into another fit of laughter.

That was just what he needed. Max telling Kia his friends gave Max a whoopee cushion in the middle of a busy restaurant. She'd been hesitant to let him take Max out alone at all and now he'd be going home with stories about the loud fart his dad let rip in a restaurant. He glared at Gonzo, then turned to Max. "Maybe we don't tell your mom?"

Max's forehead wrinkled. "But that's lying."

"No, I'm not saying lie to your mom. I'm just..." Shit, this was just getting better and better.

"I gotta pee," Max declared.

"But I just asked you if you had to go."

"I didn't have to go then." Max bounced on the seat. "I gotta go," he whined.

"You know what buddy, I gotta go too," Ryan stated.

"I could pee," Gonzo added.

Jeff pinned him with a glare. "No, you don't." He turned to Ryan. "You mind taking Max so I can talk to Gonz for a second?"

"Sure no problem." Ryan stood up from the table. "Alright Maxie, let's hit the head."

Max's nose wrinkled. "The head?"

"Yeah, you know the can, the john, the head."

Jeff scrubbed his hand over his face. "Can we maybe not teach him every slang for the bathroom on the first day?"

Ryan winced. "Sorry." He turned to Max and bowed slightly. "Maxwell, would you like to accompany me to the lavatory?" Ryan asked in the most ridiculous English accent he'd ever heard.

Max giggled. "You're funny. I just have to go pee."

Ryan chuckled. "Let's do it."

"I'll come too." Pete eyed Gonzo. "Sorry man, you're on your own."

Max jumped from the table and followed Ryan and Pete across the restaurant. As soon as he was out of earshot, Jeff turned to Gonzo.

"I can't believe you gave my kid a fucking whoopee cushion. I'm trying to get Kia to trust me with Max and you're over here having him make people fart in restaurants. That shit doesn't help, man."

"How does it not help? Kids are supposed to have fun uncles. That's like a whole thing."

"Fun uncles?"

"Yeah, you know every family has them. There's creepy Uncle Sal with the lazy eye who you're never quite sure if he's looking at your face or your boobs."

"Jesus, that's oddly specific," Jeff muttered.

Gonzo smirked. "And then there's cool Uncle Gonz who gives you whoopee cushions."

"Why are you Uncle Gonz and not just Gonzo exactly?"

He shrugged. "I want to be the cool uncle."

"Dude, you have like twenty siblings. Be their uncle."

"I have five siblings and none of them have kids. I want to be the cool uncle now," he whined.

"You're a loser."

"Loser? Or fucking coolest uncle ever?"

"I think we both know the answer to that." Jeff shook his head at his friend. They both knew the answer, but he was sure as shit they weren't thinking the same thing.

The sound of Max's voice drew his attention across the room. He smiled as he watched his son animatedly talking to Ryan and Pete. The trio wove their way back to the table.

Gonzo nudged his shoulder. "I'm sorry about the whoopee cushion, man. I thought it would be funny."

When they returned to the table, Max eyed the seat as he climbed up and frowned when he saw the empty chair. Disappointment etched across his face.

"It's fine," Jeff told Gonzo. Seeing the disappointment on his son's face, he understood why his friend had done the gag. The pure joy on Max's face when the cushion had gone off had been pretty incredible. Maybe Gonzo was right and it had been worth facing Kia's wrath.

Gonzo turned to Max. "Sorry buddy." He nodded to the table of women beside them. "I didn't think they'd be able to handle another explosive fart from our table while they're eating." He leaned over and stage whispered, "They'd probably make me pay for their dinner cuz they'd lose their appetite, and I'm saving my pennies for a house."

Max's forehead wrinkled. "You don't have a house?" He turned to Jeff. "He should stay with you, Dad."

Damn, the kid was cute. "No, he has a house, buddy. He's just looking at buying a different place."

Max turned to Gonzo. "How come?"

Gonzo leaned back in his chair and crossed his hands over his belly. "Well, now that's a story."

Pete groaned. "Don't get him started, Maxie."

"Why not?"

Jeff draped his arm over the back of Max's chair. "Because once he starts talking he doesn't shut up and I told your mom I'd have you home for dinner."

Max's eyes boggled open. "Can you really talk that long?" he asked Gonzo.

"You ain't seen nothing, kid." Gonzo rubbed his hands together. "Where to begin?"

CHAPTER EIGHT

Kia dumped out the load of laundry on the bed and began sorting. The doorbell rang. She eyed the clock. Max would be home any minute. She wandered to the front door and pulled it open. "Max, why'd you ring the bell?"

"Dad said he wasn't allowed to just barge into your house."

"True, but this is your house, so you don't ever have to knock, no matter who you're with."

"Okay." He glided past her and kicked his shoe off his foot. The sneaker smacked against the wall.

"Dude, easy," she warned, eyeing the dirty shoe mark on the wall.

"Sorry." Max grinned.

She shook her head. The kid wasn't sorry at all.

"So how was your day?" she asked.

"Good." Max dug into his backpack and pulled out a flat, round red object. "Look what Gonzo gave me."

Jeff groaned audibly beside her. She flicked a glance at him, and he mouthed sorry. Narrowing her eyes, she looked back at the object in Max's hand. "What is that?"

"A whoopee cushion." Max's eyes gleamed. "You shoulda heard dad's fart with it."

Turning, she raised her eyebrow at Jeff. "Seriously?"

He held up his hands, palm up. "First, it was Gonzo, not me, that set it up."

"Yeah, but you farted," Max said.

"Not helpful, buddy," Jeff grumbled.

"And just where did you let this giant ripper go?" she asked. At the mortification on Jeff's face, she couldn't help but smile. His cheeks turned pink as the blush worked its way up his face.

"In the restaurant."

She sputtered a laugh. "Oh God. That's awful."

"Are you seriously laughing?" he asked. "There was a table of women beside us. I think one of them gagged a little."

Max bent over, laughing. "Gonzo said next time we should have stink bombs too."

"No," Jeff growled, then turned to her. "Look, I know it's not great. I talked to my friends, and they understand why that wasn't appropriate."

"Relax, Jeff, it's totally fine. His cousins have taught him a lot worse."

Jeff visibly sagged beside her. "You're not mad?"

"No, of course not. It's a whoopee cushion. You didn't teach him how to rob a bank."

"Can dad stay for dinner?" Max asked.

"Um…" She eyed Jeff. Did he want to stay? "If he wants to, he can."

"What are you having?" He cocked his eyebrow and looked at her. "It's got to be something with vegetables, right?"

"Ha-ha, but yes, I'm making a stir-fry."

"Can I go play with Marco?" Max asked.

"Let me check with his mom and make sure they're home." Kia grabbed her phone and quickly fired off a text to Miriam.

"Who's Marco?" Jeff asked.

"He's the little boy next door."

"Nice. I didn't know you had a friend next door. That's cool."

"Yeah." Max bounced on his feet. "So can I go over?"

Kia glanced at her phone and saw the three little dots that showed Miriam was replying. When the text popped through, she fired off a quick reply, then said, "Yep, looks like you're ready. I'll walk you over."

"Can Dad do it?"

A jolt of annoyance slashed through her before she quickly masked it. It wasn't Jeff's fault that he was the shiny new parent. "Of course." She glanced at Jeff. "They live right next door." She pointed to the left side of the house. "Marco's mom is Miriam. I texted her we'd be right over, so she'll be waiting."

Jeff stared at her for several seconds, then his eyes warmed with sympathy. Somehow, he saw through the mask that most people didn't see.

"Alright, you got everything you need?" Jeff asked.

"Yeah." Max dropped onto the floor and slid his feet into his sneakers, then hopped back up.

She crouched so she was eye level with Max. "We're eating soon, so when I say it's time to come home, it's time to come home. No arguments. Deal?"

"Yeah." Max nodded in agreement.

"I mean it, Max." There was nothing worse than having the whiny kid who didn't listen. She'd learned how much she hated that when Max was little and had quickly learned if she set the stage ahead of time, she could usually avoid most of the conflict.

"I know, Mom," he groaned. Reaching up, he grabbed Jeff's hand. "Come on, Dad."

The two walked out the front door hand in hand. Weird emotions collided in her ribs. Jealousy, warmth, fear, happiness. How could she be feeling all of these things at once? Why did she feel threatened by Jeff's relationship with Max? That didn't make sense. She loved the idea of Max having a solid relationship with Jeff. Of Max having a strong male role model, he could turn to. From everything she'd seen from Jeff so far, Max was lucky to have him in his life, so why did she have this little niggle of jealousy? What kind of mother was jealous of the other parent? If this was happening to one of her friends, she'd say what she was feeling was normal, understandable even. But it didn't feel normal. It felt awful.

A few minutes later, Jeff lightly rapped on the screen door just before he pushed it open. He wandered into the kitchen and leaned against the kitchen counter. "Your neighbors seem nice."

"Yeah, Miriam is a good mom. I don't know how she does it with four kids. I struggle with just having Max."

"She's got four kids. By herself?"

She nodded. "I can't imagine. Her ex left before we moved in, so I never knew him."

"He doesn't see the kids?"

"Not that I'm aware of. From my understanding, he just decided one day he was done and walked out, never to be heard from again."

"Jesus," he muttered. "That's rough. Sounds like she's better off without him. Her kids deserve better than an asshole like that in their life."

"Yeah, they do." Guilt dragged across her chest. He was right. Kids deserved everything, and so far, that's what Jeff was trying to do with Max. He was the exact opposite of Miriam's ex. How Jeff was with Max was exactly what she'd always dreamed about for him.

"Can I help with anything?" He eyed the stack of vegetables she'd set on the kitchen counter.

"No, I'm good. You want a drink or anything?"

"Yeah, that would be great."

"Beer? Soda? Water?"

"Beer would be great."

She reached into the fridge and pulled out two long neck bottles, cracked the tops and slid one toward him.

"So how did it go today other than the whoopee cushion?" She leaned her butt against the counter and faced him.

"Good. It's different hanging out with him alone without you."

"How so?"

He scrubbed a hand through his hair. The movement drew her eye to the flex of his biceps, and she brought her bottle up to her mouth to distract herself. She shouldn't be looking at him like that. Okay yes, he was obviously a gorgeous man, but come on, ogling her baby daddy was such a cliche. Besides, she was dating Austin. And yes, maybe looking at Austin's arms didn't zap her lady bits the same way Jeff's did, but that was beside the point. The man was a professional athlete. Of course his body was fit.

He was paid to look after it. That was all this was, just an appreciation of the human form. Nothing more.

"You make it look so easy to do the whole mom thing. You're doing ten things at once and somehow you always are perfectly homed in on where Max is and what he's doing at every moment." He shook his head. "I was so conscious of what Max was doing I could barely function to drive my car. I don't know how you do it."

She slid a pepper out of the bag and set it on the chopping block. "Well, I'm glad I make it seem so effortless. I feel like I look like a hot mess most of the time."

"You definitely don't look like a mess," he mumbled.

Something about the tone of his voice made her look up. A flash of awareness sizzled between them. Quickly followed by guilt. God, what was she doing? She had a boyfriend. Jeff wasn't just some guy. He was Max's dad. Even thinking lusty thoughts about him complicated things.

"So—" He cleared his throat. "My parents are coming into town next weekend to meet Max."

Her head snapped up. "Excuse me?"

"Yeah. They're pretty stoked to be grandparents, and I've held them off as long as I can. Obviously, I'd like you to be there when they meet him, but I'd understand if you think that's weird or uncomfortable or whatever."

"Do your parents actually want to meet me?"

"Of course they do. Why wouldn't they?"

She picked up pieces of sliced pepper and dropped them into the bowl. "I don't know. I mean…" Pain lanced through her chest. How could Jeff's parents be so excited to be grandparents when hers had practically disowned her when she'd gotten pregnant?

Jeff stood up and walked closer to her. "You mean what? Why wouldn't my parents want to meet you?"

She sniffed as tears welled up behind her eyes. Shit. Her throat clogged as she tried to swallow.

He stepped in closer and tilted her chin up, forcing her to look at him. "Talk to me, Kia. What's going on in that head of yours?"

She sniffed. "Nothing. I just think it's cool that your parents want to get to know Max."

"Well yeah. First grandchild and all." He laughed. "They really want to meet you, too. I've told them all about what a great job you've done with Max. My mom says if he was anything like I was at that age, you deserve an award for handling it by yourself. She needed my dad and grandma to wrangle me under control."

"They don't hate me for getting pregnant and keeping him from you?" Her chest tightened with emotion.

"First, you didn't get pregnant alone, so they can't exactly be mad at you for that one. And second, I explained you tried to find me, but I'd moved."

She slapped her hand over her mouth. "Oh God, they know it was a one-night stand?"

"Well yeah, of course."

"Oh my god, I can't even imagine what they must be thinking of me." She could hear her mother's voice calling her shameful. Embarrassing. A slut. Tears welled in her eyes. God damn it, where had this come from? She'd gotten over all this shit with her family years ago. Or so she'd thought. Even the idea of meeting Jeff's parents and suddenly she was back in her family living room being told how ashamed of her they were. And every day in Tucson they reminded her. All that pain and fear suddenly swamped back to her, making the room spin.

"Hey, Kia." Jeff's voice cut through the noise in her head, and she blinked to clear her brain. Her gaze landed on Jeff's worried face.

She closed her eyes. Of course she had to have her little meltdown in front of him.

"Sorry," she muttered, trying to take a step away from him.

His hand clamped on her arm. "Nope." He held her still. "Talk to me. What just happened there?"

Clearing her throat, she looked around the room. Her gaze landed on a platter she'd bought at the dollar store for Max's first birthday. She'd painted it so it didn't look so plain. She hadn't wanted him to look back at his birthday photos and be embarrassed by how sparse everything looked. "Let's just say my family had a different reaction than yours to becoming grandparents."

"What do you mean?"

She cleared her throat again. "Um..." She pushed out a long breath. "My family is pretty conservative."

His finger traced the line of the tattoo on her forearm. "Yeah, you mentioned they weren't big fans of the direction your art went."

She snorted out a humorless laugh. "That's one way to put it." Needing to put some space between them, she picked up her bottle of beer and took a sip. "You want to sit?" she asked, gesturing toward the sofa.

"Sure." Jeff followed her over to the sofa and sat beside her.

Shoot, she'd been hoping he would sit in the opposite chair to give her a bit of breathing room, but it seemed he had other plans.

He tapped her knee. "Talk to me."

She dropped her head back and looked up at the ceiling. "My family isn't like yours."

"Okay." He waited.

"I told you I was a disappointment to them, what with getting pregnant and dropping out of art school."

"A little yeah."

"I have a complicated relationship with my parents." She tapped her hand nervously against her thigh. "In a nutshell, when I got pregnant with Max they kicked me out."

Jeff's brows knit together. "I thought you said they were your support system in Tucson."

"Yeah, they were sort of. Thus the move to San Diego." She waved her hand around the room. How was she supposed to explain a family like hers to someone like him? Someone whose parents would fly halfway across the country the minute they learned about their grandchild. "So um...like I mentioned, my parents kicked me out when I got pregnant. I dropped out of school and got a job, but occasionally I still needed some help from friends and my brother. When Max was about three years old, I got sick and ended up in the hospital for a few days."

"Jesus, Kia," Jeff muttered.

"It was fine." She tried to brush it off. "A little surgery, some antibiotics and rest, and I was good to go."

"A little surgery?"

"My appendix ruptured, and I got pretty sick because I didn't go to the hospital."

"What do you mean you didn't go to the hospital?" His eyes widened with horror.

She raised her eyebrow and looked at him. Had he not been listening about the whole single mom, dropout, struggling to make ends meet part of the story? "Insurance is expensive, so..." She shrugged. "Anyway, I asked my brother to take Max. He panicked and took him to my parents, who I hadn't spoken to in three years." Memories of that time assaulted her. It had been the most terrifying time of her life. "After that, we came to an agreement that they could babysit now and then, and I'd take Max to church." She ran her tongue along her teeth like she'd be able to clear the foul taste in her mouth. "Max and I spent a lot of time at church." She looked at the tattoos on her arms. "Unfortunately, it didn't take."

"Hang on. I feel like you're leaving a lot out here." Jeff shifted on the couch, so he was facing her fully.

She didn't want to tell him all this. She'd worked so hard to leave all that shit behind her. "God, this is—When I went to pick up Max from their house, they took one look at me, and my tattoos, and they didn't want to give him back."

Jeff's head snapped backwards. "What do you mean they didn't want to give him back?"

She rubbed a hand across her face. "It was a messed up time in my life."

"What does that mean?" Jeff asked. "Jesus, spit it out."

"To my parents getting pregnant was shameful—getting tattoos, unforgivable." She sighed. "I don't know how to explain this in a way that makes sense to someone on the outside."

"Try."

She rubbed her lips together. "I was a sinner, in league with the devil." She rolled her eyes. Even saying it out loud sounded stupid, but there it was. "My parents gave me an ultimatum. I could either let them help take care of Max or they'd report me to Child Protective Services."

"For what?" he snarled.

"Who knows? They could have made anything up, but..." She paused. Memories swarmed in. "It was a very real fear. It didn't matter that I hadn't done anything wrong. That I was a damned good parent. It would have been my word against theirs, and I couldn't afford to fight a custody battle against my own parents. So, I tried to keep the peace."

"Holy fuck, Kia."

"I know, right?" She scoffed. "So for about six months, I let them help a bit with Max. Thankfully, my hours were such that I didn't need to call them very often. They stopped by a couple times a week, berated me, and went on their way. Thankfully, this opportunity came up here, so I jumped at it."

"And your parents were cool with you leaving?"

"God, no, but what could they do? I'm an adult. Plus, Vika lives here, and they trust her not to let me run amok." She smiled to herself as she thought about her ferocious sister. She'd practically had to jump in front of Vika's car to stop her from killing their parents. "Moving here was the best thing I could have done for Max and I."

"Do you still talk to your parents?"

"Not really, no. They don't like to travel, and conversation isn't really our thing."

"Does Max talk to them?"

"Nah, he doesn't want to and according to my mom, one of my glaring faults is that I let him make his own decisions on things like hugs and spending time with people."

"How is that a fault?"

Her chest warmed at the support from Jeff. "You know children should be seen and not heard and all that stuff." She clicked her tongue. "They hate I don't make Max hug them when he sees them if he doesn't want to. And he usually doesn't want to. My mom and I got into quite a few fights about it. At first Max wanted to hug them just to keep them happy, then he didn't, so he doesn't have to."

"Good," Jeff declared. "Is it shitty to say I'm glad your parents don't live here?"

She laughed. "Nope, cuz I am too."

He nudged her with his knee. "I'm just going to lay it out here that your parents were wrong, Kia, really fucking wrong in how they treated you."

She nudged his knee back. "Thanks."

"I mean it. I've never met a better mother than you, and I had a pretty great one. If I could pick anyone to be my kid's mom, it would be you."

Her chest tightened and her eyes welled again, but this time it wasn't shame battling to get out through the tears. "Thank you," she whispered.

"I appreciate you telling me about your family. Your reaction to meeting mine makes a lot more sense now." He grabbed her hand. "You have nothing to worry about with my family. They would have loved you regardless because you gave them Max, but once they meet you, they'll love you because how could they not?"

"Damn it," she muttered as a tear escaped down her cheek.

"Come here." He wrapped his arm around her and pulled her into him. She rested her head on his shoulder, absorbing the strength of his body. "You don't have a single thing to worry about with me regarding Max. I'm so fucking grateful to you for everything." He pressed a kiss against the top of her head, and she stilled.

Had he just kissed her? Suddenly, it felt like the air had been sucked out of the room and she held her breath. Everything in her wanted to turn her head and look up at him. Instead, she forced herself to pull away. She shifted away and stiffly sat upright. "Thanks, I really appreciate you understanding."

Jeff cleared his throat. "Yeah, sure, no problem." He clapped his hands together. "So how about I help you cut up those veggies for dinner?"

"Can you be trusted to cut them evenly?" she teased. And just like that, the awkwardness that had been floating around them evaporated.

He bumped her with his hip. "Woman, I'm known for my precision."

"Oh, okay, hotshot. Let's see what you've got."

CHAPTER NINE

MAX BOUNCED ON HIS feet beside her in the kitchen.

"I'm staying all night at Dad's, and you aren't going to come get me early, right?"

She was thrilled that Max finally had a father in his life, but did he have to be so excited about spending the night with him? Glancing at him, she couldn't help but smile. Max was practically vibrating with excitement. Jeff was going to have his hands full tonight.

"Yes, you're staying all night just like we agreed." She rubbed the top of his head. "Now have a seat and eat your snack, otherwise your dad will think he has a hyena staying with him instead of a little boy."

Max giggled. "Oh Mom." He slid onto the chair and pulled his plate of apple slices and cheese string closer to him. The apple crunched as he took a bite. "Do you think he's excited for me to come over?"

"Swallow before you talk, bud. No one wants to see your food."

"But do ya?"

"Yes, sweetie, I think he's super excited to have you sleep over."

He threw another chunk of apple into his mouth and chewed rapidly. "When's he comin'?"

How many times had he asked this question today already? "He should be here in less than half an hour. So just enough time for you to eat your snack and brush your teeth."

Max ripped open his cheese string and instead of pulling it apart like he normally did, he took a huge bite.

"Max, relax, you've got time. You don't need to inhale your food. If you aren't ready when he gets here, he'll wait."

"But I gotta be ready. You said it's rude to make people wait. If you make plans, you should care enough to be on time." He shoved another bite of cheese into his mouth.

Well crap. That little life lesson had seemed like a good idea and now it was biting her in the ass. "That's true, but he's your dad, so it's a bit different. It's like when I say put your shoes on and you want to finish what you're doing. You still do it fast, but sometimes I have to wait a minute before you get your butt in gear."

He nodded thoughtfully. "Kay, but I shouldn't make him wait cuz it's still rude, right?"

"Yeah, it's still rude."

Max placed two slices of apple together into one big piece and bit them both in half. He grinned at her, and a piece of apple poked out of the hole where his teeth were missing. He smiled wider and pushed the piece back in his mouth through the hole. His eyes sparkled mischievously.

"Max, seriously, manners, dude."

He giggled and pushed the last two bites of apple into his mouth.

The doorbell rang, and Max let out an ungodly squeal. "I'm not ready." He jumped off his chair and raced toward the bathroom. "I gotta brush my teeth."

"Max, relax, he'll wait." Kia shook her head as she walked toward the front door. With her hand on the door-knob, she took one steadying breath, then pulled it open.

"Hey." Jeff smiled. "What was all the commotion?"

She rolled her eyes. "You're early, and Max isn't quite ready. So I was given specific instructions to make sure you wait for him."

Jeff laughed. "Where else am I gonna go?"

"Who knows?" She gestured for him to come inside. "He's super excited about this sleepover."

"Me too." Jeff stuck one hand in the pockets of his jeans, his other held a small paper bag. "I'm glad he's excited. I was a little nervous he'd change his mind."

"God, no. He's been talking about this nonstop." She glanced down the hallway when she saw a streak as Max dashed from the bathroom to his bedroom.

"Wow, he can really move."

Kia sucked in a breath when she looked at him. The way his eyes sparkled with amusement looked exactly the same as Max's did. Before this moment, she hadn't realized just how similar they looked. Previously, she'd always seen herself in everything Max did.

"You okay?" Jeff stepped toward her.

"Yeah, of course." She waved him off. "What's in the bag?"

Jeff glanced down at his hand and held out the bag to her. "It's for you. I don't know. I figured tonight might be hard for you and I wanted to let you know I'd be thinking of you so—"

She took the bag and opened it up and saw a pint of ice cream. He'd brought her comfort food. Why did he have to be so sweet? "Ice cream?"

"Yeah. What's better when you're having a tough night than that?"

She pulled the container out of the bag and read the label. "Netflix and chill'd?"

He shrugged. The sexy smirk on his face said he knew exactly what the term meant and had chosen the ice cream on purpose. "What?"

"Really?"

"Kia, get your mind out of the gutter," he teased. His blue eyes twinkled with amusement and a little heat as he looked at her. "It wouldn't be appropriate for me to offer you that kind of comfort. I figured ice cream was the next best thing. Besides, Max said you loved peanut butter, so I figured it was a double win."

His sweet gesture combined with the playful flirtation was exactly what she needed. How had Jeff known she'd be feeling out of sorts about the night ahead?

When her stare connected with his again, it was clear if the situation were different, it wouldn't be the ice cream either of them would want. She cleared her throat. This attraction between them could be trouble. Needing to put some space between them, she wandered into the kitchen to put the ice cream in the freezer. When she turned back around, Jeff had followed her. He rested his hip against the doorframe.

Kia took a deep breath to try to get her hormones under control. She just needed to focus on Max. "So what do you have planned for the day?"

"I thought we'd check out the science center." He rocked back on his heels. "I'd thought about Legoland since he's so into Legos and he's never been, but thought that might be something you wanted to do with him so—" He shrugged.

As a single mom, her budget didn't exactly extend to things like Legoland. She hated that Jeff could so easily give her son the things she couldn't. She winced. What the hell was wrong with her? She should be happy that her son would get to experience things she couldn't give him instead of being jealous. "Yeah, he'd love Legoland, but it's probably best to save that for a full day."

When she raised her head, she found Jeff watching her. After several seconds, he finally spoke, "Would you be interested in going with us one day?"

She mentally ran through her bank account. Could she swing it? If she picked up a few extra clients when Max was spending time with Jeff, she could probably make it work. "Maybe."

"My treat, since I'm the one asking you guys to go with me."

"I couldn't ask you to do that."

"You're not, I'm offering. I'd really like to go there with you both."

"Go where?" Max asked as he ran down the hall from his bedroom. He skidded to a stop in front of them.

Jeff winced, and he looked at her like he was unsure if he should answer.

"Your dad was talking about taking us to Legoland one day," Kia answered.

"Today?" Max's eyes widened.

"No, not today, buddy. We'd need a whole day to do that one."

"Tomorrow?" He pinned her with his pleading stare.

"I gotta work tomorrow, bud, so you're spending the afternoon with your cousins."

Max's shoulders dropped. "You always gotta work."

That comment may as well have been a knife in her stomach. She worked so hard to balance work and being a mom. Tattooing wasn't always the best hours since the shop didn't open till eleven. In order to not miss out on dinner and bedtime most nights, it meant she couldn't work full time. She'd sacrificed earning more money to be home more and still, sometimes, it didn't feel like enough. She crouched. "I know, honey, but I gotta take my turn on the weekends. Otherwise it's not fair, right?"

He scuffed his foot on the floor. "Yeah."

"What about next weekend?" Jeff asked.

"What about it?" She glanced up at him from her crouched position.

His jaw clenched and she thought his eyes darkened for a moment and then the look was gone. "Do you work next weekend?"

"No, I'm off."

"Cool, so maybe we could go next weekend?"

"To Legoland?" Max squealed.

"Max, inside voice." Kia winced and stood up from her place on the floor. "Um, yeah, we could do that."

Max threw his arms around her waist and squeezed. "Thanks, Mom."

She hugged him back and laughed. "Don't thank me. It was your dad's idea."

He let go of her and launched himself at Jeff. "Thanks Dad, you're the best."

Air lodged in her throat as she watched Jeff. The look on his face had morphed from shock to one of such peace and contentment, all in the blink of an eye, as he embraced his son.

Jeff cleared his throat. "You ready?"

"Yep." Max turned around and grabbed the handle of his wheelie suitcase.

Jeff crouched to look at the picture on the suitcase. "Cool, an astronaut on a dinosaur. I like it." He stood back up. "I guess I picked the right place going to the science center today."

"That's where we're going?" Max began bouncing on his toes again.

"You bet."

"Cool." Max grabbed the handle and pulled the bag toward the door.

"Hold up, buster. Where's my kiss?" Kia placed her hand on her hip and pretended to scowl at her son.

"Sorry." Max giggled and ran back and planted a loud kiss on her cheek. "Bye, Mom."

"Bye, sweetie. Have fun." She turned and eyed Jeff. "Please make sure somewhere in the mix there's some dairy or a vegetable or something."

He nodded. "Don't worry, I'm on it. Vanilla milkshakes it is."

Max giggled again and Kia narrowed her eyes. He seemed to be embracing the whole dad jokes schtick.

"Kidding, kidding, we'll have strawberry." Jeff winked at Max.

The toothless smile on her son's face clenched her gut. God, he was so happy.

Kia chewed her bottom lip as a zing of nerves slid down her spine. Letting him stay the night was harder than she'd expected. "I'll pick him up around ten tomorrow morning?"

Jeff's mouth curved up slightly as he looked at her. "Sounds good. It's totally cool if you want to call or stop by later to check on him."

Damn, so much for the poker face. "Thanks, but I think that would be more for me than him."

"Nothing wrong with that." Jeff winked at her, then strolled toward the door. He paused beside the booster seat resting beside the door. "I bought one, so you didn't have to move yours back and forth."

"Really?" Why did that seem so sweet? He was Max's dad. He should want to have his own booster seat. What was the matter with her?

He scooped up the suitcase with one hand. "Alright, buddy, let's do this."

"Bye, Mom," Max called as he hopped down the front steps and raced toward the car.

Unable to stop herself, she followed them out to the car to inspect the booster seat.

Jeff looked over at her and smirked. "Didn't believe me?"

"No, of course I did. I just wanted to buckle him in so I could get one last snuggle before you leave."

"Right, sure." Jeff's eyes twinkled as he teased her.

Kia narrowed her eyes at him, then wrinkled her nose before turning to Max and making sure he was strapped into his booster seat properly. She leaned in for one last hug and kiss. "Have a great time, sweetie. I'll see you tomorrow. Love you."

"Love you too," Max said absently as he fiddled with the controls on the armrest between the seats.

And just like that, she was forgotten. Ahh, the attention span of little boys. Kia closed the car door.

"He's safe with me, Kia. I'm not going to let anything happen to him," Jeff said, cutting through her introspection.

She shook off her thoughts and turned to him. "I know that. I wouldn't let him stay overnight if I didn't."

"Good, just making sure."

"Sorry, this isn't about you. It's just..." She paused. "It's a big step. He's only ever stayed with family overnight."

Jeff's jaw tightened. "I am family."

"Shit." She closed her eyes. "That didn't come out right. I meant people he's known forever."

"Not really my fault that I just met him, Saskia." Jeff's jaw clenched like he was keeping his anger in check, and she winced again.

"Sorry. Shoot...just let me take my foot out of my mouth. What I meant was it's hard for me to let him stay anywhere, including with my family, that's all."

Jeff's tongue clicked against his teeth. "Don't worry about it. We'll see you tomorrow."

Nicely done. As she watched him round the car and slide into the driver's seat, a wave of sadness rushed through her. Why did it feel like she was being left behind? Shaking off her melancholy, she raised her hand and waved at Max in the backseat as the SUV pulled away from the sidewalk.

With a deep sigh, she strolled back inside. She glanced at the clock. Austin wouldn't be there for their date for another couple of hours. How sad was it that Max had only been gone five minutes and already she felt lost? Maybe her sister was right, and she needed more alone time when she wasn't on mommy duty.

Kia picked up her sketchbook and curled up on the couch and set an alarm on her phone. Over the years she'd learned, next to her son, nothing cured her of a bad mood better than drawing.

The buzzing on her phone pulled her attention off her sketch pad. Kia blinked and looked at the time. How could it already be 6:30 pm? She'd really been lost in drawing. Austin was going to be there in half an hour.

Setting her sketch book aside, she stood and stretched her back. She glimpsed her reflection in the mirror over the mantle and winced. Yikes. She was going to need every minute she had to make herself look presentable.

Kia switched on her curling iron as she walked past the bathroom on her way to get dressed. She stood in front of her closet and stared aimlessly inside. What did it say that she really didn't want to go out with Austin tonight? They were lucky to see each other once a week, and going out on a date was even less frequent. Most of the time, their dates consisted of meeting Austin for coffee during the day while Max was at school because she didn't like getting a sitter. Maybe that was why their relationship hadn't progressed much over the past six months.

Reaching into the closet, she pulled out a pair of jeans and slipped into them. She chewed her bottom lip as she looked at her tops. What kind of vibe did she want for tonight? Realistically she should go for sexy, but what she really wanted to do was put her sweatshirt on and watch a movie. Maybe she should just cancel. It had to say something that for the first time in she didn't know how long they had a night to themselves, and she was having a hard time getting pumped about it.

She pushed her hair off her face and grabbed a soft, long-sleeved shirt. The way it hung off her shoulder gave it a bit of an edge, but the fabric felt like loungewear. Pleased with her compromise, she pulled it over her head as she wandered toward the bathroom to do her hair.

The doorbell rang as she was putting the final touches on her makeup. With one last fluff of her hair, Kia walked to the front door and pulled it open.

Austin's gaze swept over her body. "You look hot." He leaned in and placed a kiss against her mouth. "You want to skip dinner and stay here?" His lips brushed against her neck.

Honestly, that was the last thing she wanted to do.

What was her issue? An image of Jeff popped into her mind. *Stop that,* she told herself. Being around Jeff had rattled her brain. That's all that was. It didn't mean anything.

Austin and she just needed some time alone on a date to get her mojo back. She placed her hand against his chest and pushed back. "Nope, I never get to go out, so I'm not missing it."

"You sure?" He leaned back toward her, and she braced her hand against his chest.

"Yep. I got all dressed up." She pretended to bat her eyelashes. "I need to be wined and dined."

The dimple in Austin's cheek deepened as he smirked at her. He really was a good-looking guy. What was her problem?

"Alright babe." He glanced around the living room. "But Max is gone for the night, right?"

She fought the urge to roll her eyes. "Yes. I pick him up in the morning."

"That mean you're going to let me stay over?"

Did it? No. Not necessarily.

Man, she really needed to get her head out of her ass and knock this shit off, like now. They were in a relationship. She should want to spend the night with him. Shouldn't she? Pretending to be coy, she tapped her finger against her lip and looked him up and down. "Undecided."

Austin's smirk turned into a sexy, predatory grin. "Well, I guess I have my work cut out for me."

If only he knew just how true that statement was. She patted him on the chest as she walked past him to the front door. "Wouldn't want to be too easy."

He snorted. "No one would ever accuse you of that, Kia."

CHAPTER TEN

AFTER LOCKING THE FRONT door, she followed him down the path to his truck. Grabbing the handhold, she hoisted herself up into his enormous truck.

Austin cranked the engine, and music blasted through the speakers. He winced and adjusted the volume. "Sorry about that."

"No problem." She shifted in her seat to get comfortable, then grabbed the buckle and snapped her seatbelt into place.

Austin pulled away from the sidewalk. He clamped his hand on her thigh, and she fought the urge to remove his fingers. She rolled her shoulders. She just needed to relax and unwind. Forget about Jeff and Max and everything else and just focus on the evening ahead.

"So how was your week?" she asked.

"Eh, it was there. Same ol'shit, different week."

"Was the shop busy?"

"The usual."

She rolled her eyes. He could give her something to work with here. "What are your plans for the weekend?"

He flicked a glance at her and smiled. "I don't know. You think Max's fancy dad will want to take him again?"

Kia bristled. Why did he say it like having Max was a chore? "That's not why I was asking."

"But he could take him, right? I mean, it'd be nice for us to get some more alone time. Although I guess, realistically, we could get a lot of alone time pretty soon."

"What do you mean?"

He eased the truck into a parking spot outside the restaurant. "Let's go," he said as he opened the truck door and jumped out.

Kia's mind raced. What had he been talking about more alone time?

She hopped out and rounded the front of the car. "What did you mean?"

Austin's gaze tracked down her body, and he bit his bottom lip. "Man, I wish you would have agreed to stay home." He pulled her against him and pressed a kiss to the side of her neck. "It's been so long since we got to spend any time alone."

"Sorry, it's been a bit of an adjustment helping Max get to know his dad."

Austin pulled open the door to the restaurant and waited for Kia to enter. She stepped up to the hostess station. "Two please."

The hostess looked up at Kia, then scanned behind her. When the woman's eyes landed on Austin, she licked her lips and straightened her spine.

Kia didn't miss the little smirk on Austin's face. He caught Kia looking and winked, then shrugged. The little aww shucks look used to be cute. Tonight it just irritated her. Couldn't he just ignore the girl checking him out like a normal person?

Once they were seated, they both quickly ordered a drink. As the server left, Austin steepled his hands on the table. "How's it been going with Wonder Boy?"

"Stop calling him that, please."

"Sorry. Smitty," he grumbled the name like it left a foul taste in his mouth.

Kia's back stiffened. "What is your problem with Jeff?"

"Nothing. I just—" He shrugged. "I don't know…" He trailed off, distracted by a woman walking past their table.

"Oh my god, seriously?" She laughed.

Austin's head snapped off the woman's ass and back to her. "What?"

"You know how you were hoping to go home with me tonight? That won't be happening, especially if you can't be a little more subtle about checking people out."

"I wasn't checking her out."

Was he for real? She snorted. "Okay. The sear marks on her ass from your eyes say otherwise."

He winced. "Sorry."

"It was a good ass and I'm not into girls. If I noticed it, I can't expect you not to, but seriously you could learn to be just a little subtle. The whole gobsmacked thing is disrespectful."

Austin stared at her. "You know it's really screwed up that you don't care if I check people out."

"Why?"

"What do you mean, why? It's weird."

"I disagree. We both have eyes. Of course we're going to notice if someone is attractive. There's a big difference between noticing and doing something about it. One is understandable, the other is a deal breaker."

His forehead creased as he stared back at her. "Most people get pissed if their partner looks at someone. It sure as hell would piss me off if you did it."

"Okay, now that pisses me off. It's okay for you to look, but not me? That's some bullshit."

"It's not okay for either of us."

Kia sputtered out a laugh. "Oh my God, do you hear yourself? The whole reason we're even having this discussion is because I busted you gawking." She eyed the man across the table from her. Was he right and she was the weird one for not caring? She didn't think so. She cared that he'd been disrespectful in the way he'd checked the woman out for sure, but not that he actually looked. "Look, you know how I feel about cheating and jealousy and all that."

He sat forward in his chair. "I would never cheat on you. I was just looking."

"I know, that's what I'm saying. So can we just agree that if you're gonna look, be respectful not only to me but to the other woman as well? No one wants some rando dude eye fucking them without their consent."

"I wasn't eye fucking her. I glanced at her ass."

She arched an eyebrow at him. "Eh." Taking in the look on Austin's face, she fought back the lick of annoyance. Somehow he was making her into the bad guy here because she had different views when he was clearly the one in the wrong. "Do you really want to fight about this, or can we just agree it was disrespectful and you'll knock that shit off?"

The muscle on the left side of Austin's jaw twitched. "Agreed." He picked up his menu and opened it. "For the record, you know how sexy I think you are. That chick didn't even come close."

"Now you're just full of shit." She laughed.

"Nope, I much prefer a woman who'll order a burger and get her hands dirty." He waggled his eyebrows suggestively.

The fact he thought that might work just made her laugh, but props for effort.

The server stopped at their table and set a beer in front of each of them. She looked at the beer in front of her. Damn, he wasn't wrong. That woman probably ordered fancy cocktails with umbrellas or some shit. She was a beer girl who drank wine to class it up. "You're still not getting invited over." She picked up her beer and took a long pull.

Austin threw back his head and laughed. "We'll see."

Kia set her beer back on the table. "So what were you saying earlier about me having more alone time?"

Austin leaned back in his chair. "I don't know. I just assumed now that Smitty is doing some sleepovers it won't be long before Max wants to be over there all the time."

"Why would Max want to be there all the time?"

"Big baseball player, he probably has pretty swanky digs. Makes sense Max would rather be there than your place."

"What's wrong with my place?"

"Nothing, for regular people. But come on, you can't tell me a kid wouldn't rather spend time at a house with an Xbox and a pool."

"Jeff doesn't have a pool," she muttered. But he had a big gaming room and Max was already bugging her that they should get something for their place.

"Come on, babe, this is a good thing. You've been doing the single mom thing for so long I figured it would be nice for you to have someone take over half time."

"Half-time," she screeched. The man at the table beside them glared at her, and she lowered her voice, "Half-time. Max isn't living with his dad half-time. It's one sleepover." She caught the way her voice rose again, and she winced. Holy crap, what if Austin was right and Max wanted to live with his dad half-time? Her heart pounded in her chest. There was no way in hell that was happening. Jeff had never even hinted at anything to do with custody. Besides, with his work schedule, it wouldn't even be an option for most of the year. Her mind raced.

"Babe, relax."

She blinked at him. "Sorry, what did you say?"

"I just said chill a bit. You look like I just told you to kill a puppy."

"You may as well have," she muttered.

He reached across the table and squeezed her hand. "Who knows? Once the novelty wears off, maybe he'll be like all those other athletes you always read about and lose interest. Just some deadbeat dad who throws a little cash your way every now and then."

Clearly, he didn't know Jeff. That was never going to be the kind of dad he was. Which had seemed like such a good thing just this morning. Now she wasn't so sure.

"I really blew my chances of getting invited to stay over tonight, didn't I?" Austin asked.

"Yeah, you really did." She picked up her menu. "Looks like you're in the clear to order something with lots of garlic or onions."

CHAPTER ELEVEN

JEFF HAD NEVER FELT so helpless before in his life. The sight of his son weeping in his bed was more than he could bear. He'd heard the saying his heart hurt before, but until this moment he hadn't known what it meant. This being a dad thing was hard.

He crouched beside the spare bed he'd made up for Max to sleep in. "Max, talk to me. Why are you crying?"

Max burrowed his face deeper into his pillow and shook his head.

"I don't know how to help you, Max, if you don't tell me what's going on." This was his first night with Max and already he was failing miserably.

"I want my mom." Max's face remained buried in the pillow, making it hard to hear him speak.

"You want me to call her?"

Max peeked at him over the mound of blankets and pillows and nodded slightly.

"Okay." Jeff dug into his pocket and pulled out his cell-phone. He flicked through his contacts for Kia's number and hit the call button. He eyed Max while the phone rang in his hand. What the hell was he going to do if she didn't answer? What if she answered? Would she regret letting him take Max for the night? What if she didn't let him take his son again?

"Hello," Kia's voice broke over the line.

"Hey Kia, it's Jeff."

"Is everything okay with Max?"

"Honestly, I don't know." He eyed his son on the bed. Max wiped his nose with his sleeve as he watched him. The tears continued to stream down his little face. "He's crying and he's asking for you. I'm sorry to ask you this, but any chance you can come over?"

"Can I talk to him?"

Jeff sat on the edge of the bed. "Your mom's on the phone, Max." He held the phone out toward the boy.

Max shook his head. "She'll be mad," he whispered.

He stared at his son. "Why would she be mad?"

He could dimly hear Kia speaking from where he held the phone out toward Max but couldn't make out what she said. Pushing the speakerphone button, he spoke, "Kia, I put you on speaker."

"Hey buddy, what's going on?"

Max sucked in a sob. "I forgot Pickles."

"Oh, Max, I thought you checked to make sure you had him."

"I did, but..." His voice broke on a sob.

"Alright, bud, do you want me to come get you and bring you home or just bring you Pickles?"

Jeff held his breath as he waited for Max to answer.

"Can you stay here, too?" Max asked her.

"I can't, Max, it's not my house." Kia paused. "Your dad will understand if you want to come home."

"No, he won't," Max sobbed.

The fist around Jeff's heart tightened. "I totally get it Max, it's weird staying in a new place."

"No, I...I." Max sniffed. "I...I'm a big kid."

"I'll grab Pickles and be there soon and we'll figure it out, okay?" Kia's calm voice instantly soothed them both.

How the hell did she sound so relaxed? Every muscle in Jeff's body was tense. Seeing his son crying made him want to cry, too.

"Thanks, Kia, see you soon." He flicked off the phone and dropped it on the bedside table. He ran his hand along Max's back, hoping the touch would be calming. He used to like it when his mom rubbed his back as a kid.

"Do you want me to snuggle up and read to you or something while we wait for your mom?" Kids liked that kind of thing, didn't they?

Max sat up and crawled onto his lap and wrapped his arms around Jeff's neck.

Emotion clogged his throat, making it hard to swallow.

Max blinked at him. His hazel eyes were bloodshot and glassy from the tears as he nodded in agreement.

"Do you have a favorite?"

Max nodded. "I like Junie B."

Jeff wracked his brain for what that was. "Sorry, I don't know what that is."

"She's really funny. Mom says she's sassy."

"Sassy is always good." He rooted around in the backpack and pulled out a handful of books. He sifted through them until he found one with a little girl with glasses on the front. "She looks like you." He tapped the toothless grin on the cover.

Max dragged his pajama sleeve along his nose and sniffed. "Yeah."

Jeff eyed the snotty sleeve as Max dropped his arm onto his dad's chest. Oh well, the shirt was going in the wash anyway. Jeff settled deeper into the chair and shifted Max's weight, so he was tucked up against his chest. "You comfy?"

Max nodded.

"Alright, let's see what this Junie B is all about."

As they read through the first several pages, he laughed along with Max. Kia was right, this kid was sassy. He figured they'd been reading for about twenty minutes when his front doorbell rang.

"Mom?" Max sat up straight.

"I think so. You want to come with me to check?"

Max hopped off his lap and held out his hand. The fact he wanted to hold hands to go to the front door spoke volumes about how insecure Max was still feeling. It broke his heart. When they'd planned this night, he'd expected it to be a piece of cake. Why wouldn't Max be stoked to stay at his dad's house? His place was cool. They had fun together. It'd be great. He never factored in that Max was five, sleeping in a strange house, without the one person who made him feel safest in the world. He'd been an idiot to think it would run smoothly.

He peeked through the peephole and breathed a sigh of relief when he saw Kia on the other side of the door. Pulling it open, he stepped back.

The second Max saw his mom, he burst into tears.

"Hey sweetie." She crouched and wrapped him up in a warm embrace.

What the hell? The kid had been fine two minutes ago. The way he was sobbing, Jeff would be lucky if Kia ever let him look after Max again. Dragging his hand through his hair, he looked down at the pair.

Kia glanced up at him and gave him a reassuring smile. "Can I come in for a minute?"

"Of course." He waved his arm to the side, gesturing for her to follow him into the main living area.

With Max's legs wrapped around her waist, Kia walked over to the sofa and sat. "So how was your night with your dad?"

Max mumbled against her neck, but Jeff couldn't make out what he said.

"I bet you guys had fun. It sure sounded like you did when we talked earlier."

"Yeah, we made homemade pizza."

"You did? That sounds cool. Did you get to choose your own toppings?"

"Yeah, we had meat bombs?" Max leaned back so he could look at her. His fingers absently twisted in his mom's hair while he talked.

"Meat bombs? What's that?"

"It's all the meats in one."

Kia's nose wrinkled. "Mmm, did any veggies make it into the mix?"

"Mo-om, it wouldn't be a meat bomb then."

"Right, gotcha." She pressed a kiss against Max's fore-head. "So how you feeling now?"

Jeff's chest knotted as he waited for Max to talk. He expected Max to say he wanted to go home. Why that made him feel like a complete failure as a dad he couldn't say, but it did.

Max shrugged.

Kia turned to Jeff. "You mind grabbing Pickles out of my bag?"

He eyed the big brown purse she'd set by the front door. Afraid to look inside, he picked it up and carried it over to the couch. "Do you?" He held the purse out toward her.

"You can just grab him. He's right on top."

Taking a deep breath, he unzipped the purse and spotted the stuffed animal right on top. He pulled it out and held it out toward Max.

The boy squeezed the weird green stuffed lizard tightly against his chest. After several minutes, Max yawned.

"Let's get you back to bed." She wrapped her arms around the boy and hoisted him up.

Jeff led the way back to Max's bedroom. She placed him on the mattress, tucked him in, and placed a kiss against his head. "Sweet dreams. I'll see you in the morning."

"For breakfast, right?" Max placed his palms on either side of her face to hold her in place.

"Absolutely. Your dad's buying, so I'm getting the biggest plate of waffles and whipped cream I can find." Kia flicked a glance at Jeff and winked. The knot in his chest deflated like a balloon. He didn't realize how badly he needed her support until this moment.

"I'll buy you anything on the menu," he gushed.

"Anything?" She raised an eyebrow and tapped her nail on her lip like she was deep in thought. She flashed a mischievous grin at Max. "Just this once, maybe we should have milkshakes too."

Max's eyes widened. "For breakfast?"

A laugh rumbled out of Jeff's chest. The little guy sounded so scandalized about a milkshake. "It is milk, isn't it?" Jeff asked.

"It is if you're buying." Kia rubbed her hands together gleefully. "This is going to be so good. You better get to sleep quick, Max, so morning comes sooner. I got some breakfast to eat."

Max clamped his eyes tightly shut. Kia smiled at the boy, then pressed another kiss against his forehead and stood up. "Night, sweetie."

With his eyes still glued shut, Max whispered, "Night."

Afraid if he got too close, it would shatter the safe bubble that surrounded Max and he'd want to go home, Jeff leaned against the doorframe while Kia stood up. "Night, Max, I'll see you in the morning," he said.

Max squinted open one eye to peek at him. "Night, Dad." The boy's loud stage whisper brought a smile to his face. Who knew kids were so funny?

As Jeff followed Kia back down the hallway, he broke the silence. "Sorry I ruined your night. You must be regretting letting me take him for the night."

Kia spun around. "Don't be silly. This wasn't your fault at all. I should have double checked he had Pickles. I know he can't sleep without him."

Exhausted, he sighed. "God, that was brutal."

"You did great. Honestly, he would do the same thing at Vika's house if he forgot Pickles." She squeezed his arm. "Kids cry. Their emotions are really close to the surface, so they burn hot and fast. Once it's done, it's done."

How was it possible he felt so drained when it was only 9:00 o'clock? "Yeah?"

"Absolutely." She squeezed his arm again, then dropped her hand. "If I didn't think you could handle it, believe me, there isn't a chance in hell Max would have been here tonight."

"Thanks." He finally really looked at her for the first time. His gaze scanned her outfit from top to bottom. A low whistle slid from his mouth. "Wow!"

Kia blushed and tucked her hair behind her ear.

"Sorry." He shook his head. "You just look amazing." Realizing exactly why she looked so fantastic, he winced. "Fuck, you were on a date. Weren't you?" Jealousy dug its nasty fingers into his chest and squeezed at the thought of her out with another man. He didn't have any right to feel that way. She wasn't his as much as he wished she was.

"It's fine." She waved her hand like it really was nothing.

"Is he in the car outside? He could have come in." The idea of the other guy stepping foot in his house burned, but it was the least he could do for Kia coming to his rescue tonight.

"No, no, don't worry about it. The date ended. I wasn't sure how Max would be, so we just called it a night."

"Well then, the least I can do is offer you a drink since I ruined your evening."

She tilted her head to the side, thinking over her answer. Finally, she nodded. "A drink sounds fantastic."

"Alright, let's see what we can find." He led the way into the kitchen. "You want wine?"

"Sure. White if you have it."

"Coming up."

Kia stopped at the edge of the island. "Your place is amazing. I've only seen this kind of thing on TV. I didn't think people had kitchens like this in real life."

"What do you mean?"

She pointed at the stove. "Why do you need two stoves?"

"It's not two stoves, it's really like one and a half. The left side is smaller."

She snorted. "Okay." Looking around the room, she pointed to the wall where the fridge sat. "You have a super sneaky fridge."

"A super sneaky fridge?" He laughed. "It's a regular ol' fridge."

Kia made a weird nose deep in her throat. "It matches the cabinets. If I hadn't seen you go in there, I would have thought it was a cupboard."

"That doesn't make it super sneaky. That just means it matches."

"Oh, okay my bad." Sarcasm dripped from her tongue as she mocked him.

He looked around the room, trying to see if from her perspective. Maybe it was a little over the top, but he liked to cook. He enjoyed having all his family over for the holidays. Nothing said home like a good kitchen. This kitchen was one reason he'd bought the house. That and the view.

"Sorry, that sounded a bit dickish." Kia looked at him and winced.

"It's all good."

"No, it's not." She glanced at her hand and fiddled with her nail. After several seconds, she looked up. "Truth? I'm a little jealous."

"Jealous?" He set a glass of wine in front of her. With his own glass in hand, he leaned his back against the counter and waited for her to speak.

With a sigh, she reached down and pulled out one stool from the island and sat. "Maybe jealous is the wrong word." She took a sip of wine. "Terrified would be better."

His head snapped back. "Terrified. What the hell are you terrified about?"

"Are you kidding me? Look at this place, Jeff. Look at this life that you have. The life you can offer Max."

"This is a good thing, Kia. Why would that scare you?"

She looked up at the ceiling and laughed. "You would say that." Her head lowered and she pursed her lips. "I can't offer him anything close to this." She swept her arm out to encompass the room.

"You don't have to."

"Don't I?" She wrinkled her nose as if she was fighting to hold in emotion.

He wanted to step toward her, to hold her and take this pain, but he didn't have that right. So instead of doing that, he simply said, "No, you don't."

When her eyes met his, they were filled with pain. Fuck it. He walked around the island and pulled out the stool beside hers. "Talk to me."

She shook her head. "It's nothing. I'm just being stupid. Something Austin said earlier just got in my head."

What the hell? Wasn't her boyfriend supposed to help, not make her feel insecure? What kind of douche was she dating? "What did he say?"

"It doesn't matter." She picked up her glass of wine and stood. Her gaze lingered on the deck outside. "Is that a heat lamp?"

"Yeah."

"Cool. Want to sit outside?" Without waiting for an answer, she wandered to the back door.

Grabbing his own glass, he followed her outside. Kia sat on the L-shaped sofa and curled into the armrest. He flipped on the large outdoor heater, then eyeing Kia again, he reached into the storage bucket and pulled out a fluffy dark gray blanket and handed it to her.

"Thanks."

"No problem." He sat on the opposite side of the L. "So what did Austin say exactly?"

"Crap," she muttered. "I was hoping you'd forget I mentioned it."

"Sorry, I know I'm a guy and all, but my attention span isn't that short."

Kia stared out at the ocean view and sighed. "This view is amazing. Max is going to love growing up with this."

The view was amazing. So why did the idea of Max having that make her sound so sad?

She sighed audibly. "It sucks, but Austin was right. Why would Max want to live in my shitty house when he could have this?"

"What the fuck are you talking about?"

Kia's spine stiffened at his angry tone. "Exactly what I said." She glared at him. "I've fought really hard to give Max a good life and then you swoop in and it's all for nothing."

"Austin's a fucking idiot," he muttered.

"No, he's not," she snapped.

"If he's got you believing some bullshit idea that Max is going to want to live with me because my stuff is prettier, he is." He shook his head. "Kia, come on, that's just stupid."

"Don't call me stupid." She flung the blanket off her legs.

"Oh my god, I didn't call you stupid. I said the idea was stupid." Frustrated, he scrubbed a hand down his face. "You don't think too highly of me, do you?"

"What? Of course I do."

"Clearly, you don't. Because I sure as hell am not on board with us raising some kind of dickwad kid who thinks he's too good to live in a certain neighborhood. If it ever gets to a point where you aren't happy where you're living anymore, I have a couple of rental properties. Maybe one of them would work for you."

"I don't want your charity."

"My god. It's not charity to have good tenants. It's smart business. There's a difference. I've seen how you look after your place and it's a hell of a lot better than most people."

She looked at her lap. "Sorry," she mumbled.

"For what part?"

Kia looked up and wrinkled her nose. "All of it." She pulled the blanket back across her lap. "I'm not normally this insecure. I just let some doubts worm their way in and I guess it maybe festered a little."

"I'm not sure how we went from me needing to be rescued to you feeling insecure. If anyone needs to doubt themselves around here, trust me, it's not you."

The wind blew in off the water, bringing a bite to the air. He picked up the edge of her blanket and covered his own legs with it. He gave her a quick smile. "Let's just agree that we're navigating some weird terrain and leave it at that. Okay?"

"Sounds good." She wrinkled her nose. "And if we could just forget I had this little freak out that would be cool, too?"

He leaned back on the couch and took a sip of his wine. "What freak out?"

Kia twisted on the sofa, so she was facing him. Her feet brushed against his thigh, and he adjusted the blanket better over both of them.

"We haven't had much of a chance to really get to know each other. I mean, I've seen you with Max. And obviously since my kid is involved, I had to become a full-out online stalker."

"Well, obviously." He grinned at her. "Although, have to say rookie stalker mistake to like my Instagram photos from three years ago."

Kia snorted and slapped her hand over her face. With the dim backlight from the kitchen, her eyes shone with amusement as she looked at him. "Damn it. I was hoping you didn't notice." She snapped her fingers. "Shoot. I realized my mistake later that night when I was lying in bed, but I thought it would be even more obvious if I unliked them," she teased.

"You were thinking about me when you were lying in bed?"

She sucked in a breath and instantly he realized what he'd said. "Sorry. That was completely inappropriate." He clenched his hand in his lap. He'd gotten caught up in the moment flirting with a beautiful woman and instinct had taken over. He'd been so careful whenever they were together, trying to keep his attraction to her at bay.

"It's fine." She shrugged it off. Her eyes darted to him, then back out to the ocean. The air still hummed between them.

Was it fine? Was she as attracted to him as he was to her? Kia's tongue darted out, and his eyes followed the movement as she wet her lips. Bad idea.

He stood up. "I need a refill. What about you?"

"It's late. I should probably get going." Kia pushed the blanket off her lap and stood up.

"You sure?" It was probably a good idea if she left immediately, otherwise he'd be really tempted to press his luck and forget why it was a bad idea to keep his distance.

"Yeah. Thanks for the wine and everything." She gestured to the blankets piled on the sofa.

"Of course. Thanks for coming in clutch with Pickles."

"You know it." Kia winked. "Mom for the win."

"It was a thing of beauty." He chuckled. Pulling open the deck door, he stepped back to allow her to precede him inside.

Following Kia to the front door, his gaze dropped to her jean-clad ass and the way her hips swayed with each step. Jesus, he had it bad.

She stopped at the door. "Now that it's been mentioned, I'm taking you up on the offer of breakfast. So you want to pick me up?"

"You bet. Nine o'clock?"

Kia grinned. "I hope you don't think you're sleeping in tomorrow morning."

"Picking you up at nine is sleeping in?"

And damn if she didn't start laughing. Kia patted him on the chest. "Oh, you have so much to learn."

Christ, just how early did the kid get up? "Do we need to make it earlier?"

Kia pulled open the front door. "Nope, you already said nine. No take backs. I'm going to enjoy sleeping in. Have fun," she called over her shoulder.

Well shit.

CHAPTER TWELVE

THE BREEZE OFF THE ocean blew her hair away from her forehead. Kia scanned the area around her and didn't see any sign of Austin yet. She closed her eyes and let the sun warm her face. Man, she hoped this conversation went well. Breaking up was never easy. But if the past few weeks had shown her anything, it was that Austin wasn't the right guy for her. If he was, she wouldn't be so drawn to Jeff.

After a couple of minutes, she opened her eyes and glanced to her left. Austin wandered toward her down the walkway, skirting past people on the sidewalk. A smile spread across his face when he saw her, and he lifted his hand in acknowledgment. Shit. This was going to completely blindside him.

Kia's shoulders tightened. She pasted a smile on her face and waved back.

Austin strolled up and leaned down to kiss her. At the last second, Kia turned her face slightly, so the kiss landed on her cheek.

Austin's brow wrinkled in confusion. "Everything okay?" he asked.

"Um, yeah. You want to sit, or do you want to walk?" Kia looked back out at the ocean. Afraid that if she made eye contact with him, she'd just blurt out she wanted to break up rather than easing into it more delicately.

Austin sat on the bench beside her. "What's going on, Kia? You seem tense."

Shifting her weight, Kia slid on the bench and brought her knee up so she could turn and face Austin properly. "Um... So we need to talk."

His face fell. "You're breaking up with me, aren't you?"

"I'm sorry." She winced. "I just don't think this is working anymore."

Austin stood up. Waves of anger pulsed off his body. "Why? Because you have a fancy meal ticket now?"

Pissed, she jumped to her feet. "Are you kidding me?" How dare he imply she was a gold digger! She worked her ass off for everything she had. That was one thing they both had in common. He knew how important it was to her to pave her own way.

"What? Come on, Kia. I know how hard things have been for you as a single mom. You can't tell me you aren't interested in his money."

"Screw you, Austin. This has nothing to do with money and you know it." She stared at the man who she'd spent the last six months with. "Every time we talk lately, it's snippy and uncomfortable."

"That's because I've heard the way you talk about Smitty. You get this stupid look on your face like you're picturing a picket fence and shit."

"I'm not picturing anything with Jeff. Do I like seeing my son happy? Yes. Of course I do."

"And how much he makes has nothing to do with that smile."

"Don't be a dick." She crossed her arms over her chest as she watched him.

His face dropped. "Sorry. That was an asshole thing to say. But come on, Kia. He's a professional ballplayer. They date supermodels and shit. And you're hot obviously, but there's a big difference between the kind of women those guys' date and a single mom who tattoos people for a living."

"What the hell is that supposed to mean?"

"Come on, Kia. They hire people like us. They'll fuck 'em but they don't marry 'em."

Was he right? Probably. Hell, when she'd met Jeff all those years ago, she'd thought he was blue collar. Turned out he'd been slumming it for the summer. He'd grown up upper-middle-class, while her family was definitely working-class.

"Jeff has nothing to do with this, Austin. Okay, maybe he does, but not in the way you're thinking." She sat back on the bench and Austin sat beside her. "Nothing is more important to me than my son."

"I know. All of our dates have revolved around his schedule," he grumbled.

"And that right there is the problem, Austin. It annoys you that your life revolves around my kid. And I get it. He's not yours. Watching Jeff with Austin made that difference painfully obvious. And this is nothing against you at all. I've stopped you from having a relationship with Max because I didn't want him confused." She tilted her head as she struggled to find the words to soften the blow. "I think if I had felt like we were really going somewhere, I would have wanted you around Max more. I liked how we kept things separate, and I think that speaks to our relationship and why it's not going to work."

"So I was good enough to fuck, but not good enough to have a relationship with your son?"

"No, that's not what I'm saying." Kia winced. Except that was what she was saying. She knew things with Austin weren't going anywhere and she hadn't really cared. She'd kept her life separate for a reason. Austin was hot and fun. And sometimes she needed a night out to forget she was a mom and he'd always been up for that. But watching Jeff with Max, she realized just what she'd been missing by having someone else to take some of the weight off. There was something to be said for family outings.

"Sure sounds like it to me." Austin sat quietly and pinched the bridge of his nose. Finally, he looked up. "You're kidding yourself if you think he's going to stick around, Kia. Sure, it's all fun now, but what's it going to look like when the season starts and he's on the road? You'll be back to being a single mom. Alone."

"Again, this isn't about Jeff. This is about you and I, and there's just something missing between us. I've realized we're never going to get there. I'm sorry." She reached out and placed her hand on his arm to soften the blow.

He snatched his arm back. "Yeah, I'm sorry too. I think you're making a huge mistake here."

"Maybe I am." She sighed. "But right now I have to follow my gut and it's telling me it's not fair to you to keep dating when I don't see us being a long-term thing."

"Right." The muscles in his jaw ticked as he stared out toward the ocean.

"I hope we can still be friends."

Austin laughed. "We weren't friends before, Kia. Why the hell would we be friends after?"

Sucking in a breath, she pursed her mouth. "Okay, fair enough. I hope we can at least be civil when we see each other. I mean, you work with Ty, so we're going to run into each other."

"I'm pretty sure we can avoid each other. You managed to do a good job of it whenever Max was around before." Disappointment clouded his eyes as he looked at her. "I could have made you happy if you'd just given us the chance." He stood up. "See you around."

Exhaling an audible breath, she watched him walk away. *Well, that went well.* She stared out at the water. Was he right? No. She knew breaking up with Austin was the right thing to do. They'd been dating for six months. Everything about their relationship was superficial, and she had no interest in deepening it. That said something and once he was over feeling hurt, he'd realize it too. He hadn't been any more interested in getting to know her than she had in getting to know him.

She closed her eyes and let the sun shine down on her face again. Her watch buzzed and she peered at it. Time to get to work.

After tucking Max in, Jeff wandered back down the hallway. He found Kia in the kitchen, wiping down the counters.

She looked up. "You all done?"

"Yeah, he's conked out."

"I'm not surprised. You guys had a full day." She set the rag on the edge of the kitchen sink. "You heading out?"

"I was actually wanting to chat with you about something if that was okay."

Kia eyed him warily. "Sure. Do I need to sit down for this?"

"What? God, no, it's nothing bad. I just wanted to talk to you about maybe getting some ink done."

"Really? Sure, I'd be happy to talk to you about that." She walked over to the fridge. "You want a drink?" she asked with her hand on the fridge door.

"Beer would be great."

She pulled two bottles out of the fridge, cracked them both, and handed him one. "Shall we?" She tilted her head toward the living room.

As he followed her to the other room, he tried to keep his gaze from dipping to her ass but failed miserably. He was far too attracted to her for his own good. The smart play would be to go home as soon as Max was in bed each night, but he found himself finding reasons to stay each time.

Kia sat down on the end of the couch and curled her legs up beneath her. "So, you're thinking of getting some work done?"

He shifted his weight on the other end of the sofa. "Yeah. Being around you so much and hearing you talk about your work has got me thinking a lot about getting another tattoo. A couple of my teammates and I got to talking about how it would be cool to do some kind of tattoo to celebrate." Unsure what the right word was, he wrinkled his nose. "More like commemorate winning the World Series this past season. Is that something you'd be into doing?"

Kia's eyes brightened. The interest on her face was clear as she turned fully toward him. "Yeah, absolutely. Did you have something in mind?"

"Not really. I'm hoping that's where you'd come in." He glanced at the intricate design on her right arm. "The four of us are pretty tight and we thought it would be cool to all get something together. We might not always play together in the future, but we'll always have this and it's not something many people can say they have."

She nodded thoughtfully. "Were you thinking baseball theme or—" She picked up the sketch pad that always sat on the little table beside the couch. Flipping open to a new page, she tapped her pencil against her lip. "—were you thinking more along the lines of something with a hawk?"

"Honestly? I have no clue." He chuckled. "Lame I know. You'd think we'd have some idea of what we want."

"Not lame at all. Getting something like this is a big deal. You want to make sure it's meaningful and appeals to all of you."

"Yeah, exactly."

Her hand started flying across the page. He couldn't take his eyes off her as she worked. He'd never seen her like this. Watching her draw reminded him of how he felt when he stepped out on the diamond. The sense of calm he got knowing he was doing something he loved mixed with the excitement of what was to come. He didn't realize her art gave her that same kind of feeling.

Several minutes later, she looked up and handed the sketch pad over. "This is super rough, just throwing a couple of ideas around." Chewing her bottom lip, she eyed him. "Obviously, the hawk would look a whole hell of a lot better."

He stared in awe at the page. "How the hell did you draw something that looks like this from the top of your head?"

Her cheeks turned pink, and she seemed to be looking anywhere but at him.

He stared back down at the drawing of a hawk with a baseball bat in his talons. "I knew you were talented, obviously, since I've seen the artwork around the house, but I didn't have any clue you had all this in there. Damn."

"Thanks." She smiled shyly. "Is that sort of what you were thinking?"

"Kind of yeah, but..." He looked around the room as he tried to see if something would help him explain his thoughts.

Kia stood up and returned a minute later with several books. Some looked like photo albums, and some were sketch pads. She set them down on the coffee table. "There's no rush to come up with a design. We've got lots of time and you want to make sure you've got the right thing." She pushed the books his way. "This is some of my work. Maybe something in there will give you some ideas that we can work with."

Watching her, he took a sip of his beer. "You don't mind doing this with me? I don't want to take up a ton of your time."

"I'm more than happy to spend as much time as you need to get this right for you." She smiled. Their eyes locked. The air between them shifted. His eyes drifted to her lips. When her tongue darted out to lick them, he hit back a groan. He wanted to kiss her. Clearing his throat, he tore his gaze off her mouth. Trying to get his wayward thoughts under control, he took a sip of beer. He set the bottle back down on the table and picked up one of the binders. "Alright, let's see what you've got."

This had been the week from hell. Kia glanced up at the clock on the wall. The shop had barely been open for an hour and already she wanted to call it a day. She set her sketch pad down on the counter and crossed her arms over her chest and stared at the customer sitting in the consult chair in front of her. "Yeah, no, I'm not doing that."

"You have to. The customer's always right."

She let her gaze scroll over the heavily inked idiot. He had some stupid ass tattoos already but come on. This one took the cake. "Not this time he's not. Seriously, dude. No one wants to see your dick as a pickle."

The guy's face scrunched up as he gawked back at her like she was the baffling one. "It's funny."

They definitely had different definitions of funny. "I guess it's funny if you want to be celibate for the rest of your life."

He rolled his eyes. "Are you honestly saying if a woman is into me she'd stop because of my sock tattoo?"

"Yes? That's exactly what I'm telling you." She nodded her head vigorously.

"Fine." He crossed his arms over his chest like a petulant child. "What if you put it on my ass?"

Kia narrowed her eyes. God, this just kept getting better and better. "Where were you thinking?"

He stood and turned so his back was to her. With his hand, he gestured to where he was thinking.

Kia snorted. "Yeah, that would be a no. I'm not doing that either. A month from now you'll be trying to get the damn thing removed."

"What do you mean? It's funny." His beady eyes flicked around the shop like he was looking for someone to back him up.

She pinned him with a look, making sure her face left no question about how asinine she thought the idea was. "It would look like you were going to be fucked by a pickle. No."

The guy bounced in his seat. "That's why it would be funny."

There was not enough money in the world. There was no way she was attaching her name to this shit. "No."

"No?"

"No." She stared him down. What an idiot. People did this all the time. Thought a tattoo was a great idea, then they realized it was permanent and had made a big mistake. The last thing she wanted was for one of her tattoos to show up on some redo show. Nope.

"You seriously won't do the ink?"

"I won't do it. If that's what you have your heart set on, you're going to have to find another artist." She leaned back in her chair and crossed her foot over her knee to settle in.

"Fine." He shoved his chair back as he stood. The metal legs scraped against the floor with a loud screech. "This shop sucks anyway." His loud, angry voice drew all eyes toward him.

Kia looked over at Viper and shrugged. So much for that consultation. Nice start to the day.

She glanced up at the clock. The thigh piece she had next would take up most of the day, then Jeff and his friend would be there around four. Hopefully, that consultation went better.

CHAPTER THIRTEEN

JEFF PULLED THE DOOR open to Freedom Tattoo and wandered over to his friends as the three of them stood looking at the wall of drawings. "Hey guys."

They all turned around when he spoke.

"Did you check in already?" He nodded toward the vacant front counter.

"Nah, we were waiting for you." Gonzo wrapped his arm around Jeff's shoulder. "You're lucky I love you. I wouldn't mar my body for just anybody you know."

"Says the guy who has a tattoo of a piece of bacon on his thigh."

"That's different. I lost a bet."

"No shit." Jeff walked up to the front counter and glanced toward the back of the shop. A dark-haired man with tattoos covering half of his face stepped out from the back. "Hi, what can I do for you?"

"Hey, we have a consult with Kia."

"Kia," the guy called.

A moment later, Kia walked out and just like every other time he saw her, Jeff was instantly struck by how incredibly beautiful she was.

"Damn, no wonder you guys made such a cute kid," Gonzo murmured.

"Shut up." Jeff elbowed his friend in the ribs before turning his attention back to her. "Hey, Kia."

"Hi, Jeff." She smiled at his buddies. "And you must be the teammates."

Pete stepped forward and held out his hand. "Hi, I'm Pete."

Ryan thrust out his hand. "Ryan."

Gonzo brought up the rear. "Gonzo."

"I'm sorry, Gonzo?" Kia asked.

"Well, Ramon, but everybody calls me Gonzo."

"Alright then, Gonzo it is. Why don't you guys come on back?" She walked past the counter and hung a right, taking them into a room with couches and a fancy-lit drawing table. This place was a hell of a lot nicer than the tattoo places he'd been to previously.

Gonzo looked around. "Nice."

"Yeah, we just put this in about a month ago. Before that we didn't really have a place to do consults, so this is nice to have, especially for multiple people." She walked over to the drawing table and hit a button and a picture flashed up on the TV screen on the wall. "So I just did a few preliminary sketches based on what Jeff said you wanted. I'm happy to adjust anything or go a completely different direction, if this isn't what you had in mind."

Ryan stood up and walked over to the screen. "Is that a Hawk attacking a globe?"

"Yeah, you know the Hawks killing the world series." She smiled shyly. "Too literal?"

"No, it's fucking awesome." Ryan's hand lifted like he was going to touch the screen.

"Glad you like it." Kia turned to Jeff. "What about you?"

"This is different than what you showed me the other night."

Kia nodded. "I still have those drawings too, but I did this one up last night after we talked again."

He grinned. "It's perfect."

Gonzo wandered over to her station. "Any chance you could weave my number into it somehow?"

"Of course. What's your number?"

"55."

"Last name?"

"Gonzalez."

Kia bent over and drew a band along the hawk's ankle with the number 55 on it. She continued to draw. It looked like the backside of the band that was hidden from view had Gonzo's name on it because all you could see was the G on one side and the EZ on the other. The 55 was the only fully clear thing on the band.

"Yeah, that's perfect." Gonzo said.

"That looks badass. I want my number too," Pete told her.

"I think it's numbers all around, Kia." Jeff looked up at the screen. Somehow she'd made the hawk look majestic and fierce as it shredded the world. How could her parents think she was wasting her talent when she could draw something like that? If what ended up on his skin was even half as good as what she'd drawn, he'd proudly wear that tattoo.

"Absolutely." Ryan nodded.

"Cool. Color or black and gray?"

Jeff looked up at the drawing on the screen. "Black and gray, just like that."

"Agreed," Gonzo said, followed by sounds of agreement from Pete and Ryan.

"Well, that was easy." Kia laughed. "Now when Jeff and I talked, he'd mentioned you all wanted the same tattoo to celebrate winning the world series together, but what about location?" She turned to Jeff. "I know you and Max were all hopped up about a chest tattoo. Is that still what you're thinking? Right pec?"

"Absolutely. I told him he could pick where it went. I'm not going to disappoint him."

Kia smiled at him. Her eyes warmed as she held his stare. His fingers twitched to pull her closer to him, but he didn't have that right.

The sound of a throat clearing pulled their attention away from each other. Kia blushed and looked down.

"My back is totally open, so right shoulder blade would work for me," Pete said, breaking the awkwardness in the room.

Kia pulled up her calendar on the screen. "I blocked off time for one of you to go today if you want to get started right away or if you need to think about it some more. You can call and schedule something."

Jeff looked at the clock on the wall. 4:30. "I thought you normally got off around now."

"I do, but Max is doing a sleepover at my sister's tonight, so I can work late if you want to get started."

If anyone was going tonight, it was going to be him. Maybe afterwards he could talk Kia into grabbing a bite to eat or something. "I'm good with going now."

"Great, give me half an hour to tighten this all up and make the stencil, and we can get started."

"Can we stick around and see you get started?" Ryan asked.

"Of course."

Gonzo leaned against the edge of the drawing table. "What's your schedule like coming up? I know we all want to get this done before the season starts."

"Gonzo's a pussy so he'll probably need to break his up over several sessions," Jeff joked.

"Fuck you. I can sit longer than you can."

"Bullshit. There's no way you wouldn't tap out before I did."

"Okay boys, this isn't a competition. There's no shame in needing to go slow."

Pete burst out laughing. "You clearly don't know us at all."

Ryan threw his arm around Pete's shoulder. "Everything's a competition."

"Awesome. You're those kinds of guys." Kia rolled her eyes.

"What do you mean, those kinds of guys?" Jeff pinned her with a look. The way she said it, being one of those kinds of guys didn't sound like a compliment.

"Oh, you know. The ones who talk all big. Then they tap out after twenty minutes with some lame excuse about how they don't normally react like this. It must have been something they ate that isn't sitting right." She raised one eyebrow as she looked around the group, daring them to be that guy.

Gonzo puffed up his chest at the challenge. "Not happening."

Kia patted him on the chest. "We'll see. The bigger they are, the harder they fall."

Gonzo growled, which only made Kia laugh harder. Jeff smiled as he watched her interact with his friends. She fit well with them, bantering easily. It was cool. And fuck if it didn't make him like her even more. Damn it. He wasn't supposed to be thinking about her like that. Things were complicated enough without him lusting after the mother of his child.

After several minutes of schedule manipulation, they all had appointments booked for the initial session.

"We're gonna go grab something to eat and then we'll be back in half an hour. You want me to bring you back anything?" Jeff asked.

"An iced coffee, sweet with oat milk, would be great. Thanks."

"No problem. Be back in a bit."

Twenty minutes later, Jeff and his friends strolled back into the shop. She took one last cursory glance at her station, then wandered to the front.

Jeff smiled as she walked up, and he held out a to-go cup.

She made gimme-gimme hands and grabbed the drink. "Ah thank you. Just give me five minutes to chug this down and we'll be ready."

"You don't have to chug it."

Kia pointed to the sign. "No food or drink."

"That goes for you guys, too?" he asked.

"At the stations, yeah. Water only."

He looked around the shop. "I guess that makes sense."

Kia took a long sip of her drink and closed her eyes as the sweet coffee slid down her throat. Damn, that was good. When she popped her eyes open, four sets of eyes stared at her. "Sorry." She chuckled. "Clearly I don't get out much."

Gonzo eyed her almost empty coffee cup. "That was impressive. I bet you rock at boat races."

"I rock at everything I do. Especially tattoos." She winked. "You all sticking around to see your boy get inked?"

"No," Jeff declared.

Ryan slapped Jeff on the back. "We're gonna stay for a bit to make sure he doesn't puss out or faint or something."

"Bite me, dickhead." Jeff hip checked his friend. "They aren't staying."

It was nice seeing Jeff with his friends. The way they laughed and joked with each other like brothers spoke of the strong bond between them. And once they all got this tattoo together, that bond would only be stronger. Ink was a powerful medium. It was one of the things she loved about tattooing. Marking a moment in time forever on someone's skin. Good or bad, it became a piece of them. And for Jeff and his friends this experience would be amazing. She'd make sure of it.

She downed the last sip of her coffee and dropped the cup into the recycle bin. "Alright, come on back."

Leading the way through the shop, she stopped in front of her station. She always had one extra chair for guests but needed a couple more if everyone was staying. At times like this, she really loved the open floor area in Viper's shop and how much room was allotted for each section. It gave clients the illusion of privacy without making the staff sacrifice the bonding that happened when you worked closely with a team.

"You ready?" she asked Jeff.

"Yep. How do you want me?"

Her eyes snapped up to his face. Now that was a loaded question. His eyes narrowed as he looked back at her. What was wrong with her? He was a client. Just like any other client. Whatever little whispers of attraction she felt every time she was around him, she needed to lock that shit down. She prided herself on being a professional and being damn good at her job. This was no different from any other tattoo.

"I'm gonna need your shirt off."

Jeff peeled his t-shirt off and turned to face her. Her eyes lingered on his chest. She licked her lips as she let her gaze trail over his pecs, then down over his washboard abs. The way his V-cut, drew her eyes made her mouth water. Okay, this definitely didn't feel like any other tattoo.

"Did you just flex your pecs?" Gonzo asked.

"What? No." Jeff glared at his friend.

"You totally did." Gonzo stood and struck a pose. "Oh Kia, look at my big strong muscles," he pitched his voice into a ridiculously high noise.

Jeff threw his t-shirt and hit Gonzo in the face and laughed. "You're an idiot."

Suddenly, everything shifted, and it felt like any other tattoo. Kia grinned over at Gonzo. His antics were exactly what she needed to get back on steady ground. She pointed her finger at him. "If I let you stay, keep the shenanigans to a minimum. I can't have him turning to smack you in the middle of a line." She flicked her thumb toward Jeff.

Gonzo brought his hand up to his forehead and saluted her. "Understood."

She quickly ran a razor over the area to be inked. Kia picked up the stencil and carefully positioned it on Jeff's chest. She stepped back to eye the placement. Satisfied, she said to Jeff, "Take a look and make sure you're happy with it."

He strolled over to the mirror and looked at himself from several angles, turning each way before finally walking back. A lot of people just quickly glanced but didn't really look. She liked how he took the time to make sure he was happy with the way it was placed on his body because once she started, there was no going back.

"Looks good," he said when he returned to her station.

"Alright then, let's do this." She sat on her stool as Jeff lay back on her table. "You comfy? If you need me to stop and go to the bathroom or you just need a break, let me know. There are no awards for suffering. So let me know what you need."

He shifted his body a bit on the table. "I'm good."

Gun in hand, she rolled her chair up to the edge of the table. "I'll just make a small test line, so you get a feel for the pressure and then we'll go."

"Sound good."

Kicking on her gun, she drew a small line at the edge of the tattoo.

He flashed her a thumbs up. "We're good."

"Awesome." She began outlining the tattoo, listening to Jeff and his friends laughing and talking in the background. Now and then, she'd add something to the conversation, but she just relaxed into the work.

"So Kia," Gonzo said.

"Yes?"

"How'd you get into tattooing? Smitty said you were in art school when he met you."

It probably made sense that he'd talked to his friends about her, but hearing it was still a little weird. "Yeah, I was. We had an artist come into class one day and give a lecture. Then, when I got pregnant with Max, taking a job at a shop was a good fit. The rest as they say…"

Jeff's pec muscle flinched slightly. She glanced up and found Jeff staring back at her. "You good?" she asked.

"Yep."

"Okay." She continued lining.

"And you were in Tucson then?" Gonzo continued.

"Mm hmm."

"That's wild you both ended up here."

"Yep, small world."

"You dating anyone?" Gonzo asked. Jeff's chest twitched. She glanced up at his face again. He didn't appear to be in any discomfort physically, but his jaw clenched slightly.

"Nope," she responded.

"What?" Jeff's body jerked.

"Hold still," she growled. Eyeing the outline, she breathed a sigh of relief that his reaction hadn't screwed up the line.

"What do you mean you're not dating anyone? What about Austin?"

Afraid of what she'd see in his eyes if she looked up, she kept her head down and focused on the work. "We broke up."

"When?"

"I don't know, a couple of weeks ago."

"A couple weeks and you didn't think to tell me?" Jeff's entire body tensed.

Unable to continue tattooing, she flipped off the machine. "No, I didn't think to tell you because who I date isn't really your business."

One part of her had been afraid to tell him because of what would happen without that barrier between them. The other part was afraid that needing it had all been in her mind. She wasn't sure which was worse.

His jaw clenched. "I absolutely think it's my business if you're dating someone or not."

And from his angry reaction, she still didn't know what way he was leaning. He was being a jerk. She set the tattoo gun on the tray, so she wasn't tempted to stab him with it. "Oh, and why is that?"

"Yeah, so—" Gonzo stood up. "I think we're just gonna go." He pointed his thumb toward the front door. "And we'll meet up with you when you're done."

Pete and Ryan stood as well and shifted toward the door.

"We'll all see you later for our tattoos, Kia," Ryan added.

Forcing herself to remain professional, Kia tore her glare off Jeff and glanced at his friends. Her clients. "Sounds good. I'm looking forward to it. I think you guys will love them when they're done."

The trio slunk toward the front door.

"Sorry," Jeff mumbled, drawing her attention back to him.

"For what?"

"That was out of line."

"Mm hmm."

"I'm serious, I'm sorry. I was just surprised you hadn't told me you'd broken up."

"I didn't think it mattered."

"It matters." Something in the tone of his voice made her look up. She sucked in a breath at the heat in his eyes. Guess she had her answer.

She licked her lips, and Jeff's gaze remained glued to her mouth. Goosebumps danced across her skin, making her nipples tighten. One look from Jeff and her body was instantly on fire. Oh boy. This was exactly what she'd been afraid of.

"Uh—" She cleared her throat. What the hell was happening? She was working. He was a client. She closed her eyes and took a deep, cleansing breath.

Opening them, she picked up her tattoo gun. "What do you say we get back to this, okay?"

"Sure," he mumbled.

As the machine buzzed to life again, she tried to pull in the calm she always felt when she worked. Unfortunately, her hormones had other ideas. She'd never been so conscious of how close she needed to be to do her job. She was ridiculously aware of Jeff and the fact that her hands were on his chest.

His very naked chest.

Desperate for a distraction, something to make her feel normal, she rolled her shoulders. "So tell me about your friends."

"What do you want to know?"

"I don't know, the usual. Are they married, single? How long have you known them? Hit me."

"Ryan and Pete are both in a relationship. Gonzo is single." He chuckled. "Clearly."

She snickered. "He gives off single vibes, for sure."

"Gonz and I have been friends since the minors. We came up together. Both got called up the same year. I met Pete when I joined the team, and Ryan's been with the Hawks for a couple of seasons."

It made things so much easier that Jeff was willing to ignore the elephant in the room and let her bury her head in her work. Maybe she should have told him she'd broken up with Austin, but she'd been scared. Having a boyfriend had put a barrier between them, forcing them to ignore this attraction. It kept things from being overly complicated. But now, without that, she was afraid she wouldn't be able to fight the fact she actually had feelings for her son's father.

Finally, several hours of tattooing later, Kia turned off the machine and stretched her back. "Alright, I think we're done."

"Yeah?" Jeff glanced at his chest.

"Yep, go take a look." She pushed her wheelie stool back from the table and followed Jeff over to the full-length mirror.

He stood in front of the mirror, staring at his tattoo. His hand reached out like he was going to touch it, then he shied away and just leaned in closer. A huge smile split across his face. "Kia," he reverently said her name. Turning to her, he wrapped his arms around her waist and hoisted her up in the air, so they were the same height.

Laughing, she wrapped her arms around him and held on. "I take it you like it?"

He set her back on the floor. "Like it? Jesus. I knew you were talented, but this is next level."

Viper wandered over. "I'm guessing from all the noise over here that your boy likes the work."

Jeff glanced at Viper. "Yeah, you could say that."

Viper leaned in close to Jeff's chest and a little zip of nerves danced up her back. She knew the tattoo was good, but whenever another artist looked at her work, she always held her breath. No matter how good the tattoo was, nothing was ever perfect, and another artist would see all those imperfections.

After several seconds, Viper wrapped his arm around her shoulder. "You're gonna have to raise your rates."

She threw her head back and laughed. Her eyes landed on Jeff, and he grinned back at her. As she looked at her tattoo on his chest, a little jolt of something strange zipped through her. It almost felt like possession. Like she'd branded him in some way. Claimed him. She shook her head. That's not what her tattoo was. Hell, she was giving his friends the same one. It didn't mean anything.

She looked back at him, their eyes connected in the mirror. His nostrils flared as he held her stare.

Except it meant something. She just wasn't sure what yet.

CHAPTER FOURTEEN

LATER THAT WEEK, KIA absently flicked through the TV channels for something to watch. This shouldn't be so hard. Just because Max wasn't here didn't mean she couldn't still do something she wanted. She flicked on a home improvement show, then sighed. God, she was pathetic.

She picked up her sketch pad and flipped it to a new page. Slowly, she began sketching the outline of a random design. She had no idea what it was going to become. It wasn't about drawing a tattoo or any particular design. Tonight, she just needed to clear her head. After several minutes of drawing, she was no closer to feeling relaxed. Apparently, clearing her head was the last thing she was going to be doing. Even with the drawing only partially started, it was clear to anyone looking that she was drawing

Jeff. So much for not thinking about him. He had occupied far too many of her thoughts lately. Between how often Max talked about him, to how often she thought about him on her own, it seemed like Jeff had set up camp in her brain. How many sleepless nights had she spent lying in bed thinking of the damn man? Yes, she could pretend she was thinking about him because of Max, but her vibrator would tell a different story.

Her doorbell rang. Tossing the sketch pad on the coffee table, she headed to the front door. She peeked through the peephole and sucked in a breath when she saw the man in question standing on her front doorstep with a box of pizza in his hands.

Placing her hand on the doorframe to steady her breath, she closed her eyes and exhaled. She was a strong, confident woman. She could be cool around the man. She pulled the door open, and Jeff flashed her a boyish smile that shot directly to her clit. And cool went right out the window. What the hell? How could a simple smile make her feel like she'd just watched porn? What was wrong with her? It hadn't been that long since she'd had sex. Sure, the sex with Austin was average, but it had still been sex. But standing here looking at Jeff, the muscle in his biceps flexing slightly from holding the pizza at an angle, all she wanted to do was lick the curve of his muscle. Ridiculous.

"Hey," he said, holding out the pizza box like an offering. "I come bearing gifts."

"I see that." She glanced over her shoulder toward the empty house. "Except Max isn't here. He's having a sleep-over with his cousin tonight at Vika's."

Jeff's shoulder slumped. "Seriously? That sucks." He glanced at the pizza in his hand. "I probably should have called first."

"Probably." She chewed on her bottom lip. The polite thing to do would be to invite him in. Except in this moment she was feeling like a cat in heat and would probably rub herself all over him and send him screaming into the night.

Jeff raised his head and flashed that panty melting smile of his at her again, and her nipples instantly tightened. What the actual fuck was going on with her body?

"You eaten?" he asked. "Just cuz Max isn't here doesn't mean we can't eat."

"Um...uh."

"What? You already ate?"

"Uh, no, no, not yet."

"Awesome, then let's eat." He stepped toward her, and she jumped back. He eyed her with a smirk and took another step toward her. "Unless you're worried you won't be able to keep your hands off me if we're alone together."

She narrowed her eyes. "Dream on, hotshot."

"Oh believe me, I do, every night."

Holy crap. She sucked back a breath. Then cleared her throat. "Come on in," she said and swung her arm wide to gesture he come inside.

Jeff kicked off his shoes at the front door, then walked toward the kitchen. She shook her head. Apparently, he planned on staying awhile. "Make yourself at home," she called after his retreating form.

"I plan to," he called back. "Beer or wine with the pizza?"

"It's pizza, what do you think?" she replied as she walked into the kitchen and rested her hip against the counter. She watched him move around her kitchen with practiced ease. He set two bottles of beer on the counter.

Kia's pulse quickened. How could it feel so right to have him in her kitchen? When Max was home, it made sense. Father and son were bonding. They needed to spend time together to forge a connection, and the comfortable way they moved together had made her happy. That was exactly what she wanted for her son. But Max wasn't here. So why did it feel so right to have him in her kitchen when it was just the two of them?

"You want a plate or just napkins and the box?" Jeff raised an eyebrow as he looked at her.

"Seriously? How old are you?"

"What? You're kid free tonight. You don't have to be all proper. I thought you might want to skip having to do the dishes."

"Nope, kid or not, I want the plate."

"Weak," he teased.

She reached into the cupboard and pulled out two plates. She felt her shirt raise with the movement and she cringed. Setting the plates on the counter, she pulled her shirt back down and adjusted the waistband of her yoga pants. She worked out regularly, but her job was fairly sedentary, and she was well aware she was holding onto a few more pounds than necessary. When she turned around, Jeff's eyes snapped up. He rubbed the back of his neck.

Had he been staring at her ass?

His eyes dipped to her chest and lingered a moment before he picked up the pizza box. He hooked his fingers around the necks of the beers and scooped them both up one handed. "You want to eat in the living room?"

"Sure."

Jeff sat on the couch. He licked his lips as he looked at her. "You don't usually dress like that when I'm over?"

"What are you talking about? I practically live in yoga pants."

"Yeah, but usually yoga pants and shirts that would fit me. Not shirts that look like that?" He flicked a finger at her fitted tank top.

"What's wrong with my shirt?"

He groaned. "Not a goddamn thing. That's the problem."

"What?" She frowned as she looked at him. What was he on about?

"Shit. Sorry. Maybe this was a bad idea."

"What do you mean?" She shifted her body, so she was facing him and pulled her leg up on the couch. "You're being weird. Why's this a bad idea?"

His gaze lingered on her chest again, then back up to her face. "Fuck." He ran his hand through his hair and sighed. "Cards on the table here." He stared at her and raised one eyebrow. She nodded for him to continue. "I'm just super conscious of the fact that Max isn't here, and you look like that." He eyed her body again.

She bristled. "I look like what?"

"Key, you know you look fucking hot. That's why you don't normally dress like that around me and we both know it."

"No, we don't both know anything."

He cocked his head to the side, giving her a look that said she was full of shit.

"Seriously?" She shifted uncomfortably. "Jeff, look at you and then look at me. The reason I don't dress like this around you is because I'm very aware that my body doesn't look anything like it did when you knew me before."

"So what? My body doesn't look the same as it did then either."

"Oh my god," she scoffed. "That is so not the same thing. You're ripped now and have put on twenty pounds of muscle, while I've put on twenty pounds of whatever this is." She waved her hand at her stomach. This was embarrassing. She prided herself on being this confident woman. Bold enough to free the nip and go braless every now and then. But that was different. That was around people who hadn't seen her naked before she'd had a kid. That wasn't around Jeff.

"Saskia," his voice lowered, deep, commanding, demanding she look at him.

Chewing her bottom lip, she raised her head.

"You're gorgeous. And if you're packing twenty extra pounds, believe me, every one of them is in exactly the right place." He dragged his hand over his mouth. "This is a bad idea because when Max is around I can keep my dick under control because I feel like a fucking perv when it twitches with a kid around."

She bit back a laugh at the disgusted look on his face. It was cute that he was worried about something like that.

His gaze raked across her body slowly. Even though he wasn't touching her, she felt it on her skin like a caress.

"But with Max gone and you single now. I'm just...I...I'm just going to be honest. I really want to put my hands on you."

She shivered. That sounded amazing to her too. "Yeah?"

"Yeah. But I know it's complicated." He shook his head. "And you don't like to have guys you're involved with around Max, and I get that. Hell, I respect that about you. I just... I can't stop thinking about you. Wanting you. You're making me crazy and the more time I spend with you, the more I want you." He looked over at her, then winced. "Fuck sorry. Well... shit." He shifted and began tidying up the napkins.

What just happened? She reached out and set her hand on his arm, and he stopped moving. "Jeff?"

"What?" He kept his head down, not making eye contact with her.

"Look at me."

He shifted his weight and slid back on the couch and raised his head to look at her. "Sorry, the last thing you need is me putting the moves on you."

If only that were true. As much as her mind knew it was a bad idea for them to get involved, her body completely disagreed. But if he could admit how he was feeling, the least she could do was meet him halfway. "I'm not sure I'd say it's the last thing I need."

He shifted, leaning toward her slightly. "No? So, you're saying the fact that I'm attracted to you still isn't a bad thing?"

"It's definitely a complicated thing, but not sure I'd say bad since I'm equally attracted to you still."

"Oh, yeah?" The corner of his mouth kicked up into a cocky smile. "You saying you think about me, too? You check out my ass as much as I do yours?"

She rolled her eyes. "Of course I don't check out your ass. What kind of mother would I be if I noticed that kind of thing? Although would it kill you to wear a baggy shirt every so often?"

He laughed. His eyes twinkled when he looked at her. "Well, thank fuck you noticed. I thought I was going to have to pull out the tank tops next if I didn't start getting a reaction soon."

She smacked him on the arm. "You're an idiot."

"True." He shifted his body, so he was facing her. "So, what are we going to do about this attraction?"

She chewed her bottom lip. The smart thing to do would be to ignore it completely. Her eyes lingered on his muscular chest. Too bad she wasn't feeling too smart. "I'm not sure we can act on it without things getting messy."

"Okay, let's just talk this through. What are you worried about?"

She rolled her eyes. "Seriously? I think it's pretty clear what I'm worried about. The same thing you are."

"Okay, okay, yeah, obviously it would be a bad idea to be all grabby hands with each other in front of Max?"

"All grabby hands?" She snickered.

"Fuck off." He laughed. "You know what I mean." He held her stare. "I think if we go into this knowing that we both want to protect Max, then it'll be fine."

"So what are you thinking? Fuck. Get it out of your system and we go back to normal?"

"No." He reared back. "Is that what you want?"

Uncomfortable, she shifted her weight to her right hip and pulled up her left leg onto the couch. "I don't know. I mean...what do you want?" What was it about this man that affected her like this? Normally with guys she dated, she laid it out clearly for them in black and white exactly what the boundaries were. They were completely separate from her kid. There would be no outings together with her and Max, no coming over for dinner. But with Jeff? That boundary had already been destroyed. And because of how she felt about him, she wasn't sure she wanted any boundaries in place. Hell, he already had a relationship with Max. They already did family dinners and outings and she loved it. That was the problem. She didn't want to ruin what they had already.

He shifted so his knee hit hers. "What are you scared of, Saskia?"

"I think it's pretty obvious what I'm scared of? What if we fuck and then you decide you don't want to continue that anymore and things get weird and then you don't want to hang out with Max?"

"Okay first, nothing will make me stop wanting to be around Max. I don't give a fuck what happens between us. I will always be there for Max. No matter what." He pinned her with a stare. "I'm a grown ass man, Kia, and I can behave like a grownup for my kid, no matter what. Got it?"

Her stomach quivered. Why did that turn her on so damn much? "Got it."

"Good. Besides, who's to say you aren't going to be the one who has sex with me and then feels all awkward?"

Offended, she scowled at him. "Well, as you said, I'm a grown ass woman and I can act like a grownup for my kid."

He smirked. "Cool, then what's the problem?"

What the hell just happened? Had he maneuvered her into agreeing to have sex with him? She held up a hand. "Hold up, Romeo. It's a little more complicated than that. So let's just say we agree to have sex."

"I like where you're going here."

She shook her head. "If we agree to have sex, I think it's best if we don't let Max know."

Jeff snorted. "Yeah, I don't plan on talking about my sex life with the little guy."

"Shut up." She smacked him on the chest. "You know what I mean. I'm just saying I think if we decide to have sex we should keep everything else between us the same. We can hang out all together sometimes, but you still take Max and do stuff just the two of you. I don't want Max to wonder if we are a couple or anything like that."

Jeff winced. "Except he already does."

"What do you mean?"

"Just the other day, he asked me if we were all going to live together soon."

Kia's mind raced. "Wh...why would he ask you that?"

"I don't know. He's a kid. Isn't that what they do?"

"Okay, maybe this is a bad idea. I don't want Max to be confused."

"Breathe." Jeff placed his hand on her knee. "He's a kid. He wants his parents to be together. That's not going to change whether or not we sleep together."

"True, but it makes things more confusing."

"For whom? Him or us?" Jeff asked.

Damn him for being so insightful. She exhaled a deep breath. "For me."

Jeff squeezed her leg. "For me too. But that doesn't mean I don't want to try."

"Try? Are you saying you want to see where things could go with us?"

"Obviously." He picked up her hand. "Kia, I think you're amazing. I watch you with Max and the relationship you have, the bond. I'm just in awe of you. You're this amazing mom. But you're still this super cool, sexy woman. I enjoy talking with you after Max is in bed. You fit in with my friends. And then when we hung while you were doing my tattoo, I saw this other side of you, and I was just as much in awe of you then. Seeing you in your element like that." He shook his head. "How could I not want to see if we could have something between us?"

Warmth coursed through her chest. Is that really how he saw her? Everything in her wanted to see where things could go. But did she dare try? As much as they said they could both be adults, what if it didn't work?

She looked up to find Jeff watching her patiently. "I'm in awe of you, too."

"Oh, really?"

She wrinkled her nose, and fake sneered at him. "Yes, obviously. You stepped up with Max and honestly, that surprised me."

"Why'd it surprise you? He's my kid. Of course I stepped up."

"No, Jeff, not of course. A lot of people in your position would have run the other way. You didn't sign on for a kid from a one-night stand."

"Neither did you."

"True, but I had a lot longer to get used to the idea than you did. And then when you found out, you instantly embraced Max and being his dad." She turned her hand over and laced her fingers with his. "I can't thank you enough for how you are with Max. Seeing you two together—" Tears welled in her eyes. "—it means a lot."

Jeff reached over and gently flicked his thumb under the corner of her eye, then cupped the side of her head. Holding eye contact with her, he said, "You don't have to thank me for loving my kid, Key."

She rested her cheek on his palm and closed her eyes. Sighing, she opened her eyes. "Thank you anyway. It means a lot to me. That's part of the problem. I love seeing you and Max together. Seeing the way he's shining under your attention. He's needed that, he's needed a man in his life. A dad." She paused. "What if things don't work out between us and it's awkward? You still have a relationship with Max, but it becomes weird for us to hang out all together and I have to miss out on that part of him."

Jeff shifted closer, pulling her leg on top of his thigh so they were closer together. "What if it works out? What if changing our relationship changes everything for the better? What if we become a real family?"

God, that would be amazing. Did she dare hope for that? "But what if it doesn't?" she whispered.

"What is it you always say to Max? There's never any shame in trying?" He placed his hand on her hip and with one quick move, he pulled her onto his lap, so they were face to face. "Be brave with me, Kia. Where would you be if you hadn't gone after what you wanted?"

She thought of all the things she'd been afraid to do. Becoming a tattoo artist, having Max, telling her parents she was pregnant, moving to San Diego. As hard as the road had been, she wouldn't trade it for anything.

"Think how great we could be together," he said.

"It could be pretty amazing." But there was also a very real possibility they wouldn't work out. She shifted her weight on his lap to get more comfortable as she looked at him. Everything about him made her want to jump.

Jeff bit back a groan as his hand tightened on her hip and suddenly she became conscious of their position. What had felt like a comforting position only a moment ago now felt incredibly erotic. She could feel him getting hard. She held his stare and shifted her weight slightly, grinding against his cock.

His eyes darkened and his fingers dug into her hips, holding her in place. "Kia," he warned.

"Mm hmm," she said as she rocked against him again. "Maybe we don't tell anyone we're doing this."

"Yeah, we already agreed we wouldn't tell Max."

She chewed her bottom lip. "I was meaning more like we don't tell anyone that we are sleeping together, not your friends, not my sister. We just keep this part of our relationship private."

His eyes narrowed. "Why? I mean, I get not wanting Max to know, but what's it matter if our friends do?"

She shrugged. "I don't know. What if it doesn't work out? Then there's just more questions and drama." God, it was hard to think while sitting on his lap like this. "Having Max changes things. We'll be in each other's lives regardless of what happens, which is fine, but having other people's opinions makes an already cloudy situation really murky,"

"I can see that, I guess."

She shifted her hips, grinding her clit on his cock through their clothes. "Besides, it could be kind of fun to just be each other's dirty little secret."

Jeff's nostrils flared and a sexy smile curled up one side of his mouth. "Oh yeah? Does that mean you want to get dirty with me?"

She looked him in the eyes and licked her lips. "I want to get fucking filthy."

"Jesus," he groaned. "So are we agreed we're doing this, then?"

"Yes, but Max doesn't know. No one does. We keep things the same as they are now where he's concerned. We keep it casual."

Jeff threaded his hand around the back of her head and gripped her hair tight, holding her in place. "For now," he growled. His lips crashed against hers, leaving her with no chance to argue.

CHAPTER FIFTEEN

His tongue pressed into her mouth, claiming her.

God, she didn't know what she'd agreed to exactly and frankly, she didn't care.

His finger dipped beneath the edge of her shirt, touching her bare skin. She held her breath, hoping he would push her shirt higher.

He dragged his nose along her neck. "Why do you always smell so fucking good?"

"It's cocoa butter," she murmured.

"Hmm." His tongue ran from her collarbone up to her earlobe.

Kia dropped her head back and closed her eyes. Goosebumps danced across her skin everywhere his tongue touched. Needing more, she reached up and pushed her hair off her shoulder to give him better access to her neck.

Had it been this good between them the first time? She remembered it being amazing, but this? What was going on? A dry hump, a little tongue and her entire body was on fire.

Before this moment she'd honestly thought having a baby had short-circuited something in her brain, dulled the trigger on her libido. Well, not her libido but the partner induced orgasm button for sure. Yes, she could get there, but it was a hell of a lot easier to do it by herself. Ever since she'd had Max, her stupid mom-guilt brain never wanted to shut off when she was with a man. Hell, that's why she always used toys with her partners. No toy needed here. What was so different about Jeff?

Yes, the man could kiss, but so could lots of people. So why did it feel like if he simply flicked her clit she'd come already?

Holding onto her hips, he widened his legs. The movement dragged her clit along the length of his cock, and she moaned. Who needed toys when you had that? Wow!

Jeff gripped the bottom of her shirt and pulled it over her head. "Kia, you are so fucking sexy."

With the way he was looking at her, how could she feel anything but sexy? Her nipples beaded tightly as his eyes lingered on her chest. The lace pressed against the sensitive skin. "You ain't seen nothing yet," she said. Reaching behind her, she unhooked her bra. Maintaining eye contact, she slowly lowered it down her body and dropped it onto the floor behind her.

Jeff's nostrils flared as he stared at her naked chest. His hand wrapped into her hair, and he dragged her mouth back to his. As their tongues tangled, she ground herself down on his cock. He fucked her mouth with his tongue. Mimicking the motion of his hips.

She wanted to be naked. To feel him inside her.

Anticipation made her pulse stutter as his fingers teased the underside of her breasts. She shifted her hips, grinding against him harder, hungry for the orgasm that was already so close.

Breaking the kiss, he licked a path across her neck. He lingered on the pulse point, then bit down. She shivered and dropped her head back. The motion thrust her breast in the air.

"Yeah, that's what I wanted," he murmured a second before his mouth closed around her nipple in a firm grasp.

"Holy shit," she moaned, gyrating her hips faster and harder against him. She threaded her fingers into his hair, grinding on him as he continued to lick and suck at her nipples. "Oh, my god." How the hell could she be so close already?

On hyper-alert, she waited as his hand dipped into her pants. "Yes," she hissed. That was exactly what she needed. He paused slightly and she wanted to scream at him not to stop. He shifted his weight and his hand slipped between their bodies. The first brush of his finger against her clit felt unbelievable. She widened her legs, desperate for him to continue.

He ran his tongue up her chest and neck as he rubbed her clit. "You like that?" he asked. His breath was hot against her ear as he spoke.

"Mm hmm," she moaned.

He bit her neck, pinched her nipple with one hand and her clit with the other, and her entire body bowed as the orgasm tore through her.

As she tried to catch her breath, she dimly registered him pulling his hands from her pants. The man hit the fucking trifecta on the first try, nipple, clit, and neck all at once. How the hell did he do that while keeping her from falling off the couch? Was he a bloody octopus? My god.

"That was…" she stammered.

"Hot." He slammed a kiss against her mouth. "We need a bed. Now." Strong hands cupped her ass as he stood up from the couch and marched them down the hall toward her bedroom.

He dropped her on the bed and stepped back. Kia leaned back onto her arms and looked at him, standing in front of her fully clothed with his erection fighting to get out of the confines of his jeans. "You have far too many clothes on," she told him.

"So do you." He grabbed the waistband of her leggings and dragged the fabric down her legs. Somehow he pulled her underwear off, leaving her naked on the bed while he remained fully clothed.

"Fuck, Kia. You are even more beautiful than I remember."

She pushed her chest out further. "Glad you think so." She flicked her finger toward him. "Lose the clothes and let's see if you live up to my memories as well."

He reached behind his head and pulled his shirt off with one hand. The muscles in his abdomen rippled as he wrenched the fabric off and tossed it on the floor.

She sucked in a breath. "Nope, my memories did not do you justice."

He smirked. With confidence written on every line of his body, he watched her as he undid the button on his jeans.

She licked her lips and shifted on the mattress. Jeff raised one eyebrow at her and waited.

"Hurry up," she demanded.

"Can I just tell you how sexy it is that you want my cock so badly?"

"Good, then quit being such a cock tease and pull it out."

Jeff threw back his head and laughed. "Who am I to deny the lady what she wants?" He eased the zipper of his pants down.

"Hold that thought," she said as she sat up quickly. Reaching into her bedside table, she pulled out a condom.

Dropped it on the nightstand then propped herself back up to face him again. "Okay, resume what you were doing."

Jeff shook his head and chuckled. "Anything else?"

"Nope, carry on." She wiggled her ass against the mattress as anticipation zipped through her. The orgasm had taken the edge off, but now that they had started this, she planned to enjoy every minute.

Jeff hooked his hand on the edge of his jeans and pushed them down his muscular thighs. Standing in front of her in his black boxer briefs, his cock pressed thick and hard against the fabric. She wet her lips. "Lose those too."

"Probably best if I leave them on while we play. I'm pretty sure the second my dick touches your bare skin it'll be game over, and I'll be fucking you."

She dropped her left knee open, exposing herself to him. "Good. Like I said, lose the boxers and get over here and fuck me."

Even from where she was, she could see the arousal in his eyes, the way his jaw tensed as he watched her.

He stepped toward the mattress. "I was thinking I'd make you come again before we fucked."

She shifted her leg again, showing him more of herself. "And I was thinking you'd make me come again while you fucked me." Knowing how competitive he was, she added, "Or don't you think you are up to the challenge?"

And instantly his boxers hit the floor. Jeez, the man moved fast.

He stalked toward the edge of the mattress and grabbed the condom off the bedside table and slid it on. She followed the movement of his hands as he stroked himself hard, once, then a second time.

"On your knees," he ordered.

Kia's nipples tightened. He kneeled between her legs. His cock visibly pulsed. With the way Jeff looked at her naked body, there was no way she could feel anything but completely confident in the way she looked. The stretch marks from having a child no longer mattered in the least. She crawled across the mattress and stopped in front of him.

"Turn around," he demanded.

Getting on all fours, she backed up, so her knees were on the edge of the mattress with her ass facing him.

"Jesus," he muttered.

Hearing the torture in his voice, she felt powerful. She looked over her shoulder at him and smiled.

He trailed his finger along the lips of her pussy. "Uh?"

"What?" she asked.

"You got lube or something?"

"Lube? I soaked your hand, Jeff. I'm pretty sure we don't need lube."

"Yeah, but that was a couple minutes ago and this angle sometimes—" He shrugged.

"It'll be fine." She shifted and wiggled her ass at him.

He gripped her hips and positioned himself at her entrance. He pressed slightly and stopped.

Okay, maybe he'd been right about the lube. He was a lot bigger than she'd remembered, thicker.

"You okay?" he asked.

There was no way she was telling him to stop. "Mm hmm," she murmured.

He pressed slightly again. Then stopped and stepped back. She glanced over her shoulder in time to see him spit on his hand and slather his cock with it. Moisture instantly flooded her pussy. She bit back a moan.

He smirked at her. "You good?"

"Yep." God, what would he think of her if he knew seeing him spit to lube himself turned her on that much when it should have had the exact opposite effect.

Jeff stepped back toward her, but instead of placing his cock against her, he dipped his finger inside. "That worked. You're a lot dirtier than I remember."

Embarrassed, she ducked her head.

"Don't be embarrassed, Key, as far as I'm concerned the dirtier the better."

She flicked a look over her shoulder. "Yeah?"

"Fuck yeah."

"Show me." She dropped her head onto her forearms and pressed her ass back toward him.

Jeff stepped up behind her, grabbed her hips and drove into her. She sucked in a breath as her body adjusted to the size of him.

"Second thoughts?" He gripped her hips tightly but didn't move.

"Absolutely not." She pressed back. "Fuck me."

The growl that rumbled out of Jeff's chest was the sexiest sound she'd ever heard.

Her nipples dragged against the mattress as the force of his thrusts moved her body. His fingers dug into her hips, and he shifted her body. Holy shit, he was big.

He grabbed her leg and moved it slightly forward, and she gasped. "Oh, my god."

"Good or bad?" he asked.

"Good, definitely good." Between the angle and his size, he hit places she didn't even know a person could hit. Toys? Yes. Person? Never.

His hand clasped her hair near her scalp like a ponytail and pulled her head back.

"Yes, pull my hair," she moaned.

He thrust into her hard. The tips of his fingers dug into her hip as he held her in place with one hand in her hair and the other on her waist. She'd probably have bruises, but she didn't care. His strength dictated exactly what her body was allowed to do, how she could move. And holy hell, that worked for her.

A shudder rippled through her as her orgasm built. She was so close. He released her hair and dropped his hand from her hip and wrapped it around her waist, pulling her body against his so she was kneeling upright.

He continued to thrust into her. His finger flicked against her clit, and he bit the side of her neck. "Yes," she moaned.

Kia dropped her head onto his shoulder as her back bowed with the orgasm that ripped through her.

She wanted to collapse against the mattress, but his muscular arm banded around her waist, holding her in place as he thrust several more times. She felt his body go rigid against her as he shuddered out his own release.

He eased the grip on her waist, and she collapsed onto the mattress, unable to hold herself up.

Jeff rested his head against her shoulder. "My god, Kia."

"I know, right," she replied and sucked in a breath. Her heart pounded against her chest as she tried to regain her equilibrium.

He placed a kiss against her shoulder, then stood and walked into the bathroom. A moment later, he returned. With the condom disposed of, it was her turn. She pressed herself off the mattress and padded naked toward the washroom. She quickly took care of business. When she walked back into the bedroom, she smiled to herself. Jeff was lying on the opposite side of the bed, leaving her side open for her.

She quickly slid under the sheets beside him. Would he want to stay over? Would he want to leave right away? The sex had been mind blowing, but they hadn't exactly figured out the boundaries of this thing they were doing.

Jeff's arm wrapped around her waist, and he pulled her back against his body so she was the little spoon. "Turn off that big brain of yours and stop thinking. We don't have to figure anything out tonight, Kia." He pressed a kiss against the side of her neck. "Now get some rest cuz I have all kinds of ideas on how I want to dirty you up before Max gets home tomorrow."

"That sounds promising," she said. Maybe Jeff was right. Nothing had to be decided tonight. Because whatever this was, she wanted more of it.

CHAPTER SIXTEEN

JEFF ROLLED OVER AND eyed the empty space beside him. Damn, he'd been hoping Kia would have still been in bed. So much for that breakfast plan. Pushing the covers down, he rolled off the bed and scooped up jeans from the floor. Not bothering with his underwear, he stepped into his pants and buttoned up the first couple of buttons, so they didn't fall off. Considering he was hoping they'd be coming off shortly, there wasn't much point in doing them up all the way.

Following the sound of clanking coming from the kitchen, he made his way down the hallway in search of Kia. In the kitchen, he leaned against the doorframe and watched her as her hips moved rhythmically to some kind of beat in her head that only she could hear.

It should look ridiculous with her dancing to some imaginary music, but it was hot as fuck. She picked up a cup from the drying rack and spun in a circle, dancing to her own beat. As she whipped around, her eyes landed on him, and she instantly stopped moving. Nerves clouded her face.

Fuck that. There was no way he was letting her second guess what had happened between them last night. He stepped toward her. She took a step back and hit the counter. Crowding her, he placed his hands on the counter on either side of her body, caging her in against him.

"Morning," he said as he leaned in and placed a kiss on her lips.

"Morning."

He leaned back so he could look her in the eye. She still had that wary look on her face. Bending, he rested his forehead against hers. "What's going through that mind of yours?"

She chewed on her bottom lip. "I'm still not sure this is the best idea."

Nope. Not happening. "You and I are the best fucking idea I think I've ever had. The only thing I'm questioning, Key, is when we tell Maxie. The rest isn't even up for debate." He leaned down slightly so they were eye to eye. "Are you having regrets about last night?" He sure as hell hoped not.

"No." She smiled softly. "Not really. I probably should be, but no. I'm not regretting last night. I'm just feeling a little uneasy about being around Max with you."

"Don't be. You need us to take this slow where Max is concerned, and I respect that. Will I want to put my hands on you? Absolutely. Can I control myself? Yeah. I've been doing it for the past two months."

She smirked. "Yeah, but that was before last night."

"True." He placed a kiss against her mouth. "But you need it to be this way, so it will be. Until you say otherwise. Cool?"

"Thank you." She stood on her tiptoes and wrapped her arms around his neck. The second her body pressed against him his cock fired to life. He grabbed her hips and hoisted her up. Kia squealed as he set her ass on the edge of the kitchen counter and stepped between her legs.

She pressed her hand against his chest. "Hold up there, quick draw."

He dragged his teeth across her neck, making her moan. "I think I showed you last night I can last as long as you need me to."

She tilted her head to the side slightly, exposing the line of her neck. "Big difference between a quick draw and a hair trigger, big guy. No one is questioning your stamina." He could hear the amusement in her voice as she spoke.

He ran his tongue up the length of her neck. "Then what are you questioning?" he asked right before he sucked her earlobe into his mouth.

Kia groaned, then pressed her hand against his chest to halt his movement. "Unfortunately, as much as I'd love to continue this, I have to pick up Max in half an hour, which means I gotta get dressed."

He stepped back, adjusting himself in his jeans. "What's on your agenda for today?"

"Not much, probably go to the park, pick up some groceries, then dinner at my sister's."

"Cool, you mind if I tag along?"

Her lips pulled in like she was going to run them together, then paused. "Um."

"Kia, come on, I tag along with you all the time."

"I know but..."

He stepped back between her thighs and rested his hand on the counter on either side of her. "No screw that. I'm not hanging out with you less just because of last night." He looked at her. "Whatever this is, we'll figure it out. We agreed we didn't want anything to change for Max. But to figure it out, we gotta hang out. We clear?"

She smirked. "Yeah, we're clear."

"Good." He stepped back. "I just need to brush my teeth and I'll be ready to go."

Her gaze slid down his body, lingering on the waist of his jeans. His dick twitched and she licked her lips.

"And maybe throw some underwear on. The whole commando thing isn't really kid friendly." She raised her eyebrows at him.

Glancing down, he saw how his dick tented his jeans. The half-done buttons had dragged his pants down slightly, making his treasure trail look less like a trail and more like a lit-up runway. Okay, yeah, maybe she had a point.

"Not that I'm complaining," she said as she stepped around. She paused at the entrance to the kitchen. "And just for the record, the whole bossy thing you have going on this morning is hot."

"Oh yeah? Then get back here." He quickly took a step toward her. With a squeal, Kia jumped and raced down the hallway, looking over her shoulder at him as he chased her toward the bedroom. Just outside the door, he grabbed her, picked her up, and hoisted her over his shoulder.

"Put me down," she yelled, swatting him on the ass.

"Nope." He carried her over to the bed and dropped her on the mattress. Following her down, he pressed his hips into the V of her thighs. Her body molded around him. Everything about her fit him perfectly.

"We don't have time for this."

"I can be quick," he said as he slid his body against hers, biting her hard nipple through the t-shirt. Her legs shifted further, letting him know her body was on board with a little detour. "I had my heart set on eating you for breakfast and feeling you come apart on my tongue, but if you don't want to be late picking up Max, you better be quick."

"Then you better be ready to dig in and get dirty if you want me to be fast." She pressed herself up on her elbows and looked at him, widening her legs to create more room for him. Eyeing the black and gray tiger that covered her entire right thigh and up her hip, he wanted to lick every inch of ink on her skin. His dick twitched. That tattoo was sexy as shit. But then everything about Kia was sexy.

Looking at her panties, he could see the moisture damping the fabric as he stared at her. Already imagining her taste on his tongue, he licked his lips. "There's nothing I like more than getting fucking dirty." He dropped to his knees on the floor, grabbed her legs, and yanked her toward him. Burying his face in her pussy, he ran his tongue along her seam, soaking the fabric of her panties with his tongue.

Kia moaned, her hips bucking against his face. "Aren't you going to take my panties off?" she asked.

"Nope, I think you're a dirty kind of girl who will get off having me trying to fuck you with my tongue with this fabric in the way." As he spoke, he shifted the elastic leg of her underwear and dragged it against her clit.

Kia hissed out a breath. "Oh wow, you might be on to something there."

"Thought so." He rubbed the fabric back and forth, creating a slight friction, then sucked her clit into his mouth. As he shifted his jaw, the fabric bunched up slightly in his mouth and he let out a frustrated sound.

"Oh my god, that even sounds hot," Kia groaned. Her fingers gripped his hair as she drove her hips toward his face.

He slid his finger under the fabric and inserted it inside her. She clenched around him. Inserting another, he curled them both slightly, making a little come here motion that he knew would drive her crazy. Her moans grew louder. Nails dug into his scalp as she pressed her hips against his face and pulled him toward her at the same time chasing her orgasm. There was nothing better than having Kia fuck his face.

Her pussy clenched against his fingers, letting him know how close she was. Mmm, now that was more like it. He dragged his teeth against her clit slightly, then pulled the tight bud into his mouth and sucked. Her thighs clamped around his face as she screamed out her orgasm. His dick throbbed against his fly, demanding to be released. Ignoring it, he focused instead on dragging out Kia's orgasm.

Finally, her legs dropped away from his ears and flopped onto the mattress. "Holy shit," she said as she hung her forearm across her face. Her chest rose and fell rapidly as she tried to catch her breath.

He leaned back on his heels and watched her. His dick screamed at him again. Reaching down, he shifted it slightly, so it wasn't getting crushed by the zipper. If they had more time, he would thoroughly enjoy taking his time fucking her. He glanced at the clock. They needed to leave to get Max soon, so that would have to wait for another day.

"Oh my god, what is wrong with me that I found that so unbelievably hot?" Kia pulled her arm away from her face and looked at him. "Who knew keeping my panties on would feel all dirty? Kind of like being finger fucked in the movies in high school, but like by a guy who really knew what he was doing."

"Good to know." Jeff snorted. "You do that a lot in high school?"

"Once. It started out really hot, then got weird and I had to make him stop because the angle was wrong, and it hurt. But at first? With all those people around, and all worried we might get caught? Yeah, it was hot."

"Jesus," he muttered. It even sounded hot. He eyed her. Would she be up to doing that with him? Because yeah, he could definitely get on board with doing that.

"But this was so much better." She flashed him a satisfied grin. "You can have me for breakfast whenever you want."

He leaned down and placed a kiss against her lips. Unable to stop himself, he pressed his tongue into her mouth, tangling hers with his. Knowing she was tasting herself on his tongue.

Breaking the kiss, he looked at her. He really wished they didn't have to pick up Max till later.

She eyed him and shook her head. "Your face is covered in me."

Eyeing the moisture on her face that had transferred from his, he dragged his thumb along her chin. "Now so is yours."

Kia laughed. "My god, you really are a dirty fucker, aren't you?"

He pressed a quick kiss against her mouth. "And you love it," he said as he pushed himself off the bed.

Making a face, she whispered, "I kind of really do."

A laugh rumbled from deep in his chest. "Told ya you were perfect me, Key. How could this not work?" He swatted her on the hip. "Now get that luscious ass out of bed so we can go pick up our son."

CHAPTER SEVENTEEN

THEY'D HAD A GREAT day. He walked out of Max's bedroom and followed the sound of Kia puttering in the kitchen. His kitchen. Normally, they spent most of their time at Kia's, which made sense, but he had to admit he liked having them in his home. When he got to the end of the hall, he hung a left toward the kitchen. At the sight of Kia bent over, reaching into the bottom drawer for something, he bit his bottom lip. The woman had an ass.

Her head snapped around and she smirked. "Did you just growl?"

"What? No?" he scoffed. Yeah, he'd totally growled. He glanced over his shoulder toward Max's room. He didn't dare touch her. With his luck, Max would come ripping down the hall the second he got close to her. The kid could cock-block like nobody's business.

"Okay, whatever you say." She rolled her eyes. "But it sure sounded like a growl."

"Fine, it might have been a growl." He swatted her ass as he walked to the fridge. "But if you could see what your ass looked like in those shorts, you'd make some noise too."

Her eyes sparkled with amusement. "I'm pretty sure the noise I would make if I looked at my ass wouldn't sound anything like what I just heard out of you."

"Then you clearly aren't looking right, because what I just saw?" He slapped his hand over his chest. "Mm, mm, mm."

He stepped toward her, and she held up her hand and laughingly took a step back. "Wipe that look off your face, mister."

"What look?"

"You know exactly what look." She pointed her finger at him.

He stepped closer. His gaze homed in on her nipples as they poked out through her thin tank top. He loved that her body reacted to him just as quickly as his did to hers.

"Mom." Max ran into the room and skidded to a halt at the edge of the counter.

Jeff tilted his head back and looked up at the ceiling and laughed. "Perfect timing, buddy," Jeff joked. It was like the kid had a radar attached or something.

Max blinked at him. "Why?"

Kia looked over at Jeff and raised an eyebrow at him. Challenging him to come up with an answer to the question.

"Because your mom and I were just trying to figure out something."

Max scrunched up his face. "Why do you need me?"

"Well, because you need to be the tiebreaker."

"I love being the tiebreaker," Max cheered as he hopped up on a stool at the kitchen island.

"Since you're sleeping here tonight. We were trying to figure out what to do for breakfast tomorrow." He glanced over at Kia and grinned. "I wanted to go out for breakfast, but your mom was bragging about this stuffed French toast she makes, so she wanted to cook."

"What? I never said that?" Kia swatted him on the arm.

He raised his shoulders innocently. "That's how I remember it."

"Mom's French toast is soooo good," Max moaned dramatically.

"That's what I keep hearing, but I've yet to try it out."

Kia laughed and rolled her eyes. "Fine, I'll make French toast."

"So I broke the tie?" Max asked.

"You sure did, and it sounds like I'm in for a real treat. Now we just have to decide if your mom is cooking here or your place."

Max sat up higher on his knees and surveyed the kitchen. "Here. The stove is pretty."

Jeff glanced over at his gas range. The shiny stainless steel shimmered as the setting sunlight poured through the window.

"It's definitely nicer than our kitchen," Kia agreed, running her hand along the quartz countertop.

"Plus, dad has whipped cream." Max grinned. His eyes popped wide, and he stuck his tongue out through the gap in his teeth.

The kid was such a goofball.

"So it's agreed your mom will come back first thing and make a feast fit for kings." He eyed Kia. Maybe he could convince her to stay over if Max thought she'd just come back early enough.

"Mom could just stay here," Max said.

Jeff snapped his gaze to Kia, who stood open-mouthed, staring back at him. "Why would your mom stay here?"

Max shrugged. "You got lots of rooms."

"True," Jeff agreed. He looked over at Kia. Her mouth pursed tight and the little lines between her eyes became more pronounced.

"I'm gonna go play before bed." Max hopped off the stool and bolted from the room.

Kia slumped against the island. "Well, that was weird."

"What do you mean?"

"I mean it's weird he wants me to stay over. Do you think he knows about us?" She chewed her bottom lip.

"Yeah, I think that's exactly why he wants you to stay, so we can fuck." He rolled his eyes at her. "God, no, Kia, I don't think he knows. I think he's a kid who wants to have you here in the morning so he can eat freaking delicious French toast the second he wakes up. Don't make it more complicated than that." He stepped toward her and placed his hands on her waist. "But I think he's on to something with you staying over." He leaned in and pressed a kiss against the side of her neck. Goosebumps pooled on her skin. "If you stay, we can christen my bed."

She scoffed. "Like it hasn't been christened before."

He leaned back and looked her in the eye. "It hasn't. I don't do casual hookups at my house."

Her eyes narrowed. Kia held his stare like she was trying to figure out if she believed him or not.

"Besides, I just got a new mattress last month." He grinned and waggled his eyebrows.

Kia smacked him on the arm and scrunched up her nose. "You're an ass."

He wrapped his arms around her waist and pulled her against him. "True. But seriously. Stay. You can sleep in one of the spare rooms in case Max wakes up. But stay. I want you here." He nuzzled his nose against her neck. "Max isn't the only one that wants to wake up to have you here."

Her body melted against his. "Fine."

He tilted his head to look at her. "Yeah?"

Kia rolled her eyes. "Yes, but I'm sleeping in the spare room in case Max wakes up."

"Fantastic." He ran his finger around the edge of her waistband and dipped his hand under the edge of her shirt so he could feel her skin. "And what about the before bed activities?"

Kia shifted against him, moving her legs so hers were on either side of his thigh. "I guess we'll have to see how persuasive you can be."

Taking the hint, he pressed his thigh against the seam of her jeans, and she closed her eyes. "I think we both know how persuasive I can be when I'm properly motivated."

"And are you motivated?" she asked.

He ground his thigh again, loving the way she squirmed against him. "Fucking right I am."

"Mo-om," Max's voice called from down the hall.

Kia groaned. The disappointment in her tone matched the way he was feeling. With a laugh, he rested his forehead against hers. "To be continued."

Over the past couple of weeks, they'd fallen into a comfort-able routine. He saw them practically every day. Usually at Kia's house, but on days she worked late, he'd start-ed bringing Max back to his place and making dinner, hanging out, occasionally Max slept over. He liked it. The whole dad, family man, routine was a world away from his old life, but it fit. He was going to miss it when he headed to spring training at the end of the week.

He absently played with Kia's hair as she lay with her head on his lap while she watched some ridiculous reality TV show. He lived for these moments alone with her, after Max had gone to bed, when she would finally let him touch her the way he wanted. She still wasn't willing to put a label on what they had, but maybe with camp coming up, they should.

He picked up the remote and turned the TV off. Kia sat up and looked at him. "What's up?" she asked.

"I leave for camp on Sunday."

"Yeah." She eyed him warily.

"So I think we should talk about things."

"I don't expect anything from you if that's where you're going with this." She shifted her weight, so she was leaning against the arm of the sofa, no longer touching him at all.

His jaw clenched. "Maybe I want you to expect something."

"I thought we agreed to keep this casual." She looked at her lap instead of looking at him.

How the hell she could consider what they were doing casual was beyond him. "We also agreed that if I was fucking you, then I wasn't fucking anyone else," he growled. He knew he sounded like an asshole, but it pissed him off she was acting like what they had meant nothing to her.

Kia's head snapped up. "Yeah, that's what we agreed."

At the sign of fire in her eyes, he bit back a smile. That's what he wanted to see. "So I'm just checking that's still what you want once the season starts."

"Why? Do you want to sleep with other people?" She scowled at him.

"What? God, no." That was the last thing he wanted to do. But Kia was so jumpy about their relationship he wasn't sure what she was going to say once the season started. "I'm just trying to figure out what this will all look like once our schedule changes."

She rested her back against the arm of the sofa. "Um, I don't really know."

"What don't you know?" He studied her silently, waiting for her to give him some hint about what she wanted.

"I don't know. Everything is just so new. We're barely starting to figure out anything and now you're off to training camp and then the regular season and you'll be away all the time. From everything you've told me, and I've read, that can be hard."

"You've been reading about this?" He nudged her foot with his knee. That had to be a good sign, didn't it?

"Shut up." She dropped her head, but not before he saw the blush rise up her cheeks.

"I just need to know how you see this playing out with the season starting," he pressed.

"I don't know." She shrugged. "Why does anything have to change?"

"Well, because I'm not going to be around much."

"Exactly, so why mess things up by changing anything? Who's to say you don't start the season and remember how much you liked your single life?"

His spine stiffened. "And what, somehow, I'm just going to go back to partying every night and forgetting I have a kid at home?"

"I don't know." She shifted uncomfortably on the sofa.

"That's bullshit and you know it. When have I ever given you any indication that I'm not going to put Max first?"

Her shoulder dropped. "Max? Never but—"

"Oh, so you just think I'm going to be that guy with you, is that it?"

"I don't know, Jeff. I've never been in this situation before. I've heard the stories and I'm trying to be realistic that this could be challenging."

"Yeah, so?" He stared at her. Man, he wanted to grab her and just shake her till all the damage her family had done to her fell away. He didn't have the first clue how to get her to trust him, really trust him.

"So I just think we shouldn't label things yet. I'm not saying I don't want to try because I do. I'm just saying I'm aware it will be difficult, and just in case things are harder than either of us realizes, I don't want to change anything and have Max get hurt."

"He's not a stupid kid. He knows something is going on with us."

"What he knows is he's five and likes his parents hanging out together, isn't that what you told me? But if he sees us touch or kiss or whatever, it'll make things messy."

"It's only messy if we break up," he told her. Why was she still so adamant that they weren't going to work out? He'd been doing everything he could to prove otherwise.

"Exactly." Her head tilted to the side as she studied him. "I just think it's early days to label things."

Faking a nonchalance he didn't feel, he grabbed her foot and set it on his lap. "Okay, but we agreed we're keeping things the same between us. When I'm home, we all hang out together, and after Max is in bed, you and I hang out." He picked up her foot and rubbed it.

"Mmm, you can keep doing that." She shimmied her body, so her other foot was also on his lap. She batted her eyelashes at him and smiled as she wiggled the toes of her other foot to make sure he knew it was there.

"And I was thinking I could FaceTime with Max most nights, say goodnight, that kind of thing." He picked up her other foot and rubbed the sole. "Then maybe you could call me back later and give me my own little bedtime call?"

"Mmm, you think so, do you?"

"Yep, since we're agreed we're keeping things the same and neither of us is fucking anyone else. I'm thinking we could have some fun FaceTime calls where you put all those toys in your bedside table to good use."

"You think I should masturbate over FaceTime?"

His dick twitched. "Fuck yeah." He dug his fingers into the arch of her foot. Her head dropped back, and she moaned and sounded exactly the same as when she came. He shifted to stop his cock from being choked out by his jeans. "That means the only person who's allowed to make that sound come out of your mouth is me."

Her eyes popped open, and she smirked. She pressed her foot against the fly of his pants, dragging her toes along the length of his cock, and he groaned. "As long as we agree I'm the only one who's allowed to make that sound come out of yours."

He set her right foot on the outside of his thigh, grabbed her left ankle, and pulled. She squealed as he yanked her onto his lap, so she was straddling him. "Woman, you can do anything you want with my mouth."

She ground her hips against him. Her core lined up perfectly with his already hard cock. "Maybe you should remind me what you can do with that mouth of yours," she said.

"Gladly." He hooked his hands under her ass and stood up, taking her with him to the bedroom. If this was all she was willing to give him, he'd take it.

CHAPTER EIGHTEEN

With Jeff at training camp for the past week, she'd tried to get Max and her back into their old routine, but it felt different. Trips to the cousins' house were out of necessity again rather than just for fun. Kia looked over at Max. "You ready to go, buddy?"

"Yeah." He began picking up his toys.

God, he was a cute little guy. She smiled at her sister.

The two women both stood and slowly made their way toward the front door with Max slowly following behind her. "Thank your Aunty Vika for looking after you."

He looked up at Vika and wrapped his little arms around her waist. "Thank you, Aunty Vik."

Vika rubbed the back of Max's head with her hand. "Oh, you're welcome, sweetheart. Anytime."

"Alright, see you later. Thanks again." Kia grabbed Max's backpack and handed it to him. Together they walked out toward the car. She buckled him into the back seat.

"You okay, buddy? You look a little sad."

He shrugged. "I'm OK."

Kia watched him for a few seconds, waiting to see if he would say anything. When he didn't speak, she sighed and closed the back door. She slid into the driver's seat and put the car in gear. As she pulled away from the sidewalk, she glanced in the rearview mirror at Max. He fiddled with his hands in his lap. That wasn't like him. Normally, he was so chatty she couldn't shut him up. What was going on?

She turned down the music. "You alright? You seem quiet."

He shrugged again.

"Max, you gotta talk to me, buddy. I can't help you if I don't know what's going on."

He sat silently for several minutes. Finally, out of nowhere, he spoke, "Mom, what's a slut?"

Kia reared back. Whoa. "What do you mean? What's a ...?" She cleared her throat. "Sorry, what's a what?"

Max's head cocked to the side. "What's a slut?" he asked.

Damn, she hadn't heard him wrong. "That's um...it's not a very nice word, buddy. Why do you ask?"

His mouth drew up tight. "I don't know."

"No, you must know why." She flicked a glance in the rearview again. "Where did you hear that word?"

"At school?"

"Okay, who said it?"

"Luke."

"Why'd he say it?" she pressed.

Max looked at his lap again. "He said I couldn't play with them at lunch because my mom was a slut."

What? She took a deep breath. "He said... He said what?" she stammered.

Max raised his head. When his eyes met hers in the mirror, they were filled with tears. He didn't even know what the word meant, but he knew it was bad and he'd been excluded from playing because of it.

Max sniffed. "Luke said you were a gold-digging slut."

Kia sucked in a breath. Wow. Hearing that come out of her son's mouth was like a kick in the teeth. Even though she knew it wasn't true, it still cut. Kids don't come up with that kind of thing out of nowhere. Obviously, Luke had heard it from somewhere. His parents probably. But what the hell kind of person said something like that in the first place, let alone in front of a child?

She glanced in the rearview mirror as Max wiped his nose on his sleeve. God, this was not a conversation she wanted to have. "Um, well, that's not very nice to say about anyone. I'm sorry they didn't want to let you play with them today. That must have hurt."

Max nodded. "Why'd he call you that?"

"I don't know, honey." Because his parents were assholes, probably.

Max sniffed again. "What's a gold-digging slut?"

Kia exhaled audibly. How the hell was she supposed to answer that? How was she supposed to explain to her five-year-old son what a gold-digging slut was? "Well. honey, I'm not one."

"That's what Layla said," Max muttered.

Fantastic and now her nieces and nephew knew that's what people were saying about her.

Max met her eyes in the mirror. "Layla said Luke was stupid, but she didn't tell me what it meant. She said ask you."

Awesome. "Well, a gold digger is someone who typically dates somebody for money."

Max's forehead wrinkled in confusion. "Why would he say that you were that?"

"I don't know, honey, people can be mean sometimes."

Max just looked at her, confused. God, he was so innocent. How was she supposed to discuss this? "Honey, I'm guessing he maybe said it because of who your dad is." Oh God, she was not cut out for this. This was not a conversation she thought she'd be having today.

Max's head cocked to the side again. "But why would he call you a gold digger because of dad?"

"Um...well, um...because your dad makes a good living playing baseball."

"Don't you make a good living?" Max asked.

Her heart warmed hearing him say that. Now that Max had seen where Jeff lived, she'd worried he'd compare what he had at her house to his dad's place. But her innocent little man didn't seem to get the reality of the situation yet.

"We do okay on what I make. You have some cool toys and a nice yard to play in." She smiled. "There's always good food to eat."

"We have better snacks than Aunty Vika."

Kia laughed. "What kind of smoothie was it today?" Her sister was on a smoothie kick at the moment and was always making the kids drink a smoothie after school rather than eating crackers or junk. Since it was just the two of them at their place, Max always got his favorite snacks at home.

"I don't know, but it was green and yucky." He wrinkled his nose in disgust.

"Sounds healthy."

Max made a fake retching sound, then giggled. When he stopped laughing, he asked, "Did Luke say that 'cuz dad's house is at the beach?"

So much for distracting him from the conversation. "I don't know, baby, maybe."

Max frowned. "But...We don't. We don't live at the beach."

"I know, but because your dad does, um... sometimes people think that maybe that might be why I spend so much time with him instead of just letting you hang out with him alone." God. "That's what a gold digger is. It's a person who uses someone because they have a lot of money and can buy nice stuff and pay for everything."

Max's nose wrinkled. "Is that why you like him?"

"Of course not, sweetheart. We hang out with your dad because he's your dad. And I like him. He's a good guy and..." God. It's not like she could explain to her son the fact his dad had money was actually a deterrent to dating. That she was afraid Max would like him better because of what he could buy him and choose Jeff over her. Yes, it was petty, but that didn't mean it didn't stop her stupid brain from running overtime. "The way your dad is with us has nothing to do with money."

Max shifted in his seat. He nodded thoughtfully. "OK, that's what I thought. So what's a slut?"

Kia opened her mouth to answer, then closed it again. "Um—" Crap, she'd really hoped he'd forget all about that part of the name calling. "First off, it's an awful term and we shouldn't call anyone that word. Okay?" She pinned Max with a stare in the rearview.

"Okay," he agreed. "But what is it?"

"Um...well. It's a mean term for someone that has sex with a lot of people."

Max's mouth dropped open wide. "What? You've had sex?" he yelled.

Kia bit back a laugh. "I have, honey. That's why you're...um, that's how you were born."

His face scrunched up in disgust. "With dad?" Max's hazel eyes practically popped out of his face as he gaped at her.

This time Kia couldn't stop the laugh from bursting out loud. "Afraid so, honey. You wouldn't be here if I hadn't."

"Gross," Max mumbled. "But you said it's someone who has sex with lots of people. Who else have you had sex with?"

"That's not really anyone's business, Max." This was exactly what she'd been hoping to avoid by not telling Max they were dating. Besides Jeff, she'd always kept anyone she dated away from Max. He knew she'd gone on dates, but she'd never allowed the men to get to know Max because she didn't want that kind of confusion in his life. The last thing she'd wanted for her son was to form a relationship with a man just to have him disappear when they broke up. And with her track record, they always broke up. With Jeff, there was already so much confusion and the water was so muddy right off the bat that she hadn't wanted to confuse things more. If they didn't work out, it wasn't like Jeff was going anywhere. He was Max's dad. He was going to be in his life with or without her.

"But I'm not a slut, honey, I'm not a gold digger. So people who say that kind of thing are just being mean." Her throat tightened. Someone should tell that to her parents. "And we don't need to listen to that kind of talk, right?" That was easier said than done.

She pulled the car up in front of their house and turned off the ignition. She spun around in her seat, so she was facing him. "So when people say that you could maybe just walk away. You don't need to listen to that nonsense."

"If he says it again, I'm gonna hit him." Max smacked his fist into his other palm.

"Max, you're not gonna hit him."

"I'm gonna hit him."

"Honey, fighting is not the answer. We've talked about this. When you're angry, it's okay to be angry. It's okay to say that you're angry, but violence isn't the answer."

"Luke sucks," Max griped.

"I'm not gonna argue with you there, babe." Luke might suck, but his dad needed to be kicked in the balls.

"But... but you don't like dad, cuz of money, right? It's cuz he's nice, right?"

"Yes, honey, I like him because he's nice." Was it a bad idea not to have told Max that she was dating Jeff already? She always kept all of her relationships separate from him for this exact reason, because it was confusing. It was confusing as hell when it didn't work out. It was confusing as hell when it did. Relationships confused her.

She could only imagine what it was like for her son. And now this, dealing with this from kids at school. Freaking parents running their traps out of jealousy. This was the last bloody thing she needed.

Later that evening. Kia lay on her bed, thinking about the day. How the hell had that happened?

Her phone buzzed beside her on the nightstand. Leaning over, she scooped it up as Jeff's name flashed up on the screen. Flicking her hand along the screen, she answered.

"Hi," she said.

"Hey."

"How was your day?"

"It could have been better." Did she really want to tell him about the kids calling her that?

"Yeah, why is that?" he asked.

"Well, today Max came home from school and asked me what a gold-digging slut is." It had been hurtful enough being called a slut when her parents had said it. Having it come out of her son's mouth, even as a question, and knowing he had to deal with that had nearly destroyed her.

"Are you kidding me?"

"I wish I was. No, apparently some little shit at school told him that his mom was a gold-digging slut."

"I'm so sorry, Key. What did you say?"

"What could I say? Obviously, I told him I wasn't, but... I didn't honestly know what I was supposed to say."

"Obviously it's not true," Jeff said.

"I know, but... Doesn't make it any easier to have to answer the questions. Doesn't make it any easier to have to explain to him why somebody might say that about me." She flipped onto her back and covered her arm across her face. "It just sucked."

"Understandable." Jeff paused. The silence on the phone was deafening.

Kia sighed. "He wanted to know if you really liked me and if I really liked you or if I was just hanging out with you for money. He didn't understand why somebody would like somebody for money."

Jeff chuckled. "Oh, to be young. Does that mean you finally told him we were dating?"

"No, it didn't really seem like a good time to explain any of that. He was confused enough already." She rubbed her hands over her face. "I was hoping by not openly dating, this wouldn't even be an issue. No one even knows about us. Why would someone even say that?"

"I don't know what to tell you, Kia." He paused for several seconds, and she wondered what he was going to say. Finally, he spoke, "What we have is more than that."

Hearing him say that made her stomach flip. "I'd like to think so." Shoot, this whole thing had her emotions all jumbled up. She was all over the place. "But is that honestly what people think of me? Do people really think that's the kind of person I am? Does my kid have to deal with that shit at school?" Frustrated, she smacked her palm on the mattress. "What the hell kind of parent would even say something as stupid as that? Even if it was true, how dare they say something like that to our son?"

"I'm sorry, babe. Do you want me to talk to him? You want me to call him?"

"No, I think I handled it. It just sucks that he even had to go through that. That he heard that, period. He was so hurt. Kids don't wanna play with him because of it."

"Little fucker," Jeff said. "You know I don't think that about you, right?"

"I know." She sighed. "It still sucks that other people do. Normally, I wouldn't care what some asshole said about me. But when it affects Max, I do."

"Why don't you guys get away for a week? Come see me in Phoenix. I'm sure Viper would give you the time off."

As nice as the idea of escaping sounded, she couldn't. "I can't. Max has school."

"He's in kindergarten. I somehow don't think it will be a big deal if he misses a week of school. He's already light years ahead of everyone else in class with his reading."

"I know he is, but it's not just about that."

"What is it then?"

"I don't know. How am I supposed to teach him the value of school and the importance of not skipping and stuff if I just pull him out whenever?"

"It's one week, Kia."

"It's not just one week though, it's the principle of it. So what? I take him out for a dentist appointment because it's more convenient for me and that's okay, but when he wants to skip to go hang with his friends it's not okay?" She sighed. "No, I can't have that double-standard with him. If I want him to learn it, I have to live it. Even if it sucks."

Silence filled the line for several seconds before she heard Jeff exhale loudly. "Okay, I get it. I don't like it, but I get it."

"Thank you."

"You sure he can't start learning this lesson later, like closer to the time he wants to skip with his friends?"

If only it were that easy. "I wish." There was nothing she'd rather do than escape to Phoenix and hide away from her life.

"Have to admit it kinda sucks you're such a grownup." He chuckled. "But I think it's cool you think about that stuff when you're making decisions. I never would have."

"Thank you." She pulled up the calendar on her phone. "Max has a non-instructional day next Friday. I could talk to Viper about switching some things around and we could come out then."

"Yeah, that would be amazing. I think Max would get a kick out coming to the field. Things are a lot more laid-back during spring training. I could bring him on the field and chuck the ball around."

"I'm sure he'd love that."

"I could bring you down there too if you wanted." His voice dipped all low and sexy. "Or I'm sure I could find another way to make your visit memorable."

She adjusted the pillow behind her head to get comfier. "Just what did you have in mind?"

"Well, seeing how I didn't really get a proper look at you in that bikini you wore to Ryan's house."

"What do you mean you didn't get a proper look? You were gawking at me all day."

"Well yeah, of course I was. You looked hot. And by look at you, I mean touch because I wasn't allowed to touch you yet."

A feeling of warmth slid through her body. "Did you want to touch me?"

"More than anything."

"You hid it pretty well."

"Did I? I'm not sure how since every time I glanced at you, my dick felt like it was trying to cut a hole through my shorts."

Now that she thought about it, he had seemed like he had ants in his pants that day. She'd thought it was because his wet bathing suit was chafing. It was nice to know it was because of her. "And here I just thought you had crabs or something."

"Jesus." Jeff snorted out a loud laugh. "No." He paused. "Hang on, is that really what you thought?"

She could almost picture the look of horror on his face at the idea. Giggling, she covered her mouth with her hand. "No, I didn't think that."

"Thank god," he muttered. "But seriously, we have a pool and a hot tub at the house. You in your swimsuit? It could be fun."

"You do realize we'll have a five-year-old to entertain, right?"

"Yeah, but I have three roommates. So..."

She laughed. Three roommates made it more complicated, not less. "So...more people lingering around cock-blocking you?"

"Ha-ha. No. There will be no cock-blocking that weekend. Full disclosure? I might have told the guys we were sleeping together, and I wouldn't be hooking up with anyone else."

"That's okay, I might have told Vika, too."

"Perfect, so this weekend will just be fun, sun, and sex. Lots and lots of sex."

"Not sure how you plan on pulling that off exactly."

"I'll pay the guys to entertain Max."

"You are not going to pay your friends so we can have sex."

"Yeah, I totally am."

God, she could just imagine how that conversation would go. "How about we just leave the sex till bedtime like normal people?"

"Normal people have daytime sex too, you know."

"Not normal people with kids that don't nap." She couldn't remember the last time she'd had the privacy to even go to the bathroom without being interrupted, let alone have sex when Max was home during the day.

"Okay, that might be fair. I'll think on it, don't you worry. You just get here next week, and I'll figure out the game plan. Maybe the boys and I will take Max out for the afternoon and give you some time to yourself to just lay by the pool and relax."

"God, that sounds amazing. Sold."

"Talk to Viper and get the time off, and I'll take care of everything else."

"Kay, I'll talk to him tomorrow."

"Night, Kia,"

"Night."

She hung up the phone and dropped it on her bedside table. A weekend away sounded like exactly what she needed.

CHAPTER NINETEEN

"Mom, why can't we go inside?" Max bounced on his toes beside her as he stared toward the stadium gate. Between the early morning arrival at the airport and the flight, to say her son was wired was an understatement. She dug into her purse and pulled out some matchbox cars.

"Here bud, play with those and I'll text your dad again and see how much longer he's going to be." She pulled her phone out of her bag. Shoot, he still hadn't responded to any of her texts to say their plane had landed. She tried to peek through the fence to see if she could tell if they were still practicing.

Yes, it was cheap of her, but she didn't want to pay to get into the stadium if he was done for the morning. Jeff had said he'd get them passes for the time they were here so they could come and go as she pleased. Max drove his little car over her foot, then the other. Making a loud booming sound, his car crashed on its way over her toes. Thank God, he could entertain himself pretty much anywhere.

She fired off another text to Jeff to let him know they were waiting outside the gates for him. Her phone buzzed instantly with a text from him that he would be out shortly.

A player in Hawks' gear strolled up to them with his bag slung over his shoulder. "Hey, you're Kia, right?"

How did he know that? "I am." Had Jeff told him she was out there?

He held up his hands palm up. "Sorry, I'm not some weird creeper. I'm Brandon. I play with Smitty. You were in some pictures Ryan was showing me of the guys getting their tattoos."

"Oh right, of course."

"You do great work."

"Thanks."

Brandon looked at his foot, then back at her. His head cocked to the side as he assessed her. "I was hoping we could talk about an idea I had for a tattoo."

"Sure, did you want to do that sometime this weekend while I'm here or wait till you're back in town?"

Brandon's eyes brightened. "This weekend would be great if you have time. I don't want to take you away from your family time though. I know you guys have limited time together."

"I'll have some time tomorrow after your practice. I've already been told that they are doing some male bonding. Jeff and a couple of his buddies are taking Max someplace. So I could meet you then."

"That'd be great. Give me your phone and I'll put my number in and you can text me to firm up where and when."

She handed him her phone to exchange numbers. As Brandon was handing her phone back, Jeff walked out of the gate. His eyes narrowed on her. He nodded toward them.

Okay, not the warmest welcome she'd ever seen. Max spotted Jeff and jumped to his feet. His toys forgotten as he launched himself toward his dad. The second he reached him Jeff scooped him up. Max wrapped his little legs around his dad's waist, and Kia's heart melted.

For so long, she had wished for Max to have a dad in his life. Now here he was. In just a few months, Max and Jeff had created a strong bond.

Brandon glanced at Jeff, nodded and smiled, then turned back to her. "So I'll see you tomorrow for coffee."

"Sounds good." Kia smiled at him, then frowned when she saw the scowl on Jeff's face.

"What the fuck was that?" Jeff snapped the moment Brandon walked away.

Seriously, that was the first thing he was going to say to her after ten days? Nice way to start their visit. "Hello to you too."

"Sorry, hi." He leaned in and tried to hug her, which was virtually impossible with Max clinging to him like a monkey. "So why were you making plans with Brandon? I didn't think you two knew each other."

"We don't. We just met."

"You just met and you're going for coffee with him? What the fuck?"

Anger radiated through Kia. How dare he talk to her like that? Her spine stiffened and her jaw clenched. She glanced at her son, whose little gaze darted nervously back and forth between them. His bottom lip trembled. Kia took a deep breath and exhaled. She cocked her head toward Max. For him, she could keep her anger in check. "Now isn't the time for this discussion. All I'm going to say right now is Max and I didn't fly here to visit you for us not to be treated respectfully."

"How am I not being respectful?"

Kia closed her eyes. When she felt like she could be calm, she opened them. "Again, not the time to have this discussion. Maybe you could show us your place and Max can get settled and we can chat."

"Fine," Jeff mumbled. He squeezed Max a little tighter. "You ready to see where you'll be camping for the next couple of days?"

"Camping?" Max's little face scrunched up with confusion as he looked at his dad.

"Well yeah. Your mom said you'd be roughing it while you visited me, right?"

Max's head bobbed in agreement. "Yep, I'm on the couch."

"Alright, let's go check it out."

Max's mouth didn't stop moving the entire drive to Jeff's house. Her son talked more in those fifteen minutes than he did on a normal day. He shared everything from who played with who at lunch all the way to the color of his cousins' nail polish.

Jeff pulled into the driveway of a home in a suburban neighborhood. Kia wasn't sure what she'd been expecting, but it wasn't a family home in the suburbs. "This is your place?"

"Yeah, it belongs to the friend of a fan. The guy is away for the winter every year, so we've been renting it for spring training for the past couple of seasons. It works out really well overall."

Jeff unloaded their bags from the trunk and wheeled the suitcase up the steps. He pushed open the front door and Max peered inside. Jeff crouched beside his son. "You want to see your bunk first?"

Max nodded shyly and placed his hand in Jeff's. Kia's heart tightened as she watched the two move further into the house. As they rounded the corner into the living room, Max gasped.

"Is that for me?" Max pointed toward an elaborate blanket fort that was spread out between the living room and dining room.

"Yeah, the guys and I figured you needed a space of your own for privacy and all. And who doesn't love a blanket fort?" He bent. "Except I think you might have to fight Gonzo for it. Ever since we built it the other night, he's been dying to sleep in there."

Max's eyes widened in awe. "He has?"

Jeff flicked open the blanket door and peeked inside, then back at Max. "Absolutely. I think we'll have to leave it up for a night after you leave, if you don't mind him using it."

Max crawled into the opening of the fort. "Whoa. It's huge. Gonzo can sleep in here with me if he wants."

Jeff coughed to cover his laugh. "That's nice of you, buddy, but you don't want to sleep with him. He snores something awful."

"He does?" Max flopped back onto the air mattress on the floor. "Maybe he should wait till I'm gone then."

"Good thinking," Jeff agreed.

"Mom, come in here and look."

She slid past Jeff and crawled through the opening. It was huge inside. The guys had tied multiple blankets together. A small bean bag chair sat in one corner. A stack of books rested on a little table beside the air mattress. Jeff had gone all out to make this feel special for Max.

Well shoot, how was she supposed to stay annoyed at him when he was so damn sweet to Max?

She smiled at him. "This is amazing. Thank you."

"Of course. I know it's not ideal, but I really wanted you both to feel comfortable staying here."

"Where's Mom gonna sleep?" Max asked.

"I'm letting your mom have my bed."

"Cool. Where are you sleeping?" Max sat up on his knees and stared at Jeff.

"Up to your mom. If she's okay with it, there's a couch in my room or else I can sleep out here on the couch."

Max's eyes narrowed. "Do you snore like Gonzo?"

Jeff grimaced. "I don't know. I might."

Max's nose wrinkled up in disgust, and he turned to his mom. "You gotta let him sleep on the couch in your room, Mom."

"You think I want to sleep with someone who snores?"

Max shrugged. "You're the grownup. It's like paying taxes."

The look of confusion on Jeff's face made her giggle. "Things you don't like to do but have to because you're a grownup," she explained.

"Ah got ya." Jeff nodded at Max. "Looks like she's stuck with me then."

Max's head bobbed in agreement. "Yep, looks like," Max mimicked.

Jeff pushed himself off his knees. "You want to see where your mom will be sleeping?"

Max jumped up and grabbed Jeff's hand. Feelings she was fighting hard to keep at bay pushed to the surface as she followed the pair out of the room and up the stairs.

After a quick tour of the second floor, they made their way back downstairs. From the kitchen came the sound of men's voices. Max dropped back a step and nervously looked at his dad.

"Sounds like my roommates are home." Jeff scooped Max up onto his shoulders. "You hungry? Because, if you are, we should get in there before they eat all the food."

Kia giggled as Jeff winced when Max's little fingers dug into his hair to hold on. "We better go then."

"Hey, hey, Max my man." Ryan reached up and high-fived Max.

"Gonzo lost at vids last night, so he's cooking." Pete grinned at Max. "You like burgers, right?"

"With chips?" Max asked.

"Is there another way to eat homemade burgers?" Pete reached into the cupboard and pulled out four different varieties of chips and held them out to Max. "You think this will be enough?"

Max giggled.

Kia eyed the display of food on the island. "I thought you guys ate healthy during the season?"

"We do. We just thought Max might enjoy something different on the first night." Jeff reached up and hoisted Max off his shoulders and plopped him on the bar stool beside Gonzo.

"Which ones look good to start?" Gonzo asked Max.

Max chewed his bottom lip and narrowed his eyes as he looked at the heaping mound of chips.

Gonzo leaned over and pulled a large plastic bowl toward him, then grabbed a couple of bags. He held them up to Max. "Should we mix 'em? Then we don't have to pick."

Max's eyes gleamed as he looked at her. She noted the two bags of chips and winced. The gleam of excitement in Max's eyes dulled slightly like he expected her to say no. Which, if she was honest, normally she would have. Doritos and Dill Pickle chips mixed together sounded repulsive. She eyed the four men and her son, who all watched her expectantly. "Knock yourselves out."

"Yes." Max threw his fist in the air.

Gonzo dumped half a bag in the bowl, then half of the other bag and then began an elaborate flick and shuffle move to mix the chips all together.

Max grabbed a handful and shoved chips in his mouth. Gonzo did the same and grimaced as the flavors hit his mouth.

"Not the best combo?" Kia asked.

"No, it's freaking delicious," Gonzo said. "I just need something to drink to go with it."

Max shifted onto his knees. "Me too." Chip crumbs fell out of his mouth as he spoke.

"Wait until you're done chewing before you talk, please," Kia reminded him.

"Ah, Mom." Max rolled his eyes. "We're men."

She tilted her head to the side and stared at her son. What did that mean?

"Nah, man, you don't want to waste good chips by spitting them when you talk," Pete said as he slid a glass of juice across the island to Max.

"Right." Max nodded in agreement.

"We were thinking some BBQ then video games tonight." Ryan scooped up a handful of chips. "That work for you, Maxie?"

Her son beamed at the nickname. "Yep."

"Cool. Mario Kart tonight. Real go-karts tomorrow." Ryan held up his hands for Max to slap.

"Go-karts?" Kia turned to Jeff. "You sure that's a good idea?"

"Yeah, he'll ride with me. He'll be safe, I promise."

"Are you gonna come, Mom?"

"Nope, I was told it was male bonding time."

"Right, you're meeting Brandon," Jeff sneered.

That was enough of that bullshit. "We'll be back in a minute." She grabbed Jeff's arm and pulled him to let him know they needed to talk.

She strode upstairs and spun around when he closed the bedroom door behind them. "What is your problem?" she demanded.

"My problem? You're the one going for coffee with another guy."

"Are you kidding me right now? You're seriously jealous?"

Jeff crossed his arms over his chest. "I know we agreed to keep things low-key because of Max, but for the record, when I said we wouldn't be fucking other people, I meant dating as well."

"Oh my god, I'm not going on a date."

"What would you call it?" Jeff growled.

"A consult."

Jeff's forehead wrinkled. "What do you mean?"

"I mean he wants to discuss getting a tattoo. You had already told me you wanted to do a guys' night, so it seemed like a good time to meet."

"I saw the way he looked at you," he grumbled.

"First, I can't control how someone else looks at me. He's a client, so how he's looking at me is irrelevant. I don't mess with clients."

"You messed with me."

Kia rolled her eyes. "Not the same thing, and you know it. Second, if I was going to date someone else, it sure as shit wouldn't be one of your teammates. That's tacky."

"God forbid you be tacky," he scoffed.

The sarcastic scoffing sound just pissed her off more. "Third, I don't do jealousy. I told you when I broke up with Austin that I don't cheat. You either believe me or you don't." She stared at him. "If you don't, then we may as well stop this before we get any further, because we clearly don't have the foundation to build shit."

"It's not that I don't trust you."

"No?" She dropped onto the edge of the mattress. "What is jealousy if it's not a lack of trust?"

"It's not you I don't trust. It's everybody else."

Unimpressed, she tapped her foot on the floor in front of her. "Same thing. If you trust me it doesn't matter what anybody else does. Like I said, I can't control them. I can only control myself and I'm telling you I'd never cheat. Therefore, jealousy is a wasted emotion."

"I don't like when other guys look at you."

"Oh my god, get over yourself. You're a flippin' professional athlete. It's not like women aren't ogling you every time you go out. Do you think I care?"

"You should," he mumbled.

"Why? Do you plan on cheating on me?"

His mouth gaped. "God, no."

"Then why should I care if they look at you? You're a good-looking guy. Of course they're going to look. The only thing I care about is what you do with that attention."

"I'm not going to do anything." He stepped closer to her and crouched. "I think I've made it pretty clear how badly I want us to try to make this thing between us work."

"Exactly my point. I have zero tolerance for cheating. I don't do it and I expect the same level of respect from you. Jealousy is a waste of time. We either respect each other or we don't. If we don't, then what the hell are we doing here?"

He moved closer to her. "We respect each other."

"Do we?" She raised one eyebrow as he placed his hand on her knee.

"Yeah, we do. Sorry, you're right. My problem was with Sims, not you."

Oh, my god. Men. "Brandon wasn't looking at me like anything other than someone who was excited to get a tattoo. That's what you saw and what you heard in his voice."

"You don't know that." His jaw tightened.

"Trust me, I do. I've tattooed enough people to know what it looks like. Besides, he's your teammate. He knows why I'm here."

"That doesn't always stop people."

She leaned back to look him in the face. "Is Brandon that kind of person?"

"Nah, I don't think so. From what I know of him, he's a good guy?"

"So what's the problem?"

He shifted back on his feet. "I don't know. Nothing I guess."

"Good." She leaned over and pressed a kiss to his lips.

"Now let's go back downstairs so I can watch this BBQ mastery Gonzo was going on about."

"Or." Jeff licked his lips and stared at her. "We could stay up here and make up properly." He waggled his eyebrows at her.

"There's zero chance I'm having sex with you with your friends downstairs looking after our son."

"Why? They wouldn't care." He trailed his hand up her thigh. "If anything they'd expect me to try." He leaned in and pressed a kiss to the side of her throat. "It's been a long training camp already."

"Mom? Dad?" Max's voice sounded from somewhere in the hallway.

"My god, that kid," Jeff groaned and dropped his head on her lap. Kia burst out laughing. Max seemed to have impeccable timing. She clapped Jeff on the shoulder. "Come on, Romeo, let's go see what he needs."

"I'll tell you what I need," he grumbled.

She snickered. Men were such babies.

CHAPTER TWENTY

"You know where you're going to meet Brandon?" Jeff's lip curled up slightly as he asked the question. She didn't think he even realized he'd done it. Clearly, he still wasn't 100% comfortable with her meeting with his teammate. Well, too bad. This was her livelihood. She wasn't letting him mess with that.

Kia went back into the house and grabbed her purse and keys. She took one last look at the map on her phone. Feeling confident she knew where she was going, she headed outside.

Twenty minutes later, she pulled open the door of a funky coffee shop. She scanned the room and spotted Brandon sitting in the back corner with a mug of some kind of beverage on the table in front of him. She nodded toward him and pointed at the counter to let him know she was going to grab a drink.

Brandon stood up and walked toward her. "Let me buy your coffee."

"Don't be silly. I'm perfectly happy to buy my own."

"I know, but it's the least I can do. You're in town for a break and here I am dragging you back into work stuff."

"It's all good. I would have just been doodling or something today anyway with the guys all off go-karting."

Brandon smiled. "Sounds like fun. I'm sure your son will love it." His eyes narrowed slightly. "What's your son's name again?"

"Max."

"Right, I should know that. I've heard the guys talking about him."

She slid up to the counter and ordered a hazelnut latte and before she could even pull out her wallet Brandon was holding his card out to tap the machine to pay.

"Thank you."

"No problem."

Kia tilted her head back to look him in the eyes. "So what have they been saying?"

"Nothing bad, that's for sure. Smitty seems pretty stoked about him. Grilling the guys with kids about things he might like." Brandon grinned and shook his head. "It's been pretty amusing to watch, honestly."

Kia couldn't help but smile as she pictured Jeff questioning his teammates. "That would explain the pile of toys in the living room when we arrived."

A deep laugh rumbled from Brandon's chest. "Yeah probably. It's cool to see him so happy."

"Was he not happy before?"

"Eh, I wouldn't say he wasn't happy. Smitty's always pretty laid back and laughing, having fun. It's just now, he's... I don't know. Just different, but in a good way."

Warmth flowed across her chest. It was nice to hear that Max and her coming into his life had made a change for the better that was noticeable to his teammates.

Brandon took a sip of his coffee, then set it down and studied her for a moment. "So are you and Smitty a couple, or are you just here visiting as the mother of his child? He's pretty tight-lipped about his relationship with you."

That was a good question. What were they? Figuring things out? A couple in training? Delusional? Who the hell knew at this point? Yes, they were trying to figure it out, but so far, they weren't announcing anything to the world because of Max. Yes, she'd put that rule in place to start, but Jeff had been fine going along with it. "Why does it matter?"

A slow cocky smile spread across Brandon's face as confidence oozed out of him. "Just wondering if I had a shot or not?"

Wow, Jeff had been right about the way Brandon had been looking at her. She smiled to soften the blow. "Honestly, I'm not sure where things are at with Jeff and I, but either way I would never date one of his teammates. Or a client."

Brandon nodded. "That's cool. I can respect that." He grinned again. "I'd have kicked myself if I didn't take my shot." He reached down and pulled his backpack off the floor. After digging around inside, he pulled out a firm cardboard folder and set it on the table. Suddenly, the confident baseball star was gone, replaced by an uneasy boy. He slid the folder toward her.

Curious about the change in Brandon's posture, Kia pulled the folder closer to her but didn't open it up. "Are these ideas you have for tattoos?"

"Sort of." He rubbed the back of his neck. "Those are drawings that my mom did for me when I was a kid. I'm hoping maybe we can figure out a way for you to weave some of them together to make a sleeve."

"May I?" Kia pointed at the folder.

"Yeah, please."

She flipped open the folder and sucked in a breath. "Holy shit." Inside were pages and pages of storybook drawings. Raising her head, she looked at Brandon. "These are amazing."

"Yeah, my mom was ridiculously talented."

She flipped through several pages. Her gaze lingering on a beautiful dragon soaring over a castle. Ideas immediately began flowing through her head of how she would position the dragon on his arm. "Tell me about the drawings."

Brandon took another sip of his coffee. His cheeks turned pink as he looked at her. "Any chance what we talk about can stay between us a bit?"

"Of course."

His finger traced the edge of the dragon on the page. "As you can tell, my mom was an artist." He paused. "My... my mom, sh... she died when I was nine."

"Oh my gosh, I'm so sorry."

"Thanks." He paused. "When she got sick, she drew these pictures for me, stories really. We'd sit on her bed at night, and she'd elaborate on them, or we'd do this choose your own adventure kind of deal with them." His mouth curled up into a sad smile as he talked. "Sometimes the dragon was the good guy, sometimes the bad. Sometimes it was about love. Sometimes it was about fighting. I don't know, every night was something different. It was sort of our thing."

Without saying a word, Kia reached across the table and squeezed his hand.

"Thanks." Brandon raised his head and smiled at her. "This is embarrassing, but I've always traveled with at least a couple of her pictures with me on every road trip. She never got to see me play. Never got to see me do much of anything honestly and I don't know... just when I think of her stories and the messages, it just..." His voice broke. "It helps."

Tears welled in Kia's eyes. She blinked to hold them back as she watched this big, strong man open up and expose the raw wounds he still carried around about his mother's death. "I don't think that's embarrassing at all. I think it's sweet that you want your mom with you."

He held her stare. "Yeah?"

"Absolutely."

"Cool." He exhaled with a laugh. "Traveling with them kind of sucks. You're probably going to think I need fucking therapy or something. I become a bit of a basket case if my luggage gets lost or delayed and I can't see them. I'm OCD about looking at them. So this is my pathetic way of dealing with that." He laughed again. "And yeah, I know a therapist would probably say it's unhealthy, but fuck it."

Kia smiled. "Not my place to judge. I've tattooed people for all kinds of reasons." She fingered through the drawings again. "And I have definitely tattooed a lot worse than these beautiful drawings."

She laid a few drawings out side-by-side on the table. "So were you thinking of a full sleeve? Half sleeve?"

"Full. Obviously, I want the dragon." He pulled the pages toward himself and pulled out a picture of a sea monster. "I know the drawings were all designed for me as a kid, but if you could figure out a way to make it look a bit more badass than Disney that would be good."

She slid the sea monster picture toward herself and placed the dragon above. Flipping through the pages, she pulled out a man wielding a sword. Her mind raced as the ideas for how to create a sleeve out of the drawings swirled in her head. "I can definitely do that. We could do a couple of things. We could weave in your mom's drawings into a design that is totally unrelated, or we could do a sleeve that tells the story of your mom's designs. With the sea monster at the bottom. And work our way up to the dragon in the sky."

"Both sound cool."

Her eyes narrowed as she looked at the pictures closer. "What's this symbol? It's on every page." She pushed the sheet toward Brandon and tapped the drawing.

He smiled. "It's a little symbol my mom made that weaves together my initials, with hers and my dad's."

"I like that. I assume you want that somewhere on the sleeve?"

The muscle in his jaw flexed. "I...I... I'm not sure. My dad and I aren't really tight."

"No?"

"Nah." He sniffed, then dragged his tongue along his teeth and clicked his mouth. "He kind of disappeared after my mom died."

"Like he left?"

"No, no, he was there, sort of. He just…" He shrugged. "We just coped differently, I guess." He stared at the drawings on the table. "Yeah, probably it should be in there. I mean, it's in all the pictures, right?"

Kia's chest tightened. That poor family. "Let me see what I can do."

"Any chance we could get started on this tattoo soon? I don't know how all this works for where you'd need to set up and all that."

"You were hoping to get it done during training camp? I don't live here."

"I know and obviously I'd pay for your flight and stuff." His cheeks turned bright pink and he looked down. "With the season starting soon, I wouldn't mind getting this done, so I'm not a headcase if my suitcase gets lost."

"I could refer you to someone local. There are tons of talented artists here in Phoenix."

"I'm sure there are. I'd just feel more comfortable with you. I saw the work you did on the guys, and I don't know, it's stupid and hard to explain, but…" He blushed again. "I think my mom would like the idea of you doing the tattoo. You have a little boy yourself." He shrugged. "You just feel like the right person. Besides, I already spewed all my embarrassing shit at you. I'd just as soon not have to explain that to someone else." He rubbed a hand over his eyebrow. "I'm not exactly sure why I told you half of that."

"I appreciate it. I'd be honored to create something with your mom's art." She pulled out her phone and looked at her schedule. At the moment, she only had one client booked so far on Saturday and had Sunday off, so she and Max could probably make the trip back. She could maybe see if Christian would rent her out some space, otherwise she could do it at the house, but that was less than ideal. "Let me see what I can do. Would next weekend work?"

"Yeah, we have a Bi on Saturday, so that'd be perfect."

"That could work if Jeff can watch Max. Hopefully, I could do all the outlining that day and then we could figure out other sittings from there. It would mean a long seating, so we'll have to see how you do."

"Are you worried about whether I can handle the pain?"

"Yeah." She bit back a smile. People always thought they could handle the pain. In her experience, it was often the cockiest ones who couldn't.

"No offence, Kia, but tattoo pain is nothing compared to what I've already been through." The air shifted around him and the look on his face was haunted. "Sitting isn't going to be a problem."

She didn't understand what Brandon had experienced, but whatever it had been was dark. The steel she'd seen snap in his face made it clear this would not be a man who tapped out. The mother in her wanted to hug him. The fighter in her respected the hell out of the armor. "That's good to know. Makes my job easier. Let me grab a couple measurements if that's okay."

"Yeah, whatever you need."

She pulled out the roll of paper she'd brought with her. Looking around the mostly empty cafe, she gestured to an open area behind their table. "Can you just stand over there? And maybe push up your sleeve."

"Sure." He stood up and shoved his sleeve up over his shoulder. She wrapped the paper around his arm and put a couple marks on the page to show a few key points: elbow, wrist, shoulder cap. She added a couple of light musculature tracings so she could picture the way the drawing needed to flow.

"Alright, that should do it." She walked back to the table and set the roll with her other belongings. "Let me make a few phone calls, and I'll let you know."

He reached and shook her hand. "Cool. I appreciate you meeting me and getting this done so quickly."

"Of course." She eyed the drawings in front of her. "This is going to be fun."

CHAPTER TWENTY-ONE

HOVERING ON THE EDGE of sleep, it felt like someone was watching him. He popped one eye open and found Kia staring at him. "Jesus, that's creepy as fuck. Why are you staring at me?" With a chuckle, he rubbed his hand over his face to clear the sleep away.

"Sorry I didn't want to wake you, but I also kind of did, and I know when Max watches me, I can always feel it. Weirdly, it's less jarring to me than when he touches me. I tend to flail when I'm asleep and am likely to hit someone. I figured maybe it would be the same for you."

He dragged his hand down his face again. What time was it, anyway? "For the record, I can think of several better ways to wake me up than staring at me. And unlike you, I promise not to flail. I'll just lay there and take it like a good boy." He waggled his eyebrows at her.

"You're such a clown." Kia shoved her hand against his chest. She rolled onto her stomach and propped herself up on her elbow. "So...um...I know we agreed to keep things casual and...well obviously your friends know about us, but Max doesn't, and yesterday when I met with Brandon he asked, and I wasn't sure what to say."

Tension tightened his shoulders. "What do you mean he asked?"

"Dial it down, big guy. We were just talking, and he asked what the deal was with us, and I honestly didn't know what you wanted me to say."

He folded up the pillow behind his head, so he was sitting more upright for their discussion. "What I want you to say or what I think you'll agree to say?"

Kia scrambled up, so she was sitting upright on the bed. "What's that supposed to mean?"

"It means I know you aren't all that eager to announce to the world that we're together."

She flipped from her knees to a cross-legged position. Her body no longer screamed annoyance as she settled in on the mattress to talk. "Is that what we are? Together?"

"Kia, seriously? Before I left we were together every day."

"Yeah, but that's because of Max."

"Are you fucking kidding me?" She couldn't be serious with this. "If it was just about Max, why did I stick around every night after he'd gone to bed? Why have we talked every night since I've been here? Why do I beat off thinking about you almost every night?"

"You did that?" She looked at her lap shyly.

"How can you be so in tune with everything to do with Max and so clueless when it comes to yourself? I'm fucking crazy about you. I was when I met you six years ago, and I'm even more so now. How do you not see that?"

"I just don't want to mess this up and have Max get hurt."

"Kia, the only way we're gonna fuck this up is if we keep dancing around what we both want. In case you can't tell, I'm in. With you, with Max, with us as a family."

A smile spread across her face. "So we're doing this for real? We're telling Max we're dating."

"We are abso-fucking-lutely telling Max we're dating and every other person we see. There's gonna be no doubt we're a couple."

"I don't know that we need to shout it from the rooftops, but I'd like to tell Max."

"Does this mean I can finally hold your hand in public?"

She held up her hand. "Let's not get too carried away."

He snickered. "What's your problem with PDA?"

"I don't know, it just feels a little..." She scrunched up her nose. "Like marking your territory or something."

He sat up and hooked his finger in the collar of her shirt and jerked her toward him. "Kind of like the big hickey I left on your neck?"

She slapped her hand to the side of her throat. "Oh, my god, you did not?"

He eyed the edge of the bite mark he could just make out from his angle. "I might have." The mark hadn't been intentional, but now that it was there, he liked it. She'd probably think it made him a pig, but he didn't care. He wanted everyone to know she was his.

"How the hell am I supposed to explain that to Max?"

"Wear your hair down and no one will see it." He tapped the back of her neck where it met her shoulder.

She narrowed her eyes and gave him a mock glare. "You're lucky I can hide it."

"Am I?"

"Mm hmm." She pushed up onto her knees and hovered above him. The collar of her t-shirt gaped, giving him a perfect view of her naked breasts.

"I'm all for a little marking, but I was thinking you could maybe mark me a different way."

"Oh yeah? What did you have in mind?" He hooked his hand in the collar of her shirt and pulled her face to his, so they were just a breath apart.

"Well, first I was thinking, I really like when I ride your face, so it might be kind of fun to have you fuck mine." She leaned in and ran her tongue up his neck.

The image of him hovering above her, fucking her mouth, made his dick instantly hard as a rock. He shifted his body as his cock pulsed against the constriction of his boxer briefs.

Kia nipped his ear and whispered. "Then I was thinking when you were ready to come, you could come all over my chest."

With a growl, he wrapped his arm around her waist and flipped her onto her back. Kia let out a little squeal, then giggled. "I'll take that as a yes?"

The collar of her shirt gaped where it was all over-stretched from his fist. He grabbed the stretched-out fabric in both hands and ripped it down the middle.

Kia gasped. Her nipples hardened the second the air hit them. Her eyes heated as she looked at him.

"I love when you want to get a little dirty." His voice sounded like sandpaper as he fought to stay in control and not rut on her like some sort of animal when every cell in his body wanted to do exactly that.

Leaning down, he sucked a tight nipple into his mouth, and her back arched off the mattress. Kia threaded her hands through his hair as he licked his way over to the other nipple.

"You really are a dirty girl, aren't you?"

"Yes, and I want you to make me dirtier." She pushed the edges of her ripped t-shirt so the only part of her body it covered at all was her shoulders. Her chest was completely naked and exposed.

Jeff hopped off the mattress and kicked off his boxers, then climbed back on the bed. He leaned over and pressed his lips against hers. Driving his tongue into her mouth, hers tangled with his, as they both fought for control. When they pulled apart, they were both breathing heavily.

Holding eye contact with him, she licked her lips. "Fuck my face, Jeff."

He loved how Kia gave as good as she got. How she embraced what she wanted in the bedroom. She didn't try to be coy or pretend she needed to be coaxed into anything. She wanted it; she asked. And he was going to enjoy giving her exactly what she asked for.

His dick pulsed, demanding he listen to her. Now.

Jeff moved up the bed and set one leg on either side of her face. When he looked at Kia, she smirked back at him, clearly enjoying the power she had over him. Good, let her. He was definitely not on the losing end of this scenario.

Kia shifted her body lower on the mattress slightly. She cupped his balls a second before she wrapped her lips around them and sucked hard.

"Jesus," he groaned, gripping the headboard with both hands as his eyes rolled back in his head.

His balls pulled up tight. She ran her tongue up the length of his dick. Her heated stare never left his face, watching him as she flicked her tongue on the little spot on the head of his cock. "Yes," he hissed. She wrapped her lips around the tip and sucked her way down his shaft. When he hit the back of her throat, her eyes widened slightly before she relaxed. He tried to move back, but Kia sucked him in deeper and he groaned. His head dropped back as his hips involuntarily surged forward.

"Kia, you need to stop, or I won't be coming on your chest. It'll fire down your throat." She moaned, the sound vibrated against his dick, and it took everything in him not to surge forward again. Her eyes watered from the last deep thrust, but she didn't look like she wanted to let up.

"Baby, I'm serious," he told her, tapping the side of her mouth so she'd stop.

She released him with a pop. Tears trickled out of the corners of her eyes. She wiped the corner of her mouth and smiled at him. There was nothing hotter than seeing how turned on she was from having her face fucked.

"You jacking me off or am I?" he asked. Guess they'd see how dirty she wanted to be.

"Definitely you." She bit her lip as she stared at his throbbing erection.

Hot. A grin pulled at the corner of his mouth. Jeff shifted his body back slightly, so he was over her chest. He gripped his cock hard and roughly jerked his palm up and down the shaft. He couldn't decide if he wanted to watch the come fall on her chest or see Kia's face when it did.

Heat raced down his spine as his balls pulled up tight. With one last hard stroke, he shot all over her chest. Kia gasped as the liquid hit her body.

"Fuck," he groaned loudly when he saw the look on her face.

Her eyes popped open, and she smiled at him. Her gaze never leaving his face, she reached up and rubbed the come all over her chest. Somehow, his dick twitched, instantly alert. There was no way he could go again already, but his body sure seemed like it wanted to try.

"It is so fucking hot how filthy you are," he told her.

Kia held out her hand and gripped his arm, pulling him on top of her. "Now we both are," she said as she nipped his earlobe, then laughed.

"I'm definitely going to need a shower before the game now." He shifted his body, so his hips nestled between her legs. But maybe they had time to get her off before he got ready. Her soaking wet panties brushed against his dick. Kia wrapped her legs around his waist and lifted her hips so her clit ground against his still slightly erect cock.

A loud thumping sounded against the door. "Mom?" Max's voice called through the wood. "Why's the door locked?"

Jeff dropped his head against Kia's shoulder and laughed.

"Just a minute," Kia called back. "I'll meet you down-stairs."

She slapped an arm over her face. "I can't believe the kid just vag-blocked me."

He burst out laughing. "Jesus, no, that is not a term."

Kia peered at him. "What cock-blocking is? But vag-blocking isn't?"

He shuddered. "No, it definitely isn't. You have to come up with a better name than that."

"I'll work on it, but either way. That kid's timing." She sighed. "I'll go make breakfast while you grab a shower. I can grab mine after you leave for the field."

"You guys are still coming to the game today, right?"

She placed her hands on either side of his face and pressed a kiss to his lips. "Wouldn't miss it."

He rolled off Kia and she stood up from the bed.

"You might want to run a facecloth over your chest, so you don't smell like jizz before you go down there." As hot as it was knowing she was coated in him, there was no denying the way it smelled.

Kia wrinkled her nose, then padded toward the ensuite.

Propping himself up with the pillows, he stared up at the ceiling. Over the past couple of seasons, when he'd watched his friends fall in love, maybe a small part of him had been jealous of what they had. But mostly he thought they'd been crazy. There was no way he'd wanted to settle down. He enjoyed playing the field, hooking up with random women. Locking himself in with one person hadn't made sense when there were so many women out there.

But now? Man, now he got it.

What he had with Kia was so much better than anything he'd ever imagined a relationship could be. He never dreamed it could be like this. He understood why Pete and Ryan wanted to skip beers and go back to the room to FaceTime their girls. Why they were always getting goofy looks on their faces when they looked at their phones. Knowing Kia and Max were coming to the game today had him feeling energized in a way he hadn't experienced since he was first called up. His entire body buzzed.

A moment later, Kia walked out of the bathroom. She paused at the bed, leaned down and kissed him. He wanted to pull her back on top of him, but he knew Max was waiting.

Kia walked to the door and paused. "I'll see you downstairs."

"Count on it."

CHAPTER TWENTY-TWO

WEARING MATCHING SMITH JERSEYS, Kia held Max's hand as they stood looking out over the stadium. Her eyes scanned the field for Jeff. They'd gotten there early hoping to catch him before the game started while his team was still warming up.

"There's Dad," Max yelled, pointing out to the middle of the field.

Her heart fluttered in her chest as she watched him joking around with his teammates. Wow, the man did things for a baseball uniform. She knew women who went gaga for a guy in uniform, any uniform, and she'd never understood it until this moment.

"Come on." Max pulled on her hand, dragging her toward the field.

"Hang on, let me double check where we're sitting." Jeff said their seats were on the first base line. As she scanned the row numbers, she realized their seats were in the front row a little closer to the outfield side of first, so they'd be able to see him.

She directed Max to their seats. Max dropped his clear backpack on the ground, then stood against the rail and waved his arms around like a windmill, trying to get Jeff's attention.

"Dad," Max yelled. When Jeff didn't look, Max yelled again. Unfortunately, his little voice just couldn't carry the way he needed it to.

Kia stood up beside him at the rail. "Jeff," she yelled. Nothing. She looked at Max's disappointed face. Time to pull out the big guns. She placed her fingers at her mouth and let out an ear-piercing whistle, quickly followed by, "Smitty," as loud as she could holler.

Jeff's head snapped in their direction and a smile spread across his face a moment before he jogged across the field toward them.

When Jeff stopped at the rail, Max launched himself at him. Jeff's arms immediately opened to catch him on instinct. The laugh that rumbled from his chest as he caught their son made Kia's throat catch. Never in her wildest dreams had she ever envisioned this for Max.

"Good luck today, Dad. Hit me a homer."

"No pressure." Jeff made a face. "Unfortunately, Maxie, it's not that easy to hit a home run. How about I promise to look over here at you before I bat, and I'll adjust my helmet, so you know I'm looking at you?"

"Kay, do this." Max grabbed his own cap and wiggled it aggressively on his head.

Jeff winced. "Maybe let's go a little more subtle." He took his hat off and pushed his sandy blond hair back from his forehead, then set his hat back on his head. "How about that?"

"Kay, but scratch your nose too," Max demanded.

Jeff's lips curved up slightly as he looked at his son and nodded. "Deal." He tapped Max on the bill of his cap. "Okay, I gotta get back out there. Give me a hug."

Max wrapped his arms around Jeff's neck and squeezed. Kia placed her hand against her chest as a wave of emotion swept through her.

The pair separated. Jeff looked at her and flicked his head for her to step toward him. "Come here, Keys."

She shook her head. He knew her feelings about PDA.

"You didn't think you were getting off that easy, did ya?" He smirked.

"Yeah." She blinked at him innocently.

Jeff sighed, then in a lightning-fast move, he hooked his hand in the waistband of her shorts and yanked her forward. She fell against him. As she rested her hands on his chest for balance, he pressed his lips against hers. Her traitorous body melted into him briefly before she jumped back and stood upright. Her gaze instantly darted to Max, who stood with his eyes bugging wide open back at them.

"Are you guys in love?" Max asked in awe.

"Would you be okay if we were?" Jeff asked.

Kia's heart raced. Why would he say that? There was a big difference between admitting they were dating and saying they were in love. Did he love her? Did she love him? Holy shit.

"Yeah," Max whooped. He threw his arms around Jeff's neck again. "This is awesome."

"Agreed." Jeff's eyes locked with hers as he spoke.

The man was trouble, there was no doubt about it. The little zip in her stomach said she liked it, not that she would tell him that. Shaking her head, she waved him off. "Go play your game."

Jeff winked, his blue eyes sparkling with amusement as he blew them a kiss before running back onto the field.

"So that's your dad?" The man behind them leaned between their seats.

Max turned around. "Yeah."

"He's a pretty good player," the man responded.

Kia shifted to look at the group of older men in the row behind them. It was only March and already their darkened skin spoke of seasoned sports fans who spent hours outside soaking up the Arizona sun.

"He's the best player ever," Max told him.

"Is that so?"

"Yep." Max's head bobbed up and down.

"And is this your mom?" the man asked, nodding at her.

Max looked at her, then back at the man. "Yep."

"And you two are a couple?"

Kia's spine stiffened. How was this any of his business?

"Yeah, they're in love," Max gushed.

Kia's eyes closed. Damn Jeff. Why hadn't he corrected Max?

The stranger's gaze drifted across her body, lingering on the arm of her jersey where her tattoo sleeve covered her exposed skin. His eyebrow rose. "Is that right?"

Kia's spine stiffened. Who did this guy think he was judging her like that? "Yeah, that's right?" she snapped back, daring the man to say something else.

"Hmm, go figure," the guy muttered before picking up his beer and turning his attention back to the field.

Why had she engaged? Now she'd just as much admitted to a stranger that Jeff and she were in love. It's not like she could be mad at Jeff for telling Max that when she'd pretty much just done the same thing. Kia eyed Max, who sat perched on the edge of his chair, watching the field. "You want a hot dog before the game starts?" she asked.

"Yeah." Max jumped out of his seat.

Kia stood and wrapped her arm around Max's shoulder. "Let's go." As she walked up the stairs, she could feel the eyes of the group of men on her. Let them talk, she thought as she stood tall, walking with Max up the stairs.

In the third inning, Los Angeles hit a sky-high foul ball. Kia tracked the ball in case she needed to cover Max's head. Brandon Sims raced over from right field. Just when Kia thought she'd have to yank Max out of the way, Brandon's arm reached over and swiped the ball out of the sky in a very impressive catch.

Max leaped from his seat and cheered. Brandon grinned at Max and handed him the ball. Turning toward her, Brandon winked. "Looks like you two figured it out." He nodded his head toward center field.

Remembering their conversation the day before, she smiled. "Looks like."

"Smart man," Brandon said before he jogged off back to right field.

Max held his ball up in the air triumphantly toward center field, trying to show his dad the ball. Jeff flashed him a thumbs up, but even from this far away, Kia could see the tension in his body. What was that about?

Brandon looked over at Jeff, then the stands, then back at Jeff before tipping his hat slightly. Jeff gave him a stiff nod in return. Kia fought the urge to roll her eyes at the ridiculous display of testosterone. It was a flippin' foul ball for their son, not a bouquet of flowers. The man needed to simmer down.

Every time Jeff came up to bat, Max hopped out of his seat and stood at the rail. When Jeff took off his helmet for their signal, Max bounced up and down. Kia could practically feel the pride and excitement pulsing off Max from several feet away. Sharing this ritual meant everything to the little boy. She pictured all the bragging he'd be doing when he got back to school on Tuesday. Maybe then the little shits in his class would finally shut up about her relationship with his dad.

As Jeff lined up to bat in the fifth, she leaned forward in her seat. Who knew watching baseball was so exhilarating? Normally, she found it kind of boring. The games always seemed to drag on with not a lot happening, but it was a whole different game when you knew the players on the field.

The first pitch came in low and outside.

"Good eye, good eye," the man behind her yelled. The second pitch flew across the plate like a rocket nearly hitting Jeff. He dropped to the dirt to avoid being hit. "Holy shit," she muttered. What if that thing had hit him? It would break his face. Yes, she knew that's what that piece on the side of his helmet was for, but seriously, that pitcher had a cannon. How could he stand there so calmly when someone was whipping a ball at his head?

Jeff stood up and brushed off his pants. He lined up in the batter's box. When the ball zipped toward him, he swung and cracked the ball. Max jumped up and down as

Kia tracked the ball all the way out of the field into the stands to the right of center field.

"He hit a homer," Max screamed. "He hit a homer." Max threw his arms around her waist.

When Jeff crossed home plate, he turned in their direction, took off his helmet and did the big elaborate helmet display Max had wanted them to do as their signal. Kia burst out laughing as Max mimicked the same thing back to his dad. Jeff's grin encompassed his entire face before he turned and headed to the dugout, where he was swept up in congratulatory back slaps from his teammates. She doubted he'd be able to do that kind of thing with Max during the normal season since spring training was so much more laid back. That just made her even more glad she'd listened to him when he'd suggested they come up for the weekend. These memories would stick with Max for the rest of his life.

The rest of the game dragged by with no hits, but with Jeff's two-run homer in the fifth, it led to a victory for the Hawks.

After the game, they made their way to the agreed upon meeting area. Max jumped up in the air beside her, landed, then jumped again. "What are you doing?" she asked.

"Trying to see if Dad's coming." He jumped again.

Kia bent and hoisted him up on her hip. Normally he told her he was getting too big to be carried, but apparently today it was fine as he pushed himself up on her shoulder to get higher in the air.

"I see him," Max declared, pushing on her arms to be put down. The second his feet hit the ground he bolted toward Jeff. Dodging legs, finally the crowd parted for her just in time to see Max launch himself at Jeff. Jeff swung Max up into his arms. Gonzo fell into stride beside them. Setting the boy on his hip, Jeff strode past bystanders, his eyes honed directly on her. It was hard to swallow. Emotion clogged her throat as she watched her two guys walking toward her. No matter what happened between her and Jeff, this right here was worth taking a risk for. Having moments like this as a family.

He stopped in front of her, the look in his eyes challenging her to step into him. Feeling bold, she wrapped her arms around his waist. On tiptoes, she pressed a kiss to his lips. "Nice hit."

"You saw that, did ya?" He raised his eyebrow cheekily and stuck his tongue out slightly between his teeth.

"I might have been watching," she teased.

"You know ballpark rules say when a guy hits a home run, he should be rewarded." Jeff arched his brow at her as he spoke.

"Do they?" She smirked. Knowing exactly where this was heading.

"Yes, ice cream." Max threw his arm in the air.

Jeff snorted. "Not quite where I was going, but sure bud, ice cream works."

"Who's getting ice cream?" Pete asked as he and Ryan joined the group.

"We are," Max yelled.

"Max, not so loud." Kia laughed. Yes, the kid was excited, but holy cow, did he have to show it by deafening the group?

Jeff set Max on the ground and Gonzo immediately grabbed the boy, flipped him upside down over his shoulder and yelled, "Ice cream." Then took off running toward the parking lot.

With a laugh, Jeff slung his arm around Kia's shoulder. "Looks like everyone is going for ice cream."

Kia pulled the car up in front of her house. Shit. Why the hell was he here?

The last thing she wanted to see was Austin. She parked at the curb. With a deep exhalation, she exited the vehicle. "Hey Austin. What are you doing here?"

His eyes scanned her body. "Hi Kia." He glanced behind her at the car where Max sat in his booster seat. "Can we talk?"

"Sure." She sighed. "Let me just get Max inside."

"You're seriously not going to invite me in?"

"No, I'm not."

"Fine, but I think you're being ridiculous. We were friends, weren't we?"

"Pretty sure you said we weren't last time we talked. So it's outside or nothing." After the number of asshole texts he'd sent her over the past few weeks, he was lucky she was even willing to do that. Kia turned, popped open the back door, and unbuckled Max. "Come on buddy, let's head inside and I'll put the TV on for you to watch one of your shows."

Max eyed Austin suspiciously. "What's he doing here?"

"No idea, but I'm about to find out, so let's get you set up."

Together they walked toward the house and up the front stairs. As she opened the front door, she glanced over her shoulder at Austin, warning him not to come in. Once inside, she dragged her overnight case into the bedroom and dumped it on the floor. She'd deal with all that later.

In the living room, she turned on the TV and started flipping through the channels. "Hey bud, what do you think you want to watch?"

"Cartoons."

She paused on one of the kid's channels. "This look good?"

Max lay on his stomach on the carpet, rested his elbows on the floor with his chin in his hands, and looked up at the TV. "Yeah."

"I'm just going to go outside and talk to Austin for a minute. Okay?"

Immersed in his cartoon already, Max made some absent sound that could be anything from agreement to leave me alone.

Outside, she walked down the front steps and stood in front of Austin. "So, you gonna tell me why you're here?"

"I'm worried about you."

Worried about her? That was a new one. She couldn't help the smirk that crossed her mouth. This outta be good. "Alright and just why is it exactly that you're worried about me?"

"I saw you on TV. You and Max were at the game."

"Okay?" What did that have to do with anything?

"Yeah, I saw you guys at the game, and it looks like maybe you're trying to do the whole happy family thing with Smitty."

She rubbed her hand across her forehead. "Austin, I'm not doing this with you."

"Not doing what with me?" he asked. "I'm worried about you. Come on, Kia. It's not like he's going to end up with someone like you. We both know that."

"It's not your problem. We broke up. What I do. Who I date isn't any of your business anymore."

"Doesn't mean I don't still care about you."

"Austin, I don't want to hurt you. When we broke up, I wasn't dating Jeff, but yes, now we're dating."

"I always knew you were interested in him."

"That's not why we broke up. I told you that you and I just weren't gonna work. It just wasn't there. You didn't want to be around Max. I didn't want you around Max. Clearly this was never going to go anywhere."

Austin turned. His face marred with some weird emotion. She wasn't quite sure what it was. Anger. Jealousy. Pain. "The reason we didn't work is that you weren't willing to try. You never gave me a chance. You never let me be around Max, so I didn't want anything to do with him. Why would I? Every time I asked if we could hang out with him, you said no."

"Come on, let's not try to rewrite history. You never were interested in having a relationship with Max, and that worked just fine for both of us. That was exactly what we both wanted. What we had was fun. It worked, but now it's done."

"And you think it's going to work with Wonder Boy?"

"I don't know, maybe, I hope so." Did she think it was gonna work? Who knew? Everything in her said what Jeff and she had was worth fighting for. It was worth the risk of trying to see if this relationship would work. She'd never been willing to do that with anyone else. She'd never been willing to risk it, but for whatever reason with Jeff, she was. There was something there she'd never had with anyone else. She prayed it worked because Max deserved everything.

"Yeah, you've seen what he's like online. You see all the girls he dates. He's not going to settle down with you. You're just going to be some notch on his belt, some other woman he bangs and leaves, and you're going to get hurt."

"I'm willing to take that risk."

Austin crossed his arms over his chest. "Why weren't you willing to take that risk with me?"

God, how was she supposed to explain to somebody that it just wasn't there? She'd thought he felt it, too. They barely saw each other. Their relationship had been purely a physical thing. Sure, they went out for meals now and then, but that was just to fuel the night ahead. It meant nothing. Now he was all butt-hurt because she'd picked Jeff. His ego couldn't handle feeling like she picked someone else over him. He hadn't thought what they had was worth fighting for before, but now that Jeff actually seemed interested, suddenly she was worth fighting for. It was ridiculous, and she wasn't going to play this game.

"Look Austin, I'm sorry that you're upset that Jeff and I are trying to make this work. And that your feelings are hurt by that, but I'm not going to change my mind. I appreciate you coming by, and I wish you all the best."

Austin crossed his arms over his chest and glared at her. "That's seriously all you have to say to me?"

Exhausted by the conversation, she pinched the bridge of her nose. "Yeah." She turned and walked toward the front door. At the base of the steps, she stopped and looked at him as if to say this conversation was done, but she wasn't going inside until he left. There was zero possibility she was bringing this conversation anywhere near her son.

Austin's eyes narrowed. Anger radiated off his body as he took a step toward her.

Where the hell had that come from? Why was he so pissed off? She'd never seen this side of him. Nothing about him even hinted at this type of aggression before. Why she felt a little afraid she couldn't say. But she turned fully around, prepared for action if necessary.

"You're going to be sorry you picked him over me, Kia."

"Goodbye Austin."

Austin stormed toward his truck, hoisted himself up into the big vehicle. The engine roared to life. His tires screeched as he ripped away from the sidewalk. Watching him drive away, a sense of foreboding zipped down her spine. With a shake of her head, she brushed off the feeling. She pulled the front door open and joined her son.

CHAPTER TWENTY-THREE

Surprised by the 10:00 pm airport traffic, Jeff checked his rearview mirror as he changed lanes. After some careful maneuvering, he flew past the majority of slow drivers, merging onto the freeway. Thank god their place wasn't too far because he couldn't wait to get home.

Kia shifted in her seat as she set the water bottle in the cupholder between the two car seats. "Thanks for picking us up. We could have grabbed an Uber."

His mouth pulled tightly. Like he was going to let that happen. "Of course I'm gonna pick you up. I would have picked you up last time, but your plane arrived during a game so I couldn't get away."

She squeezed his arm. "Well, I appreciate it."

Every time he looked at her, he had the same physical reaction. Sure, part of it was chemistry, but it felt like so much more than that. Before Kia he hadn't found the whole tattooed badass thing all that appealing, but now he certainly understood it. Taking his eyes off the road briefly, he flashed her a wicked grin. "I'm more than happy to let you show me your appreciation."

"I'll just bet you are," she murmured.

His gaze flicked down to her chest, lingering on her nipples as they poked out through her shirt. The car was almost hot, so there was no way she could pretend her reaction was anything other than what it was. He raised an eyebrow at her. "You telling me you don't want to?"

Kia glanced at her chest and winced. "Shut up." She crossed her arms over her breasts.

No chance he was letting her cover that up. He grabbed her hand and pulled her arm away from her chest and set it on her lap. "Me too, babe, me too."

She shifted in her chair and looked in the backseat. "Okay Max, the second we get inside teeth brushed, pajamas on, off to bed."

"Come on." Max's shoulders slumped. "Can I at least play a video game or something with Uncle Gonzo and Uncle Ryan?"

Since when did his friends become uncles? "Uncle?"

"Yeah, they said I could call them that."

"They'll be there in the morning for breakfast with you." He had to admit as eager as he was to spend time with Max, the idea of getting Kia alone ASAP was incredibly appealing.

"But we have to play Mario Kart," Max whined.

Kia fully turned in her seat to face her son. "Max, this isn't up for discussion. It's already 10:00 o'clock. It's way past your bedtime. Let's get you ready for bed and then tomorrow you'll spend the day with the guys while I get some work done. You've got a whole boys' day planned, but if you don't get some sleep, you're not going to do it because you're going to need a nap."

"Fine." Max crossed his little arms across his chest.

As he pulled the car into the driveway of their suburban rental, it surprised him how much he loved the feeling of bringing his family home. Three months ago, he hadn't even known Max existed and now he couldn't imagine his life without him. Or Kia. When they'd started this thing, it had been a physical craving. Now the last thing he wanted was anything casual with her. He wanted it all. The picket fence. Them moving into his house. The woman beside him in the crook of his arm while he slept. A home with Max and Kia in it.

Everything between them was perfect. There were no issues, yet she was still super skittish. As he looked at her, she glanced over at him, and a warm smile spread across her face. Maybe she wasn't as skittish as she used to be.

He turned off the truck and hopped out. He pulled open Max's door. "Alright bud, let's get you inside and get to bed so we can have some fun tomorrow."

The trio trudged their way into the house. The second the front door opened hoots and hollers sounded from the couch in the living room.

"Maxie," Gonzo yelled.

"Don't get him riled up, guys. He's heading to bed," Jeff told his friends.

A resounding chorus of groans echoed from the living room.

"Don't start," Jeff hollered back.

"You're no fun, Smitty.

He could always count on Gonzo to be ready to rock n'roll. But he knew his friends would respect the rules.

He smiled to himself as he watched Max make the rounds of his friends, giving hugs and high-fives to each of them. When Jeff first found out about Max, he'd been worried things with his friends would change. But they'd embraced Max like their own.

Max stood in the middle of the living room and eyed the gaming system longingly. He sighed with his whole body. "Mom says I have to go right to bed."

The kid had the whole 'woe is me' thing down to an art already.

Gonzo sat up in the chair and looked like he was about to say something. The last thing the kid needed was help from his honorary uncles. Jeff pinned Gonzo with a look, daring him to argue about the bedtime rule. Gonzo held up his hands.

"Actually, it's almost my bedtime, too. I plan on kicking some ass at go-karts tomorrow, since I lost last time, and I want to look all fresh and pretty for my photo op in the winner's circle." Gonzo winked at the little boy, making Max giggle.

"Why do you want to look pretty? You're a boy, Uncle Gonzo."

"Boys can be pretty," Gonzo said. "Have you seen what I look like on TV?"

"Doesn't get much prettier than him," Pete agreed, his lips twitched with suppressed amusement.

"Thank you." Gonzo licked his thumbs and dragged them across his eyebrows, making Max burst into a fit of giggles again.

Kia wrapped her arm around Max's shoulders. "Let's get ready for bed."

She ushered Max upstairs. Less than ten minutes later, she hurtled him back to the living room and into his tent.

"Night Maxie." The guys called as they all stood up from the couch and made their way up the stairs to their respective rooms so Max could sleep.

"Can Dad read to me tonight?" Max asked.

"Sure, if he doesn't mind." Kia raised her eyebrow and held out the book to him.

Damn, the thing looked long. He eyed the chapter book. As much as he loved spending time with Max, he really wanted to get Kia alone. Like now.

He took the book from her and crawled into the tent. He held open the flap for her to follow him. "Let's go. You know you're gonna want to snuggle him before bed, so you may as well do that while I read."

Twenty minutes later, Jeff set the book on the floor and rolled onto his knees. Looking at Max all snuggled up with Kia on the mound of pillows, he almost hated to break it up. Almost. He wasn't a saint. There was no way he would give up the chance to have Kia in his bed for the night. He bent over Max and the little boy wrapped his arms around his neck. Damn, that felt good. He smiled as he absorbed the tight squeeze from his son. "I'm glad you're here."

"Me too. Can I play video games in the morning when I get up? I gotta practice so I can beat the guys."

He ruffled Max's head. "I need to talk to you mom about that one, buddy."

Max scrunched up his face. "She hates video games."

"I don't hate them. I just would rather see you play outside most of the time, that's all." Kia replied.

After checking to make sure the house was locked up, he followed Kia up the stairs toward his bedroom. His eyes lingered on her ass. With each step she took, his desire for her grew. Need coursed through him. The urge to claim her, mark her as his surged through his veins.

"Quit looking at my ass."

Busted. But he didn't care in the least. "Not a chance, Key. You're lucky I don't throw you over my shoulder and haul you up these stairs." He swatted her on the ass. "Now hustle it up and get this sweet ass up the stairs."

The moment she pushed open his bedroom door, he was on her. Wrapping his arm around her waist, he kicked the door closed with his foot. He pushed her chest against the door and pressed his front to her back.

"Well hello," humor laced her voice as she wiggled her ass against his already hard cock.

He wanted her aroused, not amused. Threading his hand in her hair, he pulled her head to the side and dragged his teeth along the column of her neck.

Goosebumps pooled on her skin, and she let out a long groan.

That was more like it.

"God, I've wanted to get my hands on you since the moment I saw you at the airport."

She pressed her ass against him. "Is that right? And what did you want to do with me?"

He slid his hand down her stomach and into the waistband of her pants. His fingers teased the edge of her panties and Kia's breath hitched.

"What I want to do is make you come so hard you scream down the walls, but I know you'd hate that with

Max downstairs. So I'm trying to figure out exactly how to keep you quiet for what I have planned."

She placed her hand on top of his while he kept moving teasingly close to her core, but never quite dipping where they both wanted him to go. She guided his hand further into her panties. "Why don't you let me worry about keeping quiet while you show me what you've got?" she said as she pushed his finger against her clit.

The competitor in him couldn't turn down a challenge. He shoved his hand fully inside her panties. Moisture instantly coated his fingers. "You're soaked already."

Kia widened her legs, giving him better access.

He dropped to his knees. She tried to turn around, but he gripped her hips, holding her in place. "Put your hands on the wall," he ordered.

She let out a little groan and did what she was told. He hooked his hands in her waistband and pulled her pants and panties down her legs, leaving her bare, luscious ass on full display. Unable to stop himself, he sunk his teeth into the firm flesh.

Kia moaned and pressed her ass back toward him. He pulled her back even further so he could see her pussy, forcing her to widen her stance even further to stay upright.

Inhaling deeply, he bit back a groan. "Fuck, I love the way you smell."

He should go slow, draw it out, tease her, like she'd been doing to him. Instead, he leaned in and plunged his finger inside her. Kia's head dropped against the wall and a loud, low moan ripped from her lips.

"Quiet, baby."

"A little warning next time."

"Where's the fun in that?" he asked. Allowing his breath to brush against her clit as he spoke.

She groaned. "I want you to fuck me."

"I will." He swirled his tongue around her clit.

"Now, Jeff." She pushed her hips back further.

"I'm not fucking you till you come, so if you want my dick, you better hurry up."

"Don't you want to fuck me?" She wiggled her ass back and forth in his face.

The little tease knew there was nothing he wanted more. But he'd promised her an orgasm and there was nothing like the feel of Kia coming on his face.

He sucked her clit into his mouth. Gripping her hips, he licked and sucked at the little bundle of nerves. Knowing the guaranteed fastest way to make her come, he pressed his finger at the tight rosebud of her ass and pushed inside as he sucked hard on her clit. Kia threw her head back, biting her fist as she came. Her body trembled against him as she rode out her orgasm. He flattened his tongue, scooping up her moisture. Delicious.

Kia chuckled lightly. "Oh my god."

She pressed her cheek against the wall while he stood up and took a step back. "Where do you think you're going?" she asked, glancing coyly over her shoulder. Her face flushed with arousal as she hungrily challenged him.

His dick twitched. He'd been thinking of taking her to bed, but seeing her standing there splayed against the wall, he'd be a fool not to take her up on the challenge. Letting his eyes rake down her body, he licked his lips. "Believe me, honey, I'm not going anywhere." He ripped his shirt off and tossed it to the side, then grabbed the condom from his wallet.

Kia started to turn around. "What do you think you're doing?" he asked, kicking his pants off.

"What do you mean?" She cocked her hip out seductively. She knew exactly what she was doing, but she wasn't in charge of this show. If she wanted to be fucked against the wall, they were doing it his way.

Rolling the condom on as he looked her up and down, he stroked himself once. Kia's eyes widened at how roughly he gripped himself.

"Turn around and put your hands on the wall," he ordered.

With a smirk, she did what she was told, pushing her ass out at him while she arched her back.

Yeah, that was better.

He gripped her hips, using his strength to maneuver her where he wanted her. Kia's breath hitched. The turned-on sound increased his own arousal.

He placed himself at her entrance and slowly pressed inside. At this angle, her pussy gripped him so tight he wasn't going to last long.

"Fuck me," Kia demanded.

"Gladly." He thrust into her. Kia matched him stroke for stroke. The way her pussy gripped his cock felt amazing. Each time with Kia was better than the last. This wasn't going to take long. Before he was ready, his balls were pulling up tight as the orgasm built. Reaching around, he pressed his finger against Kia's clit, needing her to come with him. He bit her neck and flicked her clit at the same time. His jaw clenched as her pussy clamped around his cock. Gripping her hips tight, he groaned as his orgasm tore through him.

Sucking in a breath, he attempted to get the oxygen back to his brain and dropped his head against her shoulder.

"How are we still standing?" Kia asked as she rested her body against the wall.

"No idea." His legs trembled. They wouldn't be for long.

He pressed a kiss against her shoulder blade, then scooped her up into his arms. Kia gasped a second before she wrapped her arms around his neck. Her body quivered against him as he carried her to the bathroom. He loved the way she relaxed in his arms, trusting him to keep her safe. He could get used to this.

Kia bent to help Max tie his shoes.

"I can do it, Mom." He grabbed the laces in each hand and made the first tie to tighten the lace around his shoe like she'd shown him. Concentrating on the task at hand, he dug his teeth into his bottom lip. His little fingers wrestled with the tie to make the first loop.

Jeff walked over and rubbed the back of Max's head. "Making some bunny ears?"

Max's head snapped up, dropping the laces as he looked at his dad then turned to her. His panicked eyes were wide as he searched her face. "Bunny ears?" he squeaked.

She smiled softly at him. "Nope, we are doing the loop swoop and pull method."

Jeff nodded. "I like it. Sounds much cooler than bunny ears."

Max's small shoulders relaxed. "Yeah, much cooler." He set his jaw and picked up the laces again and made the first loop. His tongue darted out and remained out as he focused on the swoop. When he pulled the lace and his shoe tied, he grinned up at them triumphantly.

"Good job, buddy." Pride welled in Kia's chest. Such a little thing and yet every time he battled with the laces and came out victorious, it warmed her heart.

Ryan and Pete rounded the corner and pulled up short in the mudroom. "What's up?" Ryan asked.

"Nothing, just getting our shoes tied." Kia pushed off the ground. Max stood and leaned against her leg. "You ready for your guy time?"

"Yep." Max turned to Ryan and Pete. "Dad said we whupped you at Mario Kart now we're gonna whup you on the track, just like last time."

"Oh, ho, is that right?" Ryan raised his eyebrows. "We'll see about that little man. He got lucky last time. I'm a much better driver than your dad."

"Nuh-uh, no one is better than him."

Pete shook his head. "Seriously, now you come with your own built-in cheering section. That seems unfair."

Jeff high-fived Max. "We're gonna leave 'em in our dust, right Maxie?"

"Right, Dad."

The fist around Kia's chest tightened the way it did every time she watched them together. Seeing her son like this was everything she'd ever hoped for. She'd done her best with him, but she couldn't deny this was what he'd been missing. Maybe Jeff was right, and they could make it as a couple. Try to be a real family. But what if things went sideways? The thought terrified her.

She leaned over and hugged her son. "Be good. Don't eat a bunch of junk food. Listen to your dad."

Max's arm tangled in her hair and pulled as he tried to wrap his arm around her neck. "I will." His arms tightened and squeezed.

God, she could stay snuggling him all day.

"Meet you in the car." Pete brushed past her and opened the door to the garage.

Ryan stuck his head back into the hallway and yelled, "Yo, Gonz, let's go. Get your ass in gear." When he turned around, he winced. "Sorry."

Kia bit back a smile. "It's fine. He's heard worse."

"Yeah, a lot worse. Mom said Uncle Nick swears like a trucker."

"Who's Nick?" Pete asked.

"My brother." Now that she thought about it, she hadn't talked to him in a while. She should really give him a call. It had taken a long time for them to get back to being as close as they used to be. But now that they were, she didn't want to lose it.

"You want to FaceTime Uncle Nick later?"

"Yeah." Max bounced on his toes and launched at Jeff. "You can do it too, so Uncle Nick can meet you."

Jeff made eye contact with her, holding her stare until she nodded in agreement. "Yeah, sure, bud. Sounds good."

"Alright, let's go," Gonzo said as he walked into the mudroom. "You ready to eat my dust, Maxie?"

"No." Max snorted. "You can eat mine."

"Do you want to bet on it?"

Max yelled, "Yes."

At the same time as Kia said, "No."

Gonzo, the little shit, winked at her, then tapped his mouth like he was deep in thought before finally smiling mischievously. "Winner gets to choose what flavor of ice cream the other one has to eat."

"Ew, I hate Tiger." Max's entire face scrunched up as he wrinkled his nose in distaste.

"Then I guess you better not lose." Gonzo tapped him on the head and walked into the garage.

"Bye, Mom," Max said absently as he turned to his dad. "We better not lose."

Jeff smirked at her as he walked past. "Don't worry, we're not going to lose."

"Have fun." Kia held the door open and watched while Jeff loaded Max into the booster in the backseat.

CHAPTER TWENTY-FOUR

KIA STROLLED INTO FATHOMLESS Ink and looked around. Her gaze landed on the man leaning against the counter. He eyed her up and down, his lip quirked up slightly as he watched her walking toward him. "Can I help you?" he asked.

"Yeah, I'm looking for Christian."

He eyed the case in her hand with amusement. "He know you're coming?"

"Yeah, he's expecting me. Can you tell him Kia's here, please?"

"Sure." He poked his head around the corner and yelled, "Yo, Chris, there's a Kia here for you."

A moment later, Christian strolled out with a huge smile on his face. "Kia." Christian wrapped her up in a hug. "You got your stuff?"

She nodded toward the case in her hand. "Yeah. Thanks for letting me use your shop for the day. I really appreciate it."

"Anytime. You know I'll always make room for you."

The guy at the counter snorted. "Yeah, I'll bet you will," the guy muttered.

Kia raised her eyebrow and looked at him. The asshole eyed her up and down like she was a piece of meat. Her jaw clenched. She turned to Christian and flicked a finger toward the guy behind her. "Chris, I'm not putting up with that shit." Dickheads like this guy were a dime a dozen, but she'd paid her dues and she sure as hell didn't have to put up with it anymore.

Christian's eyes narrowed as he looked at the guy behind her. "You don't have to worry about that, Kia. He's not going to be a problem."

"I didn't do anything," the guy growled.

"Keep it that way." Christian stared at the guy pointedly, then turned back to her. "Let me show you around and you can get setup."

"Seriously Chris, you're just going to let some bitch off the street come in and tattoo?"

Kia spun around. "First, I'm not some newbie off the street and second, you haven't even begun to see what a bitch I can be. Keep it up, dickhead, and I'll tie you to my fucking chair."

Christian laughed loudly and wrapped his arm around her shoulder. "Day-um, I've missed you, Kia." He spun her so they were facing the counter. "Kia, this is Saul, Saul, this is Saskia Kamen."

Saul's jaw dropped open. "Holy shit, Saskia Kamen?"

Kia smiled tightly. Amazing how fast a person could go from dipship to gobsmacked all in the space of a moment. Ever since she'd won a monster tattooing competition in Vegas a few years ago, her name had instantly garnered her respect. Her name, not the fact that she was simply a fellow artist. It sucked that until guys like him heard her name, they thought it was okay to treat her like shit.

"What are you doing here? How long are you here?" Saul pressed.

"Chris is just lending me some space to do a tattoo for a friend while I'm in town." She followed Christian deeper into the shop. He paused beside a chair against the window. "This okay? I know you like natural light."

She smirked at her friend. "And you like free advertising."

"What can I say? You pretty up the place."

"Yeah, right." And having a professional ballplayer getting tattooed in the front window sure didn't hurt either. But whatever. Christian was allowing her to use his space.

She sure as hell couldn't complain about him trying to take advantage of any perks she might bring along with her.

"Everything's clean and ready to go." Christian wheeled a cart over to her station. "Help yourself to whatever you need."

"Thanks." She opened her case and pulled out her equipment and began setting up the station the way she liked it.

She'd just finished setting up when Christian came back. "Your appointment is here."

"Great, thanks." She took one last look at her station, then headed to the front.

"Brandon, hi."

He turned from where he was looking at the prefab tattoo ideas on the wall. "Hey Kia."

"Come on back." She waved her arm, and Brandon followed her.

Brandon pulled off his hoodie. "This shirt gonna work?"

She eyed the cutoff t-shirt with the wide arm holes. "I think so. Have a seat."

He sat on the edge of the table. His long legs rested on the ground. The guy had to be six-foot-five at least. Normally people looked like Alice in Wonderland when they sat like that. She grabbed a roll of tape out of her case and used it to pull the top of the shirt into a small line so it wouldn't get in her way. "There, now we should be good."

She pulled out the drawings she'd done and gave it to Brandon to look at. While he looked at her design, she held her breath. There was no doubt it would make a killer tattoo. The only question was, did it make Brandon 'feel' his mom?

He stared at the drawing for several minutes, saying nothing. Finally, he dragged his hand over his mouth, then looked at her. "Wow! This is so much more than I was hoping for."

"Yeah?"

"Yeah." He rubbed his face as if the gesture could pull away the emotion that was betrayed in his eyes. "Is it weird that I kind of want to hug you?"

She laughed. "How about we save that for when we're done?"

"Yeah, sure." He flashed a cocky grin at her. "I mean, you could still fuck it up."

She smacked him. "I've never fucked up a tattoo in my life and I sure as hell am not going to start with this one. Now, you need to go to the bathroom or anything before we get started?"

"Nope. Let's go."

After a quick shave, Kia lined up the stencil on his arm. And paused. Shit, with the lighting in the cafe, she hadn't noticed the scar on the inside of Brandon's biceps.

"Um."

"Problem?" he asked. He watched her like he was daring her to ask about his scars.

"No, not really, just need to make a couple of tweaks." She twisted his arm and saw more of the same scars on the underside of his triceps. What the hell? They looked like cigarette burns. She eyed Brandon. He didn't say a word. Okay, clearly not something he wanted to talk about.

"I'm just going to have to freehand a little bit in a couple of places where the stencil isn't working."

"No problem."

She pulled out her colored sharpies and added some additional detail to have the scars fit into the design.

She tapped a large burn near his armpit. "Judging by your face, you don't want to talk about this and that's cool, but we need to address it. I have a couple of options for covering this, so it's up to you. I could either completely blend it in and make it virtually disappear, or I could embrace it and make it part of the fire from the dragon."

Brandon looked at his arm. While he stared at the burn, she explained to him how she could make the dragon shoot fire, turning the burn into flames. She tapped her pen on a cigarette burn on his inner elbow. "Then here I could make this singed earth since that would tie into the design."

He glanced up and her and their eyes met. When Brandon didn't speak, she continued, "Your choice. I either bury it or embrace it. Up to you."

"What the hell. I already told you to put the initials in, so why stop now?"

God. Did that mean his dad had put these burns there? It took everything in her not to ask. And he didn't volunteer.

With the stencil in place, she drew a quick test line. Brandon didn't even give any sign he felt the needle at all.

Unlike most of her clients, Brandon barely spoke as she worked. Normally people liked to chat, or the ones that didn't put earphones in and listened to music. He did neither, he just stoically sat quiet while she worked.

When she got to the first burn, he flinched slightly. "Did that hurt?"

"No."

When she got to the second, he flinched again. "You sure these areas don't hurt?" She turned off the gun while she waited for an answer.

"Yeah, not like you think they do."

"Okay."

He shifted his enormous body on the chair and cleared his throat. "Like I said, my dad and I had different ways of coping with the loss of my mom."

She'd suspected his dad had done this but hearing it out loud. Shit. She couldn't imagine a parent doing this to their child. "Your dad did this to you?"

"Yeah." He clicked his tongue against his teeth. "Why am I telling you this shit?" A harsh breath passed his lips. "What the hell is in that needle? Truth serum?"

She smiled. "Tattoo artists are like hairdressers and bartenders. People just tell us shit."

"Any chance you can be like a therapist and keep this shit to yourself?"

"Brandon, you don't even need to ask." She squeezed his arm. "After I'm done with this tattoo, when you look at those burns, you'll see the warrior from your mom's stories. And all you'll see will be her, and her love for you. You got me?" Tears burned in her eyes as she looked at him. Making that happen wouldn't be easy, but there was no way she was giving him anything else. From one mother to the other, this art deserved nothing less.

His head bobbed up and down. "Cool."

"Let's wrap this thing up." She turned the gun back on, and neither of them spoke through the rest of the outline.

CHAPTER TWENTY-FIVE

THE GAME WAS AMAZING. He played awesome. His team won. And he'd had his girl and his son in the stands watching him. What more could he want? It just sucked that they had to go home today.

Jeff hoisted his bag up on his shoulder. "You ready?" he said, turning to his roommates.

"Yeah." Ryan grabbed his bag off the floor and hooked it on his shoulder while Gonzo did the same.

"What time is their flight?" Ryan asked.

"7:00 pm. Just enough time to grab a bite to eat before I have to get them to the airport." If Pete would get his ass in gear. He looked over toward Pete's locker. "Zip, you ready?"

"Almost," Pete called back as he shoved stuff in his bag.

Johnny looked over at Jeff, then gave Gomez a little nudge. Gomez glanced over his shoulder. "Sims sure ran out of here fast," Gomez said loud enough for Jeff to hear.

"Yeah, that's because he's got a hard-on for Smitty's girl. He had to catch her before she left." Johnny stared at him the entire time he spoke.

Pete stood up and knocked Johnny on the back of the head with his bag as he walked past. "Oops, sorry." Pete grabbed the strap of his bag like he was trying to get control of the thing.

"Let's go, Smitty," Pete said as he fell into step beside him. "That guy's such an asshole."

"Yep." Asshole or not, his mind was reeling from what Johnny said. Why did Brandon need to talk to Kia? Did he have a hard-on for her?

As they rounded the corner. Jeff scanned the parking area for Kia and Max. Where were they? He spotted Sim's gigantic frame leaning against the fence with a woman. His woman. Kia's hand rested on Brandon's forearm. And he saw red.

"Smitty." Gonzo's warning tone did nothing to slow him down.

He stormed up to the pair. "What the fuck?" he snarled.

Kia's head snapped in his direction. "Are you seriously pulling some jealous guy bullshit right now?"

"I'm asking why I come out and find you out here with him?"

Kia shook her head. "I'm not even going to dignify that with a response."

"Fine, Sims, you care to explain?"

"I think you need to take a breath, man, and chill before you fuck things up more than you already are," Brandon said.

Little hands pushed against his stomach. "Don't talk to my mom like that," Max yelled.

"Shit." Max. Jeff closed his eyes as the enormity of what he'd just done sank in. He took a deep breath, then looked at his son. "I love that you want to protect your mom, buddy, but I promise I'm not going to hurt her. I just want to talk to her. Go with Gonzo for a minute," Jeff told his son.

"Let's give your mom and dad a second to talk." Gonzo leaned down. "You want to go hang out with the guys over there?" He pointed to Ryan and Pete who stood just off to the side of their group.

Max glared at Jeff. Somehow being stared down by a five-year-old was way more intimidating than facing the fiercest looking grownup. It crushed him to see his son look at him that way.

"It's okay, baby," Kia said. "Your dad's not mad anymore. And even if he was, we both know I could kick his ass, right?" She tapped her temple several times. "I've got all that good learning in here." She winked to solidify their little joke.

Max looked at Jeff, then back at her, and nodded. "Right, cuz you stayed at a Holiday Inn Express once."

Kia grinned when he got it. She stuck out her hand for Max to high-five. "Exactly."

"What?" Gonzo blinked quizzically at them.

"You know the commercial," she replied.

Gonzo shook his head. "I have no idea what you're talking about. Come on, Max, you're gonna have to explain that to me."

"You can go too, Sims," Jeff glared at his teammate. Why the hell was the guy still standing here?

Not listening to him, Brandon looked at Kia instead of his teammate. "You good?"

"Yeah, thanks." She squeezed Brandon's arm. "No more diving, okay?"

"No promises." He smiled at Kia then gave Jeff a firm, don't fuck with her glare before he walked off.

Okay, he deserved that. And maybe a little piece of him respected Brandon a little more because he was willing to go toe-to-toe with him to defend Kia if needed.

"Sorry, that was out of line," he muttered.

"You think?" Kia leaned against the fence and crossed her arms over her chest. "You want to tell me what the hell that was about?"

"Fuck, I don't know. I heard Johnny yacking in the change room about how Sim's has a hard-on for you." He hated feeling insecure in their relationship.

"Johnny, as in Knight? The guy you said is a total douche?"

"Yeah." He dragged his hand through his hair, pushing his still damp hair off his forehead.

"And why would you listen to anything he said?"

"I don't know. No one wants to hear some guy has a hard-on for his girlfriend."

He knew better than to listen to Johnny. That guy loved stirring shit up. He'd let his insecurity get the best of him because some part of him didn't trust her not to bolt.

"Oh my god, you're an idiot." She shook her head slowly, like she couldn't believe he was that stupid. "The only thing Brandon has a hard-on for is his tattoo."

"Somehow, I don't think that's what he was talking about."

"And somehow I don't think you should be listening to Johnny-Fucking-Knight. Come on, Jeff." She pinched the bridge of her nose. "This was exactly why I didn't want to tell Max we were together, because now he's over there freaking out because you can't handle me talking to a friend."

"The talking wasn't the problem," he muttered.

"Excuse me?" She turned her head slightly, like she hadn't quite heard him right.

"I said the talking wasn't the problem. It was the hand on his arm."

"I touch people all the time, Jeff."

"You don't even like to touch me in public."

"That's what this is about? Because I don't want to confuse Max with a bunch of PDA's?" She blinked, keeping her eyes closed for several seconds, then made a growly sound deep in her throat. "Let me get this straight. You're pissed I won't do some ridiculous claim my man PDA show, but somehow, I'm the type of person who would then turn around and go all gropey hands with some random guy in front of my son. Are you kidding me?"

"Well, when you say it like that it sounds pretty stupid," he grumbled.

"Because it is stupid." She glared at him. "We discussed how hard this was going to be, dating during the season. We either trust each other or we don't. So figure your shit out because I'm not doing this again." She pushed off the fence and walked away from him.

He scanned the parking lot, noting the looky-loos watching them from a distance. Awesome. If he'd had his head out of his ass, he wouldn't have had that conversation in the parking lot of the stadium. If he'd had his head out of his ass, he wouldn't have needed to have that conversation at all.

He jogged across the parking lot. He caught up with Kia just before she made it back to his SUV. Grabbing her hand, he tugged her back around. "I'm sorry. I fucked up. Again. You don't deserve that."

"You're right. I don't."

He stepped closer to her. When she didn't back away, he dipped his head, so his forehead was almost touching hers. "I'm an asshole."

"Yep."

He smirked at her. She wasn't going to give him an inch. "Forgive me?"

She stared back at him but said nothing.

He touched his forehead against hers and gave her what he hoped was his best puppy dog face. "I've never stayed at a Holiday Inn Express, so I've got a lot to learn."

Kia snorted. "You're still an idiot."

"I know, but hopefully I'm still your idiot." He batted his eyelashes the way he'd seen both her and Max do to each other when they were sucking up.

She pushed his face gently with her hand. "For now." She turned and walked the rest of the way to the car.

"I'll take it."

CHAPTER TWENTY-SIX

THE NEXT GAME SUCKED. He dropped onto the bench and dragged his bag out of his locker. Digging around, he pulled out his phone. Twenty-three missed texts, six missed calls. What the fuck?

He pulled open his texts and saw thirteen of the texts were from Kia. Shit. Max. Flicking open the texts.

Kia: *What the hell?*

That text was quickly followed by six more with links to various websites.

He didn't click the link, but continued to read her texts for some sign of what was going on.

Kia: *I didn't sign on for this shit Jeff*

Kia: *What is wrong with people? They don't know me.*

Kia: *People suck*

Kia: *And of course my parents called so....*

Kia: *I just…*

Kia: *Fuck. Call me when you get these*

What shit didn't she sign on for? What the hell was happening? Why were her parents calling her? From what she'd said, they hadn't talked at all since she moved to San Diego.

Jeff: *Sorry, just got your texts, been on the field all day. I'll call you as soon as I'm not surrounded by everyone.*

Immediately, he saw the little dots showing Kia was texting back. Shit, the fact she was obviously sitting with her phone in hand was not a good sign.

Kia: *Did you read the articles?*

Jeff: *Not yet.*

Kia: *Read them before you call*

Jeff: *You okay?*

Kia: *Just read them and you'll have your answer*

That sounded ominous. He clicked on the first link. A picture of Kia standing with her hand on Brandon's arm and him in the background looking pissed off immediately came up on the screen. His first thought was fuck was that really what he looked like? No wonder Kia had been pissed at him. His second was, oh shit, why is that picture online?

He quickly scanned the article. What the hell? This article made Kia sound like she was sleeping with half the team. It questioned Max's paternity. Made her sound like some freaking modern-day Yoko Ono. She was being blamed for everything, from the shitty way the team played, to the fact that Brandon hadn't wanted to pose for some picture with a fan. The grumpy bastard never wanted to pose for pictures with fans. This wasn't any different, but somehow if this article was to be believed Kia was to blame.

He clicked on the next link. More of the same.

The third article talked about how Kia had dumped Austin for Jeff. He continued to read. This was bad. The article did not paint either of them in a good light.

What the hell? No wonder Kia was pissed.

Fuck. She was going to bolt. This was the last thing they needed. Kia was already skittish about them being in a relationship. Worried about the effect it would have on Max. This would not help matters in the least.

He tossed his phone in his bag and scooped up his gear. He could shower at home once he talked to Kia.

Gonzo's head snapped toward him when he stood up. "Where's the fire?"

"I need to go. I'll see you back at the house?"

"You didn't drive today."

"Fuck." He slammed his bag on the bench. He needed to talk to Kia. He didn't have time to wait around for his buddies to shoot the shit like they normally did post game.

"What's going on?" Gonzo stood up and stepped up beside him.

Jeff handed his phone to his friend.

Gonzo's eyes widened as he read the article. Anger radiated off him as he handed the phone back, then yelled, "Ry, Zip, we gotta go."

"What the hell? We haven't even showered yet," Ryan yelled back as he paused on his way to the shower.

"Shower at home," Gonzo said. "We gotta go. Smitty needs to leave."

Ryan turned around and walked back to his locker. He dropped his towel and stepped commando into his basketball shorts.

Jeff hoisted his bag on his shoulder. Man, he appreciated how his friends were just so willing to do what he needed. No questions asked. "I'll meet you at the car," he called over his shoulder as he walked to the door. He knew his boys would be right behind him.

He was halfway to the car when he heard his name being called. When he turned and saw Sims jogging toward him, his first instinct was to punch the fucker in the face. But Brandon wasn't to blame for this. He was.

Brandon stopped in front of him. "I'm guessing you saw the article?"

His hands clenched into fists. "Yeah."

"That wasn't anything like that picture made it look. She was just checking the tattoo because she was pissed I did that diving catch, and she was worried I'd messed up her work." Brandon absently touched the tattoo on his forearm.

"Yeah, I know, she told me." He dragged his hand down his jaw. "That's on me. I was a dick."

"Yeah, you were." Brandon chuckled. "You have to know I'd never go after your girl. Once she said you were dating, that's all I needed to hear."

"I appreciate that."

"I'll bet she's freaking out about these articles."

He caught sight of Gonzo, Pete and Ryan walking toward him. "Yeah, you could say that."

"Don't let her run," Brandon said.

He regarded his teammate. How did he know Kia would run? "I don't plan to."

Brandon stared at him for several seconds, then slapped him on the shoulder. "Good." He walked away, then turned back toward Jeff. "If you need me to do any media shit with all this, just say the word."

Jeff's body jerked. He hadn't expected that at all. Out of all the guys on the team, Brandon seemed to be the most uncomfortable with the media.

Gonzo, Ryan, and Pete stepped up beside them. "You ready?" Gonzo asked.

"Yeah, one sec," Jeff told them. He turned to Brandon. "Why would you do that?"

Brandon rolled his shoulders, like he was uncomfortable with the discussion. "She's a... she's a special lady."

Jeff tensed.

"Jesus," Brandon growled. "Not like that. We already went over this." He looked at his tattooed arm. "We just connected as friends. And that shit matters to me. So—" He pinned Jeff with a steely look. "Don't fuck it up. And don't let her."

Jeff stared at his teammate, then finally nodded. "Thanks. I won't." He turned and tossed his bag in the back of Ryan's SUV. "Let's go."

Inside the vehicle, he scrolled through the articles on his phone again. He could only imagine what Kia's mind was doing. Looking up, he noted where they were. "Can you drive any faster?"

"Not if I don't want a ticket," Ryan replied. "I know you're freaking out, man, but a couple of minutes won't make much difference. Or just call her now."

"Yeah, Kia would love that. Me talking to her with all of you in the car," he scoffed. "I'm in enough shit already about all this. That's the last thing I need to do."

"Why would you be in shit? You had nothing to do with it. Maybe she needs to look at that loser she was dating before because that one article you showed me sure sounded like they'd talked to him," Gonzo said in his defense.

"Yeah, that fucker definitely had something to do with it." Jeff's jaw clenched so tight he was surprised he didn't crack his teeth. It was a good thing Austin wasn't in front of him right now or there was no doubt there'd be assault charges in his future. And Kia would just love that.

"The articles look bad, but Kia can't be pissed at you about them," Pete said.

He laughed hollowly. Silence lingered in the car.

"It'll be okay." Gonzo's hand clamped on his shoulder.

"Yeah." He sure as fuck hoped so.

Ryan pulled the SUV up in front of their house and he leaped out before the car was even in park. He raced up the stairs, tossed his bag in the corner of his room, and pulled up the FaceTime app. As the phone rang, he dropped onto the mattress.

Kia's face popped on the screen. His chest tightened. It broke him to see this strong woman so visibly shaken.

"Key," he groaned. What he wouldn't give to be there with her. To wrap her in his arms.

"Hey." She smiled sadly back at him. "You read them?"

"Yeah. Fucking Austin," he growled.

Her eyes flared with anger. "I can't believe he would do that to me." Her eyes welled with unshed tears. "I knew he was pissed we broke up, but I thought that was just him being all butt-hurt because he got dumped. I never dreamed he'd go to the media with some bullshit story about us." She looked up at the ceiling and blinked rapidly, like she was trying to keep the tears from falling. "I never thought this would happen."

"It's not your fault. If I hadn't been an asshole about you and Brandon there wouldn't have been any pictures for them to run with."

"What are we going to do?" she whispered.

"We're not going to do anything. We just go about our business as usual and ignore this bullshit."

"Ignore it? How the hell am I supposed to ignore it when people say shit like that about me? People at Max's school were already talking trash about me. This is just going to make it so much worse."

"I know it's hard, but it'll blow over. I saw the shit the trolls were saying about me too. How I'm a deadbeat. How I'm not willing to step up and look after my son, so you had to go elsewhere. We both know it's all bullshit. Ignore it. If we don't feed it, they'll get hungry for something else. They always do."

"What am I supposed to say to Max?"

He dragged his hand through his hair. "Tell him the truth. We're a family and nothing is going to change that."

"You make it sound so easy."

"It's as easy or complicated as we want it to be." He ached to wrap his arms around her and absorb some of this pain she was feeling. He was used to this shit. People always talked trash about players online. Some people were kind, but more often than not people were dicks just because they could be. He'd learned long ago not to pay attention to any of it. He was willing to talk about the game, and that was it. Not who designed the suit he was wearing, who his date was, none of it. Baseball and nothing else.

"Tell that to my parents." The tears she'd been trying to hold at bay slipped down her cheek.

"Baby," he groaned. "Don't cry."

She looked right into the camera. The pain in her eyes was visceral. He could feel it through the screen. And it hurt. "What did they say?" he growled.

She sniffed. "The usual. I'm a whore. I'm a shitty mom." She rubbed her nose with her hand. "How ashamed they are of me. They're embarrassed I'm their daughter. I'm going to hell." Her eyes welled again, and she pursed her lips to hold them at bay. "You know the usual."

"Oh baby, I'm so sorry." What was wrong with her parents? How could they say that to her?

"I'm used to it." Kia shrugged. "It just—"

"It still hurts."

"Yeah," she whispered. She angrily rubbed a tear that slid down her cheek. "I wish it didn't." She looked up at the ceiling again. "Gah, why did I answer the phone when they called? I know better."

What was he supposed to say? He couldn't imagine having his parents act like that. Hell, he was a grown-ass man and when things were bad, his first instinct was to pick up the phone and call his parents. Kia didn't have that. What she had with her parents was the exact opposite. "I wish I was there with you." His heart broke watching her hurting like this and knowing there wasn't a damn thing he could do to help her.

"Me too." She gave him a tight smile.

"Are we good?" He held his breath as he waited for her to answer.

"Yeah, I think so. I freaked out. It's probably a good thing you couldn't return my call till now." She gave him a tight smile and exhaled. "But you're right, this will blow over. I mean, hell, we aren't that interesting. I'm sure some rockstar somewhere will do something stupid and they'll move on."

"Exactly."

"This is a lot harder than I thought it was going to be," she admitted.

"What part?"

"All of it. Your schedule, the distance, the media, obviously." The camera angled to the floor briefly before her face came back on the screen. "I got used to having you around with Max and now you're not. I don't like feeling like this. I've worked so hard to get my life to a good place. Where I'm proud of myself, proud of what I've built with Max."

"You should be."

"I know, and it surprised me how quickly that disappeared when I read those articles."

"It didn't disappear, Kia. You still have everything you've built. What you've done is amazing. A few dickheads chirping online doesn't change that."

"Tell that to my parents."

"Fuck your parents," he growled. "They don't know shit about you and what you've accomplished. They should be ashamed of themselves, not you."

Kia's eyes warmed as she looked at him through the screen. "Thank you."

"Yeah." He stared back at her. "Do me a favor. Kill the google alerts on your phone so you stop looking at that shit."

"Tell that to Vika," she scoffed.

"I'm more than happy to call her and tell her the same thing. While I'm at it, I'll tell her to have Tyson knock some sense into that useless friend of his."

"I think Vika's already on that. And if Ty doesn't want to sleep on the couch, there will be some words being had with Austin." She sighed. "I still can't believe Austin did that. Asshole."

"Yeah, you definitely upgraded when you dumped him for me."

"I didn't dump him for you. I dumped him and then you and I hooked up."

"Keep telling yourself that, baby, but we both know you dumped his ass for me." He grinned.

"Alright, whatever you need to tell yourself."

The tension in his spine eased off as Kia relaxed in front of him. Before they'd talked, he'd been worried this was going to be enough for her to cut and run. He wasn't naïve enough to think they were out of the woods yet, but thank god for FaceTime. It wasn't as good as being able to touch her, but it was a hell of a lot better than not seeing her face. At least this way, he'd been able to reassure her. See the look in her eyes and know she was hearing him, not locked away in her own thoughts.

"How's Max doing?" he asked.

"He's fine. Completely oblivious to everything that's going on, thank god."

"Let's hope it stays that way. If some asshole kid says something let me know and we'll figure out a way to handle it together."

"What are you going to do from Phoenix?"

"You'd be surprised." If some shithead tried to hurt his kid, it wouldn't matter where he was on earth, he'd get shit done. "We're in this together. You and me." He did his best to hold her stare through the phone to ensure she heard him. "You aren't alone in this, Kia, no matter what it feels like. You feel me? I got your back. Believe it."

Her eyes welled. "I'm trying."

"Don't try. Believe it. I'm not going anywhere. I gotchu."

"Kay." She nodded. "Thank you. I'm feeling much better now."

"Good. I'm sorry for my part in all this shit."

Kia's brow wrinkled. "Your part?"

"Yeah, if I hadn't been a jealous asshole, they wouldn't have had a picture to take." He hated his actions had once again hurt her. "But you'll be happy to know that even if our conversation on my stupid jealousy hadn't done the trick, seeing those photos would have. I can promise you, lesson learned."

"I'm glad. Like I said, it's a wasted emotion."

"I get that," he agreed. "Are you feeling better now?"

"Yeah, much." She nodded.

"We're on the home stretch now. Only a little more than a week till I'm home. Spring training ends Tuesday, then we have two days off before the season opener on Friday."

"You're home all weekend, right?" She screwed up her face. "I don't know how you keep your schedule straight, home, away, my god."

He chuckled. "I'm gonna make a ball fan out of you yet."

"You can try." She wiggled her eyebrows up and down. "Oh, just a heads up. I'm doing another session on Brandon's tattoo when you get home next week."

Any jealousy he'd felt about the other man was gone. There was nothing there. "Cool. It's gonna look amazing when it's done."

She raised one eyebrow. "So, you're totally good there?"

"Yeah, I think I am. We talked today. I think I get it now. He respects you a lot."

A warm smile spread across Kia's face. "I'm glad. The feelings are mutual. He's a good guy. I think we could be friends."

"Mmm," he grunted. Okay, so maybe he wasn't 100% there yet. He trusted her, hell honestly, he trusted Brandon as well. His thoughts bashed into him like a battering ram. If he trusted them both, then there was no issue with them. So what was his problem? "Cool."

Kia smirked. "Cool?"

"Yeah, I think so. I haven't hung out with him too much. He's pretty quiet, kind of moody honestly." Brandon had stepped up today, approaching him, talking. Not everyone would have done that. "He was cool today, so yeah, maybe we could all hang out." But what about the next guy who looked at her? Could he be as calm then? Guess time would tell. But he sure as hell had learned his lesson not to have that conversation in public.

"Look at you being all grownup," Kia joked.

"I know it's wild." He winked at her through the screen. "Don't get used to it."

"Don't worry, I've seen you and your friends with Max. I know what I'm signing on for."

"Ha-ha. On that note, I'll let you go so you can grab him from next door."

"I'll say goodnight to him for you."

"Thanks. I'll call you tomorrow and do a bedtime story with him."

"Sounds good. Night."

He hung up the call and flopped back on the bed, his entire body splayed out on the mattress. Exhaustion swept through him as all the fear he'd been holding onto finally seeped away. That call could have gone a completely different way. If it had, he didn't know what he would have done. Thank god, he didn't have to find out.

He raised his arms above his head to stretch out the residual tension in his muscles and caught a whiff of himself. Shit, there was a reason he didn't usually skip the showers after a day at training camp. Between the morning weights, practice, then game, he was a little ripe. Pushing himself off the mattress, he kicked off his sweaty uniform and padded naked to the bathroom. He could already feel the hot water washing the last of the day off his body and down the drain.

CHAPTER TWENTY-SEVEN

DESPITE WHAT JEFF HAD said, the media didn't die down. They seemed to have amped up over the last week. Austin, the asshole, was taking full advantage of his thirty seconds of fame. He was talking to anyone who listened. No one seemed to care that his version of the truth and reality were night and day. His social media had blown up. From what she'd heard from Vika, he'd quit his job at the garage because he seemed to think he was going to be some influencer or some shit. Idiot.

Kia spotted her sister on the bench at the park as she sat watching the girls play some elaborate skipping game while Alex played in the sand nearby.

"Can I go play with Alex?" Max asked.

"Of course." She dropped his hand, and Max bolted toward his cousin.

Kia sauntered toward her sister. Vika held out an iced coffee drink to her as she approached. "Oh, you are a goddess. Thank you." She stretched out her arm and accepted the icy beverage. Taking a long sip, she closed her eyes as the sweet caffeine coursed through her system.

She glanced toward the playground where Max and his cousin sat on the ground, then dropped onto the bench beside her sister. "How was your day?"

Vika shrugged one shoulder. "Coulda been better. Layla's been dealing with some girl drama at school, so there were lots of tears."

Kia glanced over at her niece. The girl had grown several inches in the past couple of months, making her look like she was all legs. The preteen and teen years were rough. You couldn't pay her enough to go back and do all that over again. "She's a smart girl. She'll figure it out."

"I sure hope so. It's hard to watch." Vika dropped her head onto Kia's shoulder. "How was your day? Better?"

"Eh. People suck." She laughed. "But I did a cool zombie tattoo today, so that was fun." She grabbed her phone and pulled up the photos she'd taken. Handing her phone to Vika to check them out.

Her sister's face scrunched up. "Oh my god, that's disgusting. Why would someone want that on their body?"

Kia eyed the pictures. Pride flowed through her body as she looked at her art. It was disgusting. She'd captured the rotting flesh look perfectly. It really looked like there was an oozing open sore covering the entire thigh. She grinned at her sister. "Gross, hey?"

Vika shook her head. "I wouldn't want it, but it is ridiculous how talented you are." Vika's fingers touched the screen like she could feel the skin. "That's crazy."

"Thanks. I'm happy with how it turned out." Taking the phone back, Kia shoved it in her pocket.

"So Jeff is home tonight?"

"Yeah, he's got two days off, then the home opener on Friday." She took another sip of her drink.

"Tell him thank you again for the tickets for Sunday. We'd never be able to afford to take the kids to a game, let alone sit in those seats."

"Yeah, it should be fun. Max is looking forward to it. We had a lot of fun watching them in Phoenix, but from what Jeff says that's nothing compared to the atmosphere on opening weekend."

"Aunty Kia. Come jump with us," Layla called.

Allowing her eyes to scan over to the playground again, she smiled as she watched Max running around the jungle gym with Alex close on his heels. Knowing he was safe and having fun, she stood up and headed toward her nieces.

"Duty calls," she said to her sister.

Kia wandered across the grass to where the girls were playing. "Alright, what are we playing?" she asked the girls. After an elaborate explanation of the jumping combination, Kia hopped in.

The next thing she knew, she heard a child scream. Her heart lurched. Max. Turning, she saw Max and Alex running away from the playground. A man with a camera aimed at them ran after them.

Oh, hell no. Kia lunged out of the skipping ropes and in a burst of speed she didn't know she had, she raced toward her son. Why had she gone so far away from the boys? When she'd joined the girls, it had only felt like a couple hundred yards, now it felt like miles. Finally reaching them, she grabbed the boys and pinned the cameraman with a glare. He stopped and aimed his camera at her. No way this was happening. She stared at the boys. "Go to Aunty Vika," she told Max.

"I want to stay with you." Max's bottom lip quivered.

"I'll be right there. Go to your aunt."

Vika came up behind her. Sensing her sister's support, she said, "Max, go with your Aunty Vika, please. "

Max eyed the reporter who stood several feet away from them, still snapping pictures, then wrapped his arms around her waist. "I want to stay with you."

"I know, baby, but I need you to go with your aunt while I talk to that man."

"Come on." Vika wrapped her arms around the two boys and pulled them into her body.

Without taking her eyes off the reporter, Kia stormed toward the man. She stopped in front of the reporter. "Take my picture again, I dare you," she growled.

The reporter held up his hands. "Jeez, lady, chill."

"Chill? You just chased my son, and you tell me to chill?"

"I didn't chase him," the man scoffed.

"Give me the pictures." Kia stepped toward the man.

"No."

"Give me the pictures. They're children, and you had no right to take their picture. What is wrong with you?" Fueled by some weird maternal kickass instinct, Kia stepped in, so she was nose to nose with the reporter. "Delete the pictures, or this camera will permanently become part of your anatomy."

"Yeah, right, lady."

Without thinking, Kia reached out and grabbed the guy's balls and squeezed as hard as she could. The big man dropped to the dirt. "Delete the fucking pictures," she snarled.

The reporter hit a bunch of buttons on his camera and turned the screen toward her to show her he'd deleted the pictures. Satisfied her son's photo was no longer on the camera, she turned and walked back toward her family.

"Psycho," the cameraman yelled at her back.

Kia bristled briefly at the insult, then looked at her son. Fear had leached all the color from his normally tanned skin. She glanced over her shoulder at the cameraman one more time. He hadn't even begun to see what she could be like if he messed with her kid.

She scooped Max up, and he wrapped his arms around her waist. "Why did he do that, Mommy?"

"I don't know, baby. But you did the right thing screaming to get my attention and running to me. Exactly the right thing. I'm really proud of you."

Max nuzzled into her neck as they walked across the field. "I'm proud of you too. I can't wait to tell dad."

Kia's stomach dropped. That was the last thing she wanted to do. "Let's get out of here."

For the first time in his life, he was glad spring training was over. When the team's PR person, Kirsty, had shown him a video of Kia dropping a reporter today, it was all he'd been able to do not to leave the game and rush home immediately. Unfortunately, that wasn't an option.

Thankfully, Pete had offered to drive his truck home tomorrow with all his stuff, so he'd been able to catch a flight home instead. As the Uber driver pulled up to Kia's front door, Jeff glanced at his watch. 9:40 pm. Max would already be in bed, but Kia would still be up. Even if she wasn't, there was no way he was waiting until tomorrow to talk to her.

Conscious of Max sleeping, he knocked quietly on Kia's front door. Bouncing anxiously on her front step while he waited for her to answer, he was tempted to use the key she'd given him. But given the fact she'd been avoiding his calls and not answering his texts, he didn't figure that would go over well.

As he raised his hand to knock again, Kia pulled open the front door. With a resigned sigh, she pulled the door open further, turned on her heel and walked inside. That was not the welcome home he'd been hoping for. Shit.

Following Kia into the living room, he noted the half empty glass of wine on the coffee table.

"I guess you saw the video," Kia said as she dropped onto the sofa. She pulled the blanket up over her lap and covered her body like a shield.

His stomach knotted with dread. This wasn't the Kia he was used to seeing. This wasn't the warrior he'd seen in the video. This woman looked broken. Defeated. He hated he had anything to do with this.

"Yeah, I saw it." He stepped toward her. Kia's body tensed, and she wrapped her arms around her knees, pulling them tight. Her body language made it perfectly clear to him that touching her was not an option. "You looked pretty badass in the video."

"Gee thanks," she muttered. Sadness clouded her eyes as she looked up at him. "I shouldn't have to be a badass at the playground, Jeff."

"No, you shouldn't." He rocked back on his heels. "I'm so sorry."

"This isn't blowing over."

"It will," he tried to reassure her, but honestly, given what Kirsty had said today, he didn't know if this would blow over anytime soon. As amazing as it was to know Kia could defend Max, the fact she'd taken a reporter to his knees had just fueled the trolls online. Some people thought it was great, of course, but a very vocal few seemed to think she was a danger to society. Which was complete bullshit, but he couldn't stop people from saying what they wanted online.

"This isn't working." She nervously chewed her bottom lip. "I have to think of Max."

Needing to touch her, to be close to her, he crouched on the floor in front of her and reached out his hand. "Baby, I get that you're scared."

"I'm not scared. This isn't about me. This is about Max." She pulled away. "They chased him with cameras."

Anger bubbled up inside him. "I know."

"Do you?" She gritted out the words through clenched teeth. "Do you have any idea what that felt like? For me? For him?"

"I can imagine."

She bristled. "Well, I was there, and it was terrifying. I have never felt anger like that in my life, Jeff. I wanted to kill that guy for scaring Max. The playground is supposed to be safe for kids. How is it safe when you have some person lurking around taking pictures of your child like a fucking pervert?"

"He wasn't taking pervy pictures, Kia."

"Not the point," she snapped. "He took pictures of my kid without my consent. He chased him. What would have happened if I hadn't been there? If Vika had just been with the kids at the park alone? That's unacceptable, Jeff."

"I know." He knew. He just wasn't sure how to stop it. Being in the public eye, there was always an expected amount of media attention, granted not usually the tabloids, but it kind of went with the job. "It'll get better."

"And what if it doesn't?"

"I don't know. We figure it out." How was he supposed to answer that? He didn't have the first clue how to handle this kind of thing. And if Austin kept fueling it with his bullshit hashtags and posts all over the place, who knew how bad it could get?

"If you hadn't been all jealous, there wouldn't have been anything for them to have a picture of."

He clenched his jaw. He hated that his jealousy had anything to do with this. "I know, and that's why I apologized."

"Yeah, and then did it again the next time you saw Brandon and I together. If you'd just believed me the first time, this never would have happened." She shook her head, and angrily shoved her hair from one side to the other, like somehow having it touch the right side of her face was annoying.

"Maybe If you gave me more to work with, I wouldn't have felt jealous in the first place," he snapped.

She reared back. Fire burned in her eyes as she glared at him. "What's that supposed to mean?"

"It means I didn't know where I stood," he growled. "You didn't want Max to know about us. You didn't want my friends to know. You didn't even want to tell your sister at first." Yeah, he'd handled it badly, but having her deny what they had, what they were building had hurt and he'd reacted poorly.

"That was to protect Max. I told you that."

"Bullshit, Kia, that was to protect you and we both know it. How the hell was I supposed to feel secure about us when you wanted to keep us a secret?"

She sucked in a breath. Her eyes widened, and her mouth gaped as she stared at him. "So, this is my fault?"

Frustrated, he scrubbed his hand over his face. "No, I'm not saying that."

"It sure sounds like it." She ran her tongue along the front of her teeth. Her jaw tensed as she clicked her mouth. "Yeah, I'm not doing this anymore. I'm done."

"Kia, come on."

"No, Jeff, this isn't working. We said when we started this that we wouldn't do anything that would hurt Max, and clearly this is."

"Us being together isn't hurting Max."

"That's bullshit. If we stop dating, this all goes away."

"How? Max is still my kid. Whether we're together or not, that doesn't change."

"No, but if we stop dating, the media stops talking about me. They stop talking about me being a gold digger who's just after your money, or a whore trying to fuck up the team dynamics. They stop talking about me, and they stop caring about Max."

"Kia." His stomach knotted.

She held up her hand to stop him from talking. "No, I can't do this." Tears welled in her eyes. "Today, when I went after that reporter, I felt like everything my parents had ever said about me was true. Max deserves so much better than all of this shit."

"Are you trying to protect Max or yourself?" he asked.

"What the hell are you talking about? This isn't about me." She pushed upright on the sofa. Her protective blanket fell to the floor.

"Are you sure?" He stared at her. "You've been looking for a reason this wouldn't work since we got started."

"No, I haven't."

"Bullshit," he growled. "You have, and we both know it. This is just the perfect excuse for you to cut and run. When I saw that video of you today, I thought there's a warrior who'll fight for what she wants."

"And I am," she yelled.

"Yeah, I see that." He pushed to his feet. "I just stupidly thought what you wanted to fight for was us." Emotion clogged his throat.

"I can't, Jeff. Max is the only thing that matters."

"For the record, breaking up with me isn't putting him first. Eventually you'll realize that." There was no point in continuing this conversation when she felt like this.

Growing up, his mom had always said when fear and anger started talking, nothing else could be heard. He'd seen his parents go to neutral corners on more than one occasion. And they were still together, so maybe she was right. Who the hell knew? But with the way he was feeling at this moment, nothing nice would come out of his mouth. And he'd promised Kia after the whole jealousy thing that he'd think before he acted, so that's what he was going to do.

Turning on his heel, he walked to the front door. "Tell Vika I'll pick up Max from school tomorrow."

"I'm so...sorry, Jeff," her voice broke on the words.

"Yeah, me too," he said and shut the door behind him. She either realized they were stronger together or she didn't. All he could do was show her. Then it would be up to her.

CHAPTER TWENTY-EIGHT

Jeff stood outside the media room and glared at the team publicist. "I don't want to fucking do this tonight, Kirsty. Find someone else." His head was nowhere near where it needed to be to speak to the press. He just wanted to go home, pour himself and drink and try to forget about Kia. Giving her space was damn near killing him.

Kirsty put her hands on her hips and stared at him. "Look Smitty. I understand that what happened with that tabloid reporter and your son was not ideal."

"Not ideal? Are you fucking kidding me?" he roared. "Not ideal is when I have to wear the short ball pants instead of the long ones. That's not ideal, Kirsty. Some reporter showing up at the park and chasing my son to get a story is way past fucking ideal." Anger coursed through his veins, and he paced away from her, then back. "And don't even get me started on the fucking person who videoed the whole thing and thought they should post that shit." Given everything that had happened with the media, he'd be lucky if Kia ever let Max even come to a game and watch him play.

She hesitantly moved her arm toward him, then dropped it back down to her side before she made contact. "I know, and the situation was messed up, but that was some tabloid reporter, and some person at the park, not any of the people in the media room waiting to talk to you." She glanced over her shoulder toward the room in question, then back at him. "You hit a grand slam against your old rival tonight. That's what everyone in there wants to talk about."

The media room door opened, and a man popped his head out. "We're ready for you," he said.

Kirsty nodded to the man, then turned back to Jeff. "I don't want to be a jerk here, Smitty, but I need you to go in there and do this."

Ryan slapped him on the shoulder. "I'll be right there with you, man. I can throw myself to the wolves if necessary." Ryan scanned the area. "Maybe we need Gonzo. He's always good at distracting the media with some stupid joke or something."

"Sorry guys, you know the drill. Just be glad I don't have Brandon down here as well."

"Fuck," Jeff growled. "That's the last thing we need." Sometimes this job sucked. He couldn't go in there like this. The media would eat him alive. He rolled his shoulders to try to release the tension.

"I know that and that's why he's not here even after he made that ridiculous catch in left field to end the seventh."

Ryan squeezed his shoulder. "You got this. In and out, quick and easy."

Jeff glanced over at his friend and smirked. "If I'm going quick, it's gonna be dirty, man."

"That's fair." Ryan snickered.

"No." Kirsty pointed and wagged her finger at them. "You two will not do some stupid sexual innuendo thing that has you both snickering through the entire interview because you think you're so clever." She pinned Ryan with a glare. "Because you're not. I promise you, you're not."

"Ah, come on, Kirsty." Ryan slung his arm over the publicist's shoulder. "You know you love how we keep you on your toes. Besides, wouldn't you rather the media bugged you about that then, because Smitty here broke some poor schmuck's camera?"

Jeff smiled to himself. Breaking a camera sounded like a lot more fun than talking about some rivalry from the minors that had ended long ago.

Kirsty spun back toward him. "Don't even think about it," she snapped.

He grabbed the handle of the door and pulled it open. "I make no promises," he said as he walked past her. He dimly heard her mumble something that sounded suspiciously like fuck.

Sliding into the vacant chair beside Ryan, he pulled himself closer to the desk and adjusted the microphone and water in front of him. As soon as they sat, camera flashes began going off. He took a deep breath and let it out.

"Smitty."

He glanced at the reporter in the front row. Instantly he relaxed slightly when he realized who it was. Thank fuck. The national guys weren't going to ask him questions about his family. They knew better.

"Hey Sandy," he replied.

"So how did it feel to hit a grand slam against Campbell?"

"It always feels good to hit a grand slam, no matter who it's against."

Sandy rolled his eyes. "Yeah, sure, of course. But it has to feel a lot sweeter when you do it against someone who's made a habit out of trying to get in your head."

Campbell was a fucknob, but he couldn't say that on national TV, so instead he said, "He can try, but I think we can agree it's pretty clear he wasn't in my head tonight."

A hand shot up from the middle of the room, quickly followed by a female voice, "Angela Gaul, channel 6."

His muscles tightened as he waited for the question to follow.

"I imagine it would be hard to get your head in the game with everything going on with your family and relationship issues."

Ryan leaned forward and pulled his microphone closer to him. "So what did you all think of that snag in left field when Sim's arm grew like four feet to steal that home run from Bridges?"

Angela's eyes narrowed and a slight smile curved her lips. "Speaking of Sims. Why isn't he here today? Is it because of the animosity between you two?"

"Shit," Ryan muttered quietly beside him.

"Look, I know it doesn't make good headlines, but there's no bad blood between me and anyone. Brandon and I work great together in the field. I've got his back and he's got mine. End of story."

"Would your son agree?" Angela asked.

Jeff surged to his feet, his metal chair scraped against the floor loudly, as if it was trying to get away from him. Jeff pointed a finger at the reporter. "Don't fucking talk about my kid."

"Ah Jeff," Kirsty's voice cut in beside him.

He glared at her, then brushed it off. Turning back to face the media, all eyes were riveted to him. He knew he should shut up and sit down, but he couldn't. These people had scared his kid. They'd ruined his relationship with Kia. And they thought it was okay. Fuck that.

"Angela? Was it?" he asked, pinning the reporter with his glare. "You're new around here, right?"

"Mm hmm."

"Right. So I'm gonna tell you how it is, Angela. You want to talk to me about baseball? Let's do it. I'm happy to answer questions all day long about baseball. Because this is the media room after a baseball game and that's what we do." He looked around the room at the hungry expressions on the reporters' faces. "You want to talk about my love life? I think it's stupid, but I'll answer the odd question, within reason. Hell, me and my girl might even pose for a picture because we're adults. I took a job in the public eye and realize that there is some degree of interest in my life because of that. As does the grown-up woman I'm with." He leaned forward, pinning all of his animosity to the reporter. "But you fucking stay away from my kid."

"Jeff," Kirsty snapped beside him.

He glared at her. "No, this needs to be said and I don't care what it costs me."

Kirsty sighed and flicked her wrist as if to say proceed.

He turned back to the crowd, homing in on Angela, who was practically salivating as she waited for him to implode his career. "What the hell goes through your mind when you see footage from some tabloid vulture chasing a child? You should be appalled. You should be speaking up against that kind of shit. And instead, you show it on your network, you re-tweet it, you make it into some meme to talk about. He's a little boy. He didn't sign on for anything other than having a dad. And what did you guys do with that? You traumatized him. You did your best to humiliate his mother and make him ashamed of where he came from." He stared around the room, making eye contact with several reporters he'd known for years. It should have given him some satisfaction to see them sink into their chairs. It didn't. "He isn't the one who has anything to be ashamed of. You all do. This is baseball we're talking about. It's a game. My family is my life. And nothing is more important than that." He pushed away from the table and walked out of the room.

His heart pounded in his chest as he leaned against the wall in the hallway. "Well fuck," he muttered to himself.

The door to the media room pushed open and the team manager, Cal Schneider, stepped out. "Well, that was interesting," Cal said as he leaned against the wall. His shoulder bumped into Smitty's as he shifted.

"Yep." Jeff sighed. "How much shit do you think I'm in?"

Cal pulled his hat off his head and ran his finger along the stitching on the bottom side of the brim. "Hard to say."

The rapid staccato of heels clicking on the cement floor echoed like gunfire getting louder and louder the closer the runner came. "But it looks like we're about to find out." Cal pushed off the wall just as a petite woman in some type of business suit skidded around the corner. How she didn't break her ankle running in those heels, he had no idea. Women didn't get nearly enough credit.

"Mr. Smith, Mr. Schneider." She paused. "Mr. Hoffman would like to see you in his office."

"Shit." Jeff eyed his boss and there was no missing the resigned look in Cal's eyes. Getting summoned into the owner's office immediately following a press conference could only mean one thing. He was done.

He'd thought he'd have a few days, at least, before this conversation happened. Give his agent a chance to smooth things over a bit before he had to face the firing squad. Apparently not.

"Follow me please," the woman said before spinning on her heel and speed walking back the way she'd come.

Where's the fire? Slow your roll, lady. If he was going to be fired, he sure as shit didn't want to run through the building to do it.

As the two men fell into line behind the petite brunette, he aimed a tight smile at Cal. "I've really enjoyed playing for you."

Cal shook his head. "Let's not go there just yet."

"Come on, we both know how this conversation is going to play out."

"We don't know shit yet. Hoffman just bought the team. Nobody knows much about him. Hell, I didn't even know he was at the game tonight. This is the first one he's been at as far as I know."

"Perfect. Of course, he's at the one I decide to fire up a blowtorch directly at the press." His stomach lurched. He wasn't ready for tonight to be his last game with the Hawks. Fuck, fuck, fuckity, fuck. Maybe he should have listened when Kirsty tried to shut him up.

"It needed to be said. Bunch of vultures."

Jeff's head snapped toward his manager. "Yeah?"

"Yeah. I mean, you could have worded it differently. Maybe worked with Kirsty on some magazine interview that said the same thing, but didn't blow up your career, but what they did to Max was not okay. Even how they treated Kia was brutal. No one deserves that. But yeah, we could have done something a bit more career friendly."

His mind raced as he watched the numbers on the elevator take them up to the executive offices.

The elevator doors dinged, and he stepped forward. Shit, he wished he'd had a chance to shower before coming up to the boss's office. His nerves were making him feel like he was a sweaty beast. He lifted his arms away from his body to create some air flow.

Cal slapped him on the back. "Let's get this over with, kid."

Facing a firing squad might have felt less intimidating than meeting the new owner in person for the first time after he'd created a shit storm on national television.

The assistant led them past the opulent reception desk. She paused at the owner's door and knocked.

"Enter," the deep voice ordered from behind the door.

Enter. Who talked like that? Shit, this was going to be even worse than he'd imagined.

The petite woman pushed open the door. "Mr. Smith and Mr. Schneider are here."

"Thank you, Jenessa."

Sucking in a deep breath, Jeff squared his shoulders and stepped further into the room.

"Sit," Matthias Hoffman ordered.

Jeff slid onto the vacant seat closest to the window and Cal dropped onto the one beside him. "Matthias, good to see, sorry your first home game ended this way," Cal said.

"Me too. This is not how I planned on ending my evening."

Jeff fought the urge to slink deeper into his seat. He'd defended his kid and the woman he loved. He wasn't going to apologize for that. But he would admit he could have worded it better. "About the press conference," he began.

"No." Matthias held up his hand to stop him, then turned to Cal. "Does our press liaison prep the team during the season about how to behave in a press conference?"

"Yes, sir."

"And is she good at her job?"

Cal shifted uncomfortably in the chair beside him. "Yes, sir."

The owner turned to Jeff. "This is what, your fifth season in the majors?"

"Sixth," Jeff mumbled.

"Six." Matthias nodded slowly. "Then you've spoken to the press several times. Correct?"

Jeff cleared his throat. "Yes, sir."

"And do you think our press liaison is good at their job?"

"Yes, sir."

Matthias leaned back in his chair and crossed his arms over his chest. The guy didn't look much older than him, but somehow the way he stared Jeff down made him feel like he was a schoolboy getting scolded.

Like everyone on the team, he'd read all about the new team owners. Matthias Hoffman and his friends had purchased the team at the end of last year. From what Jeff understood, Matthias was the only owner who took any kind of active role in the team.

They'd all been holding their collective breath as they waited to see what changes the new owners planned on making. So far, they hadn't done much. The team was all waiting for the shoe to drop. He just prayed it didn't drop too hard on top of him.

Matthias stared at him for several seconds, not saying a word. Jeff tightened his core muscles to stop himself from squirming under the intense stare.

"Matthias," Cal started.

"Save it, Cal. I know what you are going to say," Matthias replied. His body never shifted from his leaned back position.

The man had the whole intimidating thing down to a science. "Mr. Hoffman, I'm..." Jeff began.

"You're the one?"

"I'm sorry?" Jeff asked. The one? The one what? The one who'd fucked up and word vomited all over the press room? The one who shit-canned his career? The one who fucked up his relationship with the most important person he'd ever met because he couldn't get his head out of his ass.

"I'm glad Saskia found you. I like you for her."

"Pardon?" Jeff's mind raced. How the hell did he know Kia?

A slight smile twitched at the corner of Matthias's lip. "I like you for her. She's a strong woman. She needs someone with the balls to stand up and be heard."

Jeff's mind reeled. What happening here? "You know Kia?"

A genuine smile split Matthias's mouth. "Yes, I know Kia."

What the actual fuck was going on? "So how do you know her exactly?" An instant flare of jealousy swirled through his gut. He clenched his jaw. Shit. He closed his eyes briefly and took a breath to tamp it down. His jealousy had fucked things up between them enough already. The last thing he needed to do was let it rear its ugly head when he was already in enough shit to bury him.

Matthias smirked. "Okay, you can control your mouth when you need to. Good to know. So going off in the press room was a choice then?"

Cal sputtered a cough that he quickly tried to cover as Jeff winced. "I'm not sure how to answer that exactly."

Matthias sat up straighter in his chair. "That press conference today was a shit show."

"Yes, sir," Jeff mumbled. His mind kept jumping back to how Matthias knew Kia. "I'm sorry. How do you know Kia?"

"Man, you have it bad." Matthias laughed. "I met her in Vegas at a tattoo convention a few years ago. The convention was at one of our hotels and I decided to get some work done. I wanted the best, and that was Saskia." He absently touched his forearm where Jeff imagined his tattoo must be. "She did my sleeve that weekend. Then I had her come back out to Vegas about a year later to do a back piece for me."

"Did you two date?"

"What? Of course not. She's my tattoo artist." Matthias stared at Jeff. "She's the most talented artist I've ever seen. I respect her. Got to know her a bit over the sessions, so I know how important Max is to her. What you did in that press conference. Defending your kid." Matthias shrugged. "I can respect that. Kia deserves someone like that for Max. For herself. From what I understand, she hasn't always had that."

"No, she hasn't." Jeff's mind raced. Why didn't Kia tell him she knew his boss? Why was she living the way she did if she had this kind of clientele?

"I'm not going to say I like the way you went about putting the press in their place, but I can respect the reason behind it," Matthias told him. "Clearly we are going to need to do some damage control." He shook his head. "This is going to be a PR nightmare."

"I'm sorry I should have talked to Kirsty first. I let my emotions get the best of me in the meeting and I know better."

"I would hope so." Matthias tapped his fingers on the top of the desk. "It might be good if you and Kia did something together. I'm sure Kirsty will know the best outlet for that."

Jeff winced. There was no way Kia would want to do an interview with him. She barely wanted to look at him at the moment, let alone do any favors for him.

Matthias raised an eyebrow. "What's the look for?"

"Let's just say she's not too thrilled with me at the moment because of all this media stuff."

"Understandable. Kia's pretty low key." He chuckled. "I can still picture her when they dragged her up on the stage at the convention after she won."

Jeff's chest tightened. He hated Matthias for sharing that experience with her. As he looked at the man in front of him, he realized he wasn't jealous of Matthias because he had a relationship with Kia. He was jealous because he'd missed seeing her success in that way. Missed seeing people celebrate how talented she was, and Matthias hadn't. The revelation nearly knocked him on his ass. He shifted in his seat. Maybe Kia was right about his jealousy. He trusted her completely. It didn't matter who she tattooed or hung out with. Kia wasn't the kind of person he needed to worry about. That wasn't who she was.

Matthias nodded toward him. "What just happened there?"

Fuck, the guy was observant. "Nothing. I just...I need to talk to Kia."

"You think you can work things out with her?"

"I sure hope so."

Matthias scowled. "You hope so? What kind of weak ass comment is that? You hope so. Is that the attitude you're going to have about the press conference, too? Because I have to tell you I'm banking a lot on the fact that you can turn this around with the media." Matthias leaned forward in his chair. "As much as I respect Saskia, I'm in the business to make money and if you're costing me money, then that needs to be changed."

Cal shifted in the seat beside him. "Understood."

Matthias tilted his head to the side, assessing Jeff. "That go for you, too?"

"Yes, sir," Jeff replied. "I'll make things right with the press, but just so we're clear, I'm not going to apologize for telling them they were out of line going after my kid."

"Of course not," Matthias replied. "Talk to the media liaison and put something together that makes them love you again. But nobody expects you to sell your soul to do that."

Jeff breathed a sigh of relief. "Thank you. I'll speak to Kirsty first thing tomorrow." Because tonight he needed to speak to Kia. He flicked a glance at his watch. If he didn't get his ass in gear, Max would already be in bed when he got there, and he needed to see him tonight as well.

"See that you do." Matthias turned to Cal. "I'll expect a full report on the plan tomorrow afternoon."

"Absolutely."

"Close the door on your way out," Matthias said. And just like that, they were dismissed. Jeff stood up and shuffled to the door behind Cal. At the door, he paused and turned back around. "Thanks again for giving me a chance to fix this."

"Don't make me regret it," Matthias replied.

"I won't." Jeff turned and walked out the door, closing it behind himself as he left the room.

Cal breathed a sigh of relief. "That went a lot better than I'd hoped."

"No shit."

"You got lucky with him knowing Kia." Cal shook his head. "Small world, hey? What are the odds?"

"Yeah." He still couldn't figure out why Kia hadn't told him she knew the new owner of the team. You'd think that would have been something she'd share with him since the guy was his boss.

"You heading there now?" Cal asked.

"Yeah. I'm going to grab a quick shower, then head over there. Assuming she'll let me in."

"She's that pissed?"

Jeff laughed, the sound without humor. "That's putting it mildly."

"Well, good luck. Either way, I'll expect you in Kirsty's office tomorrow morning 9:00 am."

"No problem." They walked toward the elevator, and he punched the button for the player's floor. His mind raced as he replayed the conversation with his boss. Who knew Matthias Hoffman would be so cool? When he'd heard a group of friends had bought the team last year, he'd expected a bunch of spoiled trust fund babies. And they'd all been waiting to see what kind of stupid shit they'd change. But Matthias seemed okay. Hell, he seemed more than okay. Thank god.

CHAPTER TWENTY-NINE

KIA LAY ON THE bed beside Max and eyed the stack of books he'd dragged onto the mattress. "Just how many books do you think we're reading tonight?"

Max grinned at her. The devilish twinkle in his eye looked so much like his dad it made her chest hurt.

It had only been a couple days since they'd fought and already she missed him. Watching the game with Max had been harder than she'd expected. Max had been disappointed they didn't go to the game. Guilt tore at her stomach. It had been petty of her to stay home. Her actions didn't just affect Jeff, they hurt her son as well. She'd promised herself when they started this thing she wouldn't let anything negatively affect Max. And yet here she was at the first sign of trouble keeping Max away from the game.

Sure, she'd tried to convince herself that it was in Max's best interest to miss the game because of the media.

But was it?

Really?

Maybe. Mostly, it was because she was a coward. Damn it. That wasn't fair.

Angry at herself, she'd turned the game off the second it was done. She hadn't been able to watch the press conference after. But when her phone had blown up with missed texts from her sister for the past hour, she wished she had.

She picked up the first book. "Okay, you need to read at least one page out loud to me, then we'll switch, and I'll read two chapters. In. One. Book." She punctuated the words to drive home the point that they would not be reading every book in the pile. Nor would she be sucked into reading additional chapters. As much as she loved the time snuggled up on the bed reading with Max every night, tonight she needed to track down the footage from the press conference Vika kept hounding her about. She hadn't allowed herself to watch it with Max just in case it created more questions than answers.

Max picked up the chapter book and flipped to the page where they'd last left off. He snuggled his head onto her shoulder and held the book in the air above his face and began to slowly read. Pride swelled in her chest as she listened to him fly through the words on the page. It didn't seem like that long ago that he could barely sound out one word, and now he was reading entire pages. Things changed so quickly.

The front doorbell rang, and she eyed the clock. Who could that be? She peeled herself off the bed. "I'll be right back," she told Max.

She adjusted her shirt as she made her way down the hall toward the front door. She peered through the peephole and sucked in a breath when she saw Jeff standing on the other side of the door. Was she ready to see him? The pounding in her chest said yes.

Steeling her spine, she pulled open the door. "Hey."

His shoulders sagged in what looked like relief as she pulled the door wider. "Hi," he replied.

Before she'd even had a chance to step back, she heard Max yell, "Dad!" A second before he flew down the hall, jumping onto Jeff.

"Hey Maxie, love the Spidey jammies. Very cool." Jeff looked at their son.

"Thanks. I watched you play tonight."

"Yeah, what'd you think?"

"Woulda been better if I'd been there," Max told him.

"Yeah, but you still could watch and that's good too," Jeff replied.

Guilt kneaded Kia's stomach. Jeff could have been a dick about her not bringing Max to the game. Instead, he wasn't. He was being really supportive of her. Which was more than she could say she'd done for him.

"You wanna hear me read?" Max asked.

"Absolutely," Jeff replied. "If it's okay with your mom."

Max's nose wrinkled up. "Is it okay, Mom?"

"Of course," she replied.

"Alright, let's go then." Jeff smiled at Kia as he followed Max down the hall to his room.

Now what? She stood in the hallway, looking around. They still needed to talk.

"Come on, Mom," Max yelled from his bedroom.

Putting one foot in front of the other, she glided down the hallway. At the bedroom door, she stopped. Her stomach whooshed as she took in the pair, snuggling on the twin mattress. Next to Max, Jeff looked so big, so solid. As she watched Max curl in tighter, it was clear how safe her son felt. Feeling like an interloper, she leaned against the wall, resting on one foot.

"Come on, Mom, lie down," Max ordered.

Jeff shifted his large body to the edge of the mattress, dragging Max along with him to create space for her on the other side.

Kia eased into the vacant space.

"Dad, you read the boy parts and mom will read the girl."

"You sure are bossy," she teased, dropping a loud, sloppy kiss on the side of her son's face.

"Mo—om, gross." Max wiped his cheek dramatically.

Jeff rolled. "Gross?" He kneeled up and tickled Max in the side. "What's gross about your mom's kisses? She gives great kisses."

"That's true. I do," Kia declared.

"Sto...stop," he gasped, squirming against the mattress to get away from Jeff's tickles. "I'll pee."

Jeff increased the tickling. "Gross, don't pee on the bed."

Max squealed and squirmed further. His legs kicked as he tried to free himself. "Mom, help," he giggled.

"Help?" She crawled to her knees. "Why would I help you? You said my kisses were gross?" She held her hands up like claws and laughed maniacally.

Max squealed louder. "I take it back."

"What's that?" she asked.

"I take it back," he yelled. He sucked in a breath and snorted, which made him giggle harder.

Geez, at this rate he really would pee. She held up her hand. "Alright minion," she said to Jeff. "Halt."

Jeff flicked an amused glance at her and held up his palms. "Minion?" he mouthed.

Kia shrugged and turned to Max. "Say I give the best kisses, or I'll order your dad to start tickling again."

Max giggled. "You give the best kisses, Mom."

"Thank you." Satisfied, she flopped back on the mattress. She looked at Jeff and nodded. "You may resume reading."

He snorted. "Gee thanks."

Max giggled again.

Together, they read three chapters in the short book before Jeff finally closed the book and set it on the bedside table. "We'll pick it up next time."

"When's that?" Max asked.

Jeff eyed her. Unable to give him any clue, she said nothing.

"I don't know Max. I have games all weekend, then I head out-of-town Monday for an away game on Tuesday, so it might be a couple days before I get back."

Max stuck out his bottom lip. "That's dumb," he mumbled.

"Language," Kia warned.

"Maybe we can FaceTime while I'm away," Jeff said. "You liked when we did that before."

Max eyed Kia. "Can we?" he asked hopefully.

Shit. She had done a crappy job with things recently. She'd let her hurt feelings and fear get in the way of what Max wanted. "Of course." See, she could do this. She could be normal with Jeff for Max's benefit. And if she felt a little nauseous, well, sometimes that was just the price of admission. For Max she'd deal.

She plopped a kiss on Max's head and pulled him in close for a tight squeeze. "I love you. Sweet dreams."

"Night, Mom." Max's little arms wrapped around her tightly and she closed her eyes to absorb the feeling. It wouldn't be too long before he didn't want to hug her goodnight. She was not looking forward to that at all.

Jeff gave Max a hug and kissed the top of his head. "Night buddy, I'll talk to you tomorrow."

"Promise?"

He rubbed the top of Max's head. "Yeah, I promise."

She followed Jeff out of the bedroom and pulled the door partially shut behind her.

Jeff stopped at the end of the hallway. "Can we talk?"

She eyed the half empty bottle of wine on the kitchen counter. "Do you want a drink?" Alcohol was definitely needed to have this conversation.

"Beer would be great," he stepped into the kitchen.

Kia pulled a beer out of the fridge for him and refilled her wineglass. She gestured toward the living room. "You want to sit in there?"

"Yeah." Jeff followed her into the living room. He sat on the chair opposite her and rested his elbows on his knees. "Thanks for letting me in tonight."

"Of course." She tilted her head slightly as she looked at him. Did he really think she would stop him from seeing his son? "No matter what happens between us, you're always Max's dad."

"Is there still an us?" he asked.

"I don't know, Jeff. I didn't expect this to all be so hard."

"Maybe that's why they say if it comes too easy you don't appreciate it."

She studied him. Gone was the cocky ballplayer she was used to. He seemed hesitant, unsure. Not at all like the Jeff she knew.

He wrinkled his nose. "Did you catch the game?"

"I did yeah." Her gut ached. "I'm sorry I didn't bring Max to the game. It was shitty of me. And not fair at all. I'll make sure we're there Sunday when my sister attends."

He took a sip of his beer and set it on the coffee table. "Understandable you didn't come tonight, given everything." He picked up the beer bottle, then set it back down without taking a sip. "Probably better you weren't there. I kind of created another shit storm with the media afterwards."

Nausea swirled in her belly. If that was true, they really were done. The reality of that hurt more than she'd imagined. "What did you do?"

"It wasn't my finest hour." He cleared his throat. "It may be best if you just watch it and then we talk."

He held out his phone toward her. She shook it off and pulled her phone out of her pocket. "I got it. Vika's been blowing up my phone ever since the game ended. I just didn't want to look at anything with Max there."

With a grimace, Jeff rocked slightly in his chair. "Probably for the best."

Afraid to look, she held the phone in front of her. "What am I going to see here?"

"Hopefully, me stepping up and showing you I'll protect my family." He rubbed his palms together nervously. "Maybe just watch it."

She tapped the link Vika had sent her. Jeff's face instantly filled the screen. She gasped as she listened to him rip into the reporter. What had he done? Her eyes drifted to Jeff. He winced as he listened to the audio.

"That sounded so much worse on replay than it did in my head the first go around," he muttered. Picking up the beer, he took a long pull, nearly finishing the entire thing in one sip. "On a scale of 1-10, how pissed are you?" he asked.

"How pissed am I?" She blinked at him. Was he serious? "How much trouble are you in for that?"

"Not as much as you'd think, honestly." He chuckled and shook his head like he still couldn't believe it. "But that's not important right now." He leaned forward and rested his elbows on his knees. "I can't change what happened, Kia, but I can own my shit. If I hadn't been a jealous prick, the press wouldn't have had anything to sink their teeth into. That's on me."

"I can't believe you did that," she whispered. "That you defended Max and I like that." Her eyes clouded with tears. No one had ever stood up for her that way before. She'd always had to protect herself, protect Max. It had always been her and Max against the world, but he'd stepped up.

Defended them at a potentially significant cost to himself. How was she supposed to respond to that?

Jeff stood up and walked over to the sofa. He sat on the edge of the coffee table, so he was close to her. "I told you when we started this thing, Kia, that I had your back."

"Yeah, but I didn't really believe you." The tears she'd been fighting to hold in leaked down her cheeks.

He reached out and wiped the tear with his thumb. "Then it's my job to show that to you. I meant it when I said in that video you looked like a fierce mama bear who would do anything to protect our son." He wiped another tear from her cheek. "You deserve me to be equally fierce in my protection of both of you."

"You don't have to protect me."

"Believe me, I'm well aware you can handle yourself and don't need me to do anything. But I want to." He sighed. "When that reporter started talking, I finally got it. I understood exactly where you were coming from and I was going to protect my family, no matter what." He grabbed her hand. "And that's not just Max, that's you too."

She turned her hand over and threaded her fingers with his. "This scares me."

"I know." He ran his thumb down the outside of hers.

"You scare me," she whispered.

"Why do I scare you?"

"Because I want it so fucking bad." She bit her bottom lip to stop it from quivering. "I've lost so much." She sniffed. "And with as hard as I've fought, this is all I have." She gestured around at her small living room in a shitty part of town.

He shifted his body, so his strong thighs bracketed both of hers and took both of her hands in his. "Kia, I know how hard you've fought. What you have—the life you've given our son—you amaze me."

He shifted his body to the edge of the coffee table and his muscular arms wrapped around her back and pulled her closer to him. His heat, his strength, encompassed her as he rested his forehead against hers. "I want all of this with you, with Max, just as bad as you do, Kia."

"Really?"

"Oh my god, yes."

She didn't even try to stop the tears from flowing down her face. "Okay."

Jeff pulled back and looked her in the eye. "Okay?"

"Mm hmm." She nodded. At the look of sheer joy on his face, she smiled.

"Holy shit, woman," he yelled. He jumped up and pulled her up with him. His arms wrapped around her waist, and he hoisted her into the air. Laughing, she wrapped her legs around his waist.

"Why are you guys yelling?"

Jeff stopped moving and turned them toward the entrance to the living room. Max stood staring at them with Pickles dangling from his hand.

"Sorry, we didn't mean to wake you," Jeff said.

"Does that mean you aren't fighting anymore?" Max looked from one to the other.

"No baby, we aren't fighting anymore." She pressed against Jeff's shoulder, so he'd set her on the ground.

"Cuz you love each other?"

Kia sucked in a breath, then looked over at Jeff. He smiled.

"Yeah bud, cuz we love each other," Jeff said.

What? She spun around to face him. "You love me?"

"Obviously." A goofy grin broke across his face.

"Tell her," Max demanded.

"Gladly." He winked at their son, then wrapped his arms around her waist. "I love you, Kia, more than I ever thought possible."

As she stared into his eyes, she realized she didn't have to be afraid anymore. "I love you too."

"And you both love me, right?" Max's little voice piped in, forcing them to look away from each other.

Jeff reached out and grabbed Max around the waist and hauled him up in the air. Max giggled with delight when Jeff stepped closer to her, pinning their son between them. "Of course we love you," she told him. She pushed her lips against his cheek in a big, noisy kiss. Jeff kissed him on the other side. The double smooch sent Max into a fit of giggles, making his entire body shake.

"I think I should get another bedtime story," Max declared.

"I think that can be arranged." Kia glanced at Jeff for agreement.

"Absolutely." Jeff winked at Max, then turned back to her. "Hey, by the way, I meant to ask, why didn't you tell me you knew the owner of the team?" he asked Kia.

"What?" Her brow furrowed in confusion. What the heck was he talking about? "How would I know the owner of the team?"

"He said you did his tattoos." He hoisted Max up higher on his hip.

She stepped back so she could look at him clearly. She'd done a lot of tattoos, but she didn't know a single person in San Diego who could afford a freaking baseball team. "Who's the owner?"

"Matthias Hoffman."

Matthias? Her eyes widened in surprise. "Seriously? Matt owns the team?"

"Well, him and a few other people, but yeah."

"Huh, that's wild. I had no idea. Last time I heard he was still living in Vegas." She smiled as she pictured the other man. From what she knew about him, he had the Midas touch. He'd certainly helped her business. The suggestions he'd given her on how to capitalize on the competition win had grown her client base exponentially back in Tucson. Any business he was involved with seemed to be incredibly successful. Matt wouldn't allow it to be any other way. The Hawks would be lucky to have an owner like him. "He's a smart businessman. I'm sure he'll be an amazing owner."

"Yeah, he seems like a good guy," Jeff responded.

Matt was a good guy. A little serious at times, but kind. When he'd found out she was a single mom, he'd given her an obscene tip and told her to take her son some place fun. They'd lost touch, but it would be good to catch up with him. "That's really cool that he's in town. I'll have to call him and grab a coffee or something."

"You should."

She raised an eyebrow at him. If he'd been jealous of Brandon, she could only imagine how jealous he'd be of someone like Matthias. So why did he seem so chill about the idea of her meeting up with the other man? "Who are you and what have you done with Jeff?"

"I deserve that." He dipped his head. "But no, no more jealousy. Lesson learned. Besides, I think you'd be crazy not to capitalize on a connection like that for your business. Viper wants you to raise your rates. Clients like Matthias could certainly afford to pay it."

"And you can't?" She smirked at him.

"Oh no, I totally can, but I figure there should be some perks to dating the artist." He stepped closer to her.

"Is that right?"

Max sighed loudly. "Guys, come on, let's go read."

"Right sorry. Priorities." Kia wrinkled her nose and grinned at her son.

Max's face scrunched up. "Priorities are me, right?"

"Absolutely baby. You're our top priority."

"Good." Max nodded once, like he was satisfied with that answer. "Let's go read."

Jeff held her gaze. The love he felt for her and Max clearly reflected on his face as he wrapped her hand in his and squeezed. "Let's do it."

EPILOGUE

6 MONTHS LATER

Kia walked up the path to her front door. What the hell was going on in there? AC/DC Thunderstruck pounded out of the speakers at a deafening level. Sounded like Jeff was going old school.

She pushed open the front door and yelled. "Hello?"

Strangely enough, no one responded over the noise. She wandered further into the house. No sign of Max and Jeff in the living room or the kitchen. She peeked her head inside Max's room. Nothing.

Just then, a loud crash sounded from her bedroom. Kia sprinted down the hall and found Max and Jeff lying in a heap on her bed, laughing their heads off. Her now broken bed.

"What is going on in here?" she yelled. No response. Why was the music so damn loud?

She stepped closer to the bed, and Jeff's head snapped up. He at least had the good sense to look embarrassed about his behavior. He waved his hand and she thought he said hi, possibly. Max launched on the broken bed, stumbling as he stepped on the bent mattress.

Jeff pulled out his phone and turned off the deafening music. "Hi, honey, you're home." He grinned like a little boy who'd been caught with his hand in the cookie jar.

She put her hand on her hip and stared around her bedroom. "What are you two doing?"

"We broke your bed," Max proclaimed.

"I can see that. I'm just a little confused about why you broke my bed."

"Now we have to move in with dad," Max declared.

She pulled on her earlobe. Surely she'd heard him wrong. "I'm sorry what?"

Max rolled his eyes. "Your bed's broke so now we gotta move in with Dad."

Okay, yep, she'd heard him right the first time. The answer still didn't make any sense. Turning her attention to the supposed adult in the room, she pinned Jeff with her best disappointed mom stare. "Care to explain?"

"So here's the thing," Jeff began. "I asked Max what he thought I needed to do to get you to agree to move in with me.

"To move in with you?"

"Yeah." He smiled.

"And you broke my bed?" She shook her head as she looked at the two mischievous peas in a pod.

Jeff shrugged. "It seemed like a good idea."

"To break my bed?"

"Well yeah. Max figured if we broke your bed, you'd have to move in with me."

"Why exactly?"

"Cuz where would you sleep, Mom?" Max scoffed.

Kia struggled to keep from laughing at her son's logic.

Jeff wasn't as good at not laughing. She narrowed her eyes and stared him down. "You know we're in trouble if you are going to take advice from a five-year-old." She raised her eyebrow at him.

"I'll be six next week," Max piped in.

"Good point, buddy." Jeff hoisted Max onto his hip. The two put their heads together. "Do you think it worked?" Jeff asked his son.

Max turned and looked at her. His eyes squinted as he stared. He tilted his head left, then right. "I don't think so," he said in a loud stage whisper. The kid really needed to work on that skill, she mused.

Jeff regarded her as well, then his mouth tightened into a straight line, and he sighed. "Time to bring out the big guns?"

"Yep," Max agreed.

The big guns? Oh boy. Kia braced herself for what these two might come up with next.

Jeff hopped off the bed and set Max on the floor beside him. He leaned down to his son. "Should we do this together?"

"Yeah, she doesn't always say yes when you ask stuff."

Jeff smirked, then quickly wiped it off and nodded. "Good point." He grabbed Max's hand, and they walked over to her. Jeff kneeled and pulled Max down beside him.

"Oh my god, what are you doing?" She gasped.

"Well, since the broken bed thing didn't work. We need to go big." Jeff reached into his pocket and pulled out the most beautiful platinum diamond ring she'd ever seen.

She covered her mouth with her hand, her eyes darting back and forth between Max and Jeff.

"Dad said if you were married you'd have to live with him," Max announced.

"I did say that," Jeff agreed. His eyes sparkled with amusement as he looked at their son. He cleared his throat. "Kia, you turned my life upside down in the best possible way when you came back into my life."

"That's 'cuz of me," Max said.

"Sure is, bud." Jeff put his finger against his lips. "This is the part where you should be quiet and let me try to sweet talk your mom. If that doesn't work, then we'll bring you in as the closer. Deal?"

Kia giggled as she watched Jeff negotiate silence from an almost six-year-old.

"Deal." Max nodded in agreement.

Jeff scooted forward on his knees and took her hand. "Where was I? Oh yeah." He cleared his throat. "I always knew I'd get married someday. Have the wife and kids. And yes, we did that a little backward."

She widened her eyes and nodded. That's for sure.

He smiled. "But I wouldn't have it any other way. Seeing you and Max. Getting to know you both made me realize how much I'd missed, and I quickly knew I didn't want to miss another second with either of you. I've never met anyone like you. You amaze me every day. You're loyal, you're fierce, and there is no one I'd rather go into battle with than you." He set the ring against her finger and looked up at her face.

Tears streamed down her cheeks, and she wiped them away.

"Will you marry me?"

"Absolutely yes."

Jeff jumped up and wrapped his arms around her. His lips lightly touched hers.

"So I don't need to close?" Max asked.

She burst out laughing. "How about we seal the deal with a family hug?"

"Kay." Max hopped up and Jeff hoisted him into the air. Max placed his hands on either side of Jeff's face. "It's a good thing you had me here to close," he whispered in his ridiculously loud whisper.

"Good thing." Jeff's blue eyes shimmered with unshed tears as he looked at her.

Kia pressed her lips gently against Jeff's mouth. "Very good thing."

"Eww," Max groaned.

She threw back her head and laughed. Breaking her bed might just be the weirdest engagement she'd ever heard of, but nothing could have been more them.

*Want to catch up with all your favorite characters from the previous books and read what happened at the pool party with Jeff and Kia. Click here to download a fun bonus scene.*http://www.laurenfraser.com/sliding-into-home-bonus-scene

I don't know about you but I'm loving Gonzo and really want to see him find his forever person. For a sneak peek at his book Hitting the Gap keep flipping the page.

SNEAK PEEK OF HITTING THE GAP

NOPE, NOT A CHANCE. There was no way anyone he cared about was living in this dump, especially not a woman. Maybe that made him sexist, but at this moment he didn't care.

Gonzo eyed the run-down apartment complex with the overflowing dumpster, the peeling paint, and big pieces of broken concrete on the path. The place looked like it should have a "condemned" sign slapped to the wall instead of "for rent".

What had Bailey been thinking, wanting to move here? This was possibly the worst neighborhood in the city. Even if money was tight, there were safer places to live.

He glanced down the street, looking for her vehicle.

Where the hell was she? She'd told him to meet her here at 1:00 to help her unload the moving truck. It was 1:30 and there was still no sign of her. But then, did he really expect anything different? His childhood best friend was notoriously late. Heck, it was such a well-known fact that his parents had let it slide when he'd missed curfew on more than one occasion because they knew he was out with her.

Finally, he heard the distinct rumble of a U-Haul truck that was a few too many moves past a repair. He couldn't see much of the driver, but from the size, he guessed it was a woman. When the truck got closer, he spotted Bailey's smiling face and red hair behind the wheel. Only Bailey would look happy pulling up in front of a shithole like this.

She double-parked the truck in front of the building and hopped out of the cab. Her feet barely hit the cement before she launched herself in his direction. Her movement didn't stop until she crashed into him. The forward momentum nearly knocked him on his ass, and he took several steps backward to keep them upright as Bailey's arms wrapped around his neck. Lush female curves filled his hands. It had been a couple years since he'd seen Bailey in person, but he sure as hell didn't remember her hugs feeling like that.

Whoa. Whatever curves she had were irrelevant. This was Bailey.

"Hey, Bay." He chuckled as he pulled her in tight for a hug. The familiar smell of citrus and something that was distinctly his childhood friend filled his senses. It was good to have her here. Until this moment, he hadn't realized just how much he'd missed her.

When Bailey had said she was moving to San Diego for a job, he hadn't known what to expect. He wasn't a fan of her boyfriend at all, but when she'd called last week to ask for his help with the move, she said they'd broken up and she was coming alone. Now that he didn't have to worry about her dick boyfriend, he was really looking forward to spending time with his childhood best friend.

Bailey glanced at the building and wrinkled her nose. "Hmm."

"You can't be serious about living here," he said.

She chewed her bottom lip, and a wave of nostalgia filled him. How many times had he seen her make that exact same face growing up?

"It looks a little different from the online picture." Her brows knitted together. "This is Sunnyvale Apartments, right?"

Gonzo eyed the graffitied sign with the word 'Sun' peeking through the paint. "That's what it says."

Bailey pulled her phone out of her pocket and swiped it open. Her lips pursed tightly, and she looked back at the building, then down at her phone and back at the building again. The lines of confusion on her face grew.

"You okay?" he asked.

She thrust her phone toward him. "Is this even the same building? I mean, even brand new, this place wouldn't have looked anything like that?"

He eyed the picture on the screen. "What the fuck? Is this seriously the ad?" The building in the ad looked modern, with clean lines and beautiful landscaping. The one in front of them looked like 1970 threw up. He could already picture the snot green shag he was gonna see inside the apartments. "There's no fucking way you're living here," he told her.

"Maybe it's better inside than out." Bailey chewed her bottom lip as she eyed the building. Even for an optimist like her, the comment was a stretch.

"It couldn't possibly be worse."

Bailey studied the building and sighed. "Let's go find the manager and look."

"The only thing we're finding the manager for is to tell him you aren't moving in here."

Bailey bristled. "Don't even start with that macho bullshit, Gonzo. I didn't let you boss me around as a kid, and I'm sure not letting you do it now." She squared her shoulders, and he bit back a groan. Damn it. He should have known better. If there was one thing destined to make Bailey dig her feet in, it was telling her she couldn't do something. The woman took independence to new heights.

"All right, let's go look." He swept out his arm to gesture she go first. He needed to have her back to make sure he could protect her if anything happened. As they stepped across the broken path toward the building, he scanned their surroundings, ready for anything.

"Hopefully we don't get shanked," Bailey mumbled.

"No shit." The hairs on his neck stood up and he looked behind him. A group of young men leaned against a car, watching them. He rolled his shoulders to loosen his neck in case he needed to get into it with these guys.

Bailey stopped and scanned the area. She turned toward the men and called, "Do you know where I can find the super?"

What the hell was she doing drawing more attention to herself?

One guy pushed off the car and sauntered toward them. His New York ball cap tilted sideways on his head. The guy couldn't even cheer for a good team. New York. Come on. As the guy scanned Bailey appreciatively, Gonzo stepped in front of her to block the other man's view.

"You moving in?" the guy asked Bailey.

Bailey nodded. "Trying to."

Just as Gonzo said, "No."

"Super's in 101. If you need anything once you're moved in, gorgeous, you come find me."

"Thanks," Bailey said.

The guy licked his lips, and his gaze trailed slowly down her body. The leer was so disgusting Gonzo needed a shower and it wasn't even directed at him.

"She won't," Gonzo growled.

The guy eyed Gonzo, then nodded to his friends, and the other four guys started walking toward them. "You look like you got somethin' to say." The guy stepped toward Gonzo.

Fuck. He flexed his hands. The last thing he wanted was to get into it with these assholes. He liked his odds one-on-one. Hell, even two-or-three-on-one. But five-on-one? Those weren't great odds. Factor that at least one of these guys probably had a piece and he was fucked.

"Holy shit, you're Ramon Gonzalez," one of the newcomers said.

"Yeah."

The guy lifted his sweatshirt to show off the Hawks T-shirt he was wearing underneath. Thankfully, the other men stopped posturing and Gonzo breathed a sigh of relief. Looked like he might get out of here unscathed yet.

"What the fuck are you doing in this neighborhood?" the guy asked.

"Just need to talk to the super for a minute."

The guy tilted his head as he assessed him, looked at his boys, then back at Gonzo. "She your girl?"

"Yeah." He felt Bailey tense behind him. What was he supposed to say? If the guys were fans, Bailey was as a hell of a lot safer if they thought she belonged to him.

The newcomer eyed Bailey speculatively and nodded his head. "If she moves in, we'll keep an eye on her."

"Thanks," Gonzo mumbled. There was no way Bailey was moving in here. When he felt her fingers wrap into the waistband of his jeans as she pressed closer to him, he was pretty sure they were on the same page.

"So how's the team looking this year?" the guy asked.

"Pretty good."

A scrawny guy walked around the side of the building and pulled up short when he saw them. The Hawks fan glanced over, then said, "That's the super."

"Cool, thanks," Gonzo said. He reached around and grabbed Bailey's hand and pulled her to his side so he could protect her if needed. Once they got a few steps from the group, he whispered, "Bay, seriously, you didn't move to some Podunk town where you sit and have lemonade on the porch with the neighbors. People here have guns."

"I know," she whispered back. "That's why I was being nice. If anyone was going to get us in trouble, it was you."

Unfortunately, she probably wasn't wrong about that assessment. "You can't seriously be thinking of moving in here." He pointed to a hole in the wall by the staircase. "That's a fucking bullet hole, Bailey."

Her eyes widened and she cringed. "Really?"

"Yes, really. Now, can we please get out of here?"

"I can't. I put down a deposit to hold the place."

Gonzo pinched the bridge of his nose. "Guess we're talking to the super." He cupped her elbow and propelled her toward the super.

"You Bailey Reynolds?" the man asked.

"Yes."

"You're late." He glared at her.

Gonzo rolled his eyes. Nice customer service. Clearly, the manager matched the shithole exterior.

The super turned on his heel. "Follow me."

Gonzo and Bailey fell in line behind him. Bailey's head swiveled from one side to the other as they walked. If she was thinking anything close to what he was thinking, they should run, not walk, to the nearest exit.

They stopped in front of apartment 213. The super pushed the door open and coughed slightly as he stepped into the room. Gonzo hadn't even taken a step and he could already see the disgusting carpet. He hadn't been far off in his guess. It was more of a mustard puke color rather than snot, but equally disgusting.

Following Bailey into the room, he pulled up short when the smell punched him in the face. Bailey's head snapped back a second before she retched, then slapped her hand over her mouth. "Oh my god, what is that?" She plugged her nose. "It smells like death. But not like good death."

"Good death?" he asked. What the fuck was good death?

Bailey's mouth gaped like a fish as she tried to suck air into her lungs. It was like the stench sucked out the oxygen from the room, making it hard to breathe. Fuck, the smell was so bad he could taste it. What was that?

Bailey flapped her hand in front of her face. "God, it's like decomposing smelly feet doused in parmesan cheese and cat piss."

That was a pretty accurate description.

She tilted her head back, then retched again. "Nope, I can't." She covered her mouth and bolted for the front door.

Gonzo walked to the door, turned, and blocked the super from leaving. "We're gonna need that deposit back."

The man narrowed his eyes and sneered. "No, she agreed to live here. If she wants to back out, that's her choice, but she's not getting the deposit back."

Gonzo stepped into the other man's space and took a great deal of pleasure in watching him back away. "We both know that ad you placed was a load of shit. That's false advertising and there's not a court in the world that would honor that bullshit." He let his derision for the little weasel show on his face. "And when my lawyer gets done with you, this place will look like a luxury condo compared to what you'll be able to afford if you don't give her back her money."

"You can't sue me."

"Watch me." Gonzo stared at the little man. He crossed his arms over his chest and continued to block the other man from leaving the apartment. Finally, the guy sighed.

"Fine, follow me to my office and I'll transfer her the money back."

Gonzo grunted in acknowledgement and stepped out of the room. He sucked in a breath of air but couldn't smell anything except the apartment. Great, that stench now lived in his nose. *Like when you puked on yourself and that's all you could smell.* He turned to Bailey. "He's gonna give you your deposit back."

The super pushed past them and stormed down the hallway. Bailey eyed the apartment and chewed nervously on her bottom lip. "I don't have a lot of options, Gonz. I gotta live somewhere."

"Well, it sure as fuck isn't going to be here. Let's get your deposit and we'll figure it out."

Grap a copy at http://www.books2read.com/hittingt hegap

ALSO BY

Playing for Keeps
Too Far   Prequel- not sports romance
Protecting the Plate Book 0.5
Everything to Me   Book 1
Throwing the Curve   Book 2
Sliding into Home Book 3
Hitting the Gap Book 4
Catching the Fly- Book 5

Cowboy Code
Rode Hard Book 1 Cowboy Code Series
Rough Stock Book 2 Cowboy Code Series
Round Up Book 3 Cowboy Code Series

Best Things are Three Series
Dani's Duo
Longing for Kayla

Flirty Forties Series

Sun, Sin and Surf

Aged to Perfection

Standalone Books

The Geek Next Door

Letting Go

Too Hot

Yielding for Him

About the Author

Lauren Fraser resides in British Columbia, Canada, with her husband, two children, and two dogs. When she's not busy writing, Lauren loves to spend time with her family outside—camping, hiking and paddle boarding.

Lauren writes about love and relationships in many different forms, but in the end, she's a sucker for a happy ending. She is multi-published and loves to hear from her readers. For the latest updates, visit her website.

Website http://www.laurenfraser.com/
Newsletter http://www.laurenfraser.com/newsletter